A SAUCY MURDER

A SONOMA WINE COUNTRY COZY MYSTERY

AJ CARTON

CONTENTS

1
———

FRIDAY AFTERNOON - SAUCE

Emma stared out of the arched triptych windows of the family kitchen at the Buchanon Estate and thought to herself, there is nowhere in the world I would rather be and nothing in the world I'd rather be doing. Quite an admission for a just-turned sixty-five year old. But, truly, you couldn't beat the view. Miles of Sonoma County, California's undulating, golden, sun-soaked hills lined with blue-green vines dripping purple Zin grapes. Like the backdrop of some famous Renaissance painting, or the score of a Verdi opera come to life. Or the Verdi Requiem.

Stop that! Emma shook her head. Trying to erase Verdi's gut-wrenching music from her brain. The image of Old Saint Mary's Church in San Francisco. Of the altar exploding in sunflowers. Of the open casket. Of Mary, her best friend since grade school, suddenly, irrevocably gone. Diagnosed in June. Dead six months later.

Emma searched the Buchanons' elegant kitchen for some wood to touch. But everything was Carrara marble and stainless steel. She settled for tapping the eco friendly bamboo spoon she was using to stir her tomato sauce. After two hours at a very slow simmer the sauce had finally alchemized from lurid blood-red into the velvety orange-gold of her grandmother's famous tomato sauce. *Salsa di pomodoro*. No one could ever call *that* a red sauce.

Why, Emma wondered, in this paradise of sun, golden hills, grape vines, spectacular wine and fabulous food did her mind still go negative? After moving to Blissburg in Sonoma County, California's wine country six months before, she should be singing the Hallelujah Chorus, not the Verdi Requiem!

Her cookbook, *Dining with the Stars*, describing her diva grandmother's favorite recipes, had just been published by a small local press. And one of the wine country's most famous wineries was featuring her signature tomato sauce recipe as the centerpiece of its annual Opera in the Vineyard fundraiser. In an hour California's richest and trendiest would join some of opera's greatest stars for music, wine and the best food Sonoma County had to offer, including hers. Yes, she was in paradise. So why did death keep popping into her head like she was the heroine of a horror movie? Or the loser in some senior game of musical chairs?

Emma shuddered, dropped the bamboo spoon onto the hand painted ceramic Deruta spoon holder the Buchanons provided next to the stove, and bent over to tap the cherry hardwood kitchen floor. Definitely more woody than the bamboo spoon. Maybe, she thought, the answer was that most people found paradise after they were dead.

"Drop something?" asked Sergio, the owner/chef of *Ristorante Sergio*, one of Sonoma County's top ten restaurants, and celebrity chef for the City Opera fundraiser. He stood in the doorway of the Buchanon family's kitchen dressed in a starched white knee-length chef's coat. With his ruddy complexion, jet black curls and chestnut brown eyes, he looked like a hunky Renaissance archangel.

"My spoon. I dropped my spoon," Emma explained.

She grabbed it surreptitiously off the counter, and poised it above the simmering pot – not wanting Sergio to know she'd been superstitiously tapping the cherry kitchen floor. The last thing she needed was for the celebrity chef to think she was a California kook who collected crystals and believed in omens, instead of an accomplished author of a cookbook on northern Italian cuisine.

"Whoa! *Signora!*" Sergio shouted, covering his face with his hands. "Do not put that spoon back in the sauce. Not after it's been on the floor. And please, wash your hands. Everything in the kitchen must be *impeccabile*, you know, clean*issimo*." Sergio remedied what he called the English language's lack of passion by adding *issimo* to any word he wanted to emphasize.

Of course, the spoon had never touched the floor. It rested solely on the ceramic spoon holder. But Emma couldn't exactly point that out after lying about dropping the spoon in the first place. Sergio was a clean freak. Now he thought she was a slob. That was all she needed from one of her daughter and son-in-law's prominent friends who'd endorsed her *Dining with the Stars* cookbook and promised to push it at his celebrated restaurant.

"*Bellissimo*," he murmured, having crossed the kitchen to stand by Emma's side over the simmering sauce. "Color, texture. All *perfetto, Signora*. Since I started featuring your sauce at the restaurant, my *tagliatelle alla salsa di pomodoro* is our best selling dish. One of my customers calls it Eatalian comfort food. Did you know that? Is just like my grandmother's."

Emma's grandmother and Sergio himself were both from Bologna, a bond the strength of which Emma was beginning to appreciate.

"And the *profumo*." He wafted great waves of the rich smelling sauce into his nostrils before picking a clean spoon out of a drawer and tasting it. "A triumph, *Signora*," he nodded, apparently dissuaded by the rich flavor from dumping the whole pot of sauce into the garbage because of the imagined sanitation violation. "Who knew Americans would love something so elegant, so simple? I'll let it simmer for a half hour longer. To kill any impurities. Then, *basta*."

He glanced at her critically. "*Signora*, you are done. You should go change into something nice for the party. I will take it from here."

Yes, Emma thought. Better go home and figure out what to wear. She'd be sitting at the fundraiser's silent auction table next to an autographed copy of her book and a sign describing her generous donation. Dinner for six. Why, Emma wondered, was the thought of preparing dinner for six strangers suddenly making her feel so tired? A year ago she'd have done it in her sleep.

Emma mechanically double kissed Sergio goodbye.

"Change into something nice," she muttered as she left the room. She wondered if he was being condescending. Or was she just too sensitive?

A hallway connected the kitchen to a small breakfast room with double doors opening onto a side garden planted with multi-colored perennials and herbs. Like the Buchanons' kitchen, their breakfast room was done to the nines. A Fortuny glass light fixture hung from the ceiling over a round antique breakfast table. The seat cushions of its eight ladder-back chairs were covered in a small yellow and white Fortuny cotton print.

But it was the artwork on the walls that caught Emma's eye. She immediately recognized the Andy Warhol soup cans and an Oldenburg ceramic fried egg. Not reproductions, she noted. Barry Buchanon owned the real thing, arranged side by side with paintings of fruit and desserts looking luscious enough to eat.

Emma let herself out of the house through the double doors into the garden where her daughter, Julie, stood deep in conversation with the winery's manager.

Julie and her husband Piers had moved to Blissburg with their toddler just three years before. Piers opened a boutique law firm specializing in family wealth. Julie started her own PR firm focusing on wineries. Emma thought her daughter worked too hard for a young mother. But Julie's business was flourishing; and Buchanon Vineyards was her biggest client.

It was after Emma's best friend, Mary, died, that Julie and Piers finally convinced Emma to retire from her job as a paralegal in San Francisco and move to Blissburg. Emma had to admit she had never felt happier. She volunteered at the Blissburg Free Legal Services Clinic twice a week. She'd finally got the cookbook published that she'd sidelined for too many years. And just the other day, the manager of Blissburg's gourmet grocery had contacted her about freezing her famous tomato sauce to sell in their market.

So why, she wondered, did her wandering mind still default to the Big D? Not Divorce, mind you. She'd already survived that. No. At 65, the Big D in her life was Death.

Emma shuddered and shook the thought away, focusing her attention on her glamorous daughter. The trim, dark eyed, dark haired young woman was dressed for Blissburg's late September Indian Summer heat in tight black jeans, an Alexander Wang T and three-inch Prada heels. Her father's good looks, Emma noted ruefully. Julie bore not a trace of her mother's once delicate, sixties, blue-eyed flower child features. Now, of course, Emma's formerly blond hair was cut in a thick, short totally grey bob.

Julie caught sight of her mother crossing the garden and motioned her over to where she and the winery's manager stood talking.

"Emma," Julie now often called her mother Emma when she was in work mode, "remember your brilliant idea to have that fortune teller client of yours from the free legal clinic read tarot cards for guests during the silent auction?"

Julie accompanied her question with a pointed stare that Emma interpreted to mean either: Do not mention that I nixed the idea, or why on earth are you wearing those dirty sweat pants?

Emma nodded cautiously. Thwarting her headstrong daughter was never a good idea.

"Well," Julie continued, "Lexie Buchanon just happened to mention that lots of her friends love tarot cards, and that since the

Opera in the Vineyard's theme this year is the Opening Night opera, *Il Trovatore*..."

Emma interrupted her daughter with a snicker. "You mean *The Troubadour*, the opera about the confused old bat who mistakenly threw her own infant son into the bonfire, instead of the little prince she'd kidnapped? Whoops! At least I never did that!"

Emma noticed Julie cringe. Her jokes, much appreciated by old friends like Mary, often sank into a dead zone between her and her highly successful daughter.

"Mom," Julie replied, "that confused old bat is one of the greatest mezzo roles in all of Opera. Anyway, a friend of Mrs. Buchanon suggested having a fortune teller at the fundraiser tonight. Mrs. Buchanon loved the idea. I told her you had a gypsy contact who might do it. We'll even..."

"Roma," Emma interrupted again.

Julie looked puzzled. "She's in Rome? Why's the gypsy in Rome?"

"Ro*ma*," Emma repeated, emphasizing the last syllable. "Do not call them the 'g' word. They are Roma. That's their name. Calling them the 'g' word is like saying the 'r' word to a Native American."

Julie jerked her head in the direction of the winery manager signaling to Emma that she was staring at them like they were crazy.

"OK. Roma," Julie backed off. "The question is, can she come? She'd need to be here by 7:00."

Emma looked at her watch. "I'll see." She couldn't help adding, "Awfully short notice," and thinking to herself that the young Mrs. Lexie Buchanon - Barry Buchanon's third - had probably only that morning turned her fragile attention span from Gaultier to Grand Opera. But whatever donors want, donors get, she reminded herself. "I'll give her a call and ask her. I know she needs the money. How much can you pay?"

Julie looked at the winery manager. "We'll only need her for about an hour."

The manager threw up her hands in a parody of surrender. "Short notice? A hundred sounds fair. Lexie will love it."

"A hundred it is," Julie repeated. "But ASAP. We need to know, so I can tell Mrs. Buchanon that her brilliant idea worked."

As Emma hurried off to her car, she was already scanning her cell phone contacts for Carmen's number. Carmen, Emma thought. Was she really named Carmen? The legal clinic where Emma volunteered as a paralegal had helped her and her family get health insurance a couple of months before. She'd listed her job then as tarot reader. Emma guessed she still desperately needed the money. Thank goodness she'd informally sounded Carmen out about the gig before even suggesting it to Julie.

"Carmen," she began when the sound of the phone ringing was interrupted by Carmen's hesitant "hello".

"It's Emma, from the legal clinic. Remember that gig I mentioned at the Buchanon Vineyards? Well, I apologize for the really, really short notice, but the party is tonight and it seems Mrs. Buchanon really, really wants a (Emma almost said the 'g' word but stopped herself just in time) a tarot card reader there for about an hour during the silent auction. The Buchanons will pay a hundred dollars for your time on short notice and, of course, it will hopefully be good advertising for you."

Carmen hesitated for only a moment. "Sure, I'll do it. What time?"

"6:45 to set up," Emma replied. "Then stay from 7:00 until 8:00."

"At the Buchanon Vineyards," Carmen repeated.

"Right. You know where that is?" Emma asked

Carmen answered, "Sure." Then added, "There'll be a lot of fancy people there. What should I wear?"

Emma thought a moment. This was way out of her job description. "Something black with a big colorful shawl?"

"And big hoop earrings, and sequin shoes, and maybe a red dot in the middle of my forehead," Carmen laughed. "Like the movies, right?"

Emma gulped back her embarrassment. "Yes, Carmen," she finally said. "You're probably right. Like in the movies."

Emma rang off and drove her silver Prius five miles south to the 1855 yellow farmhouse on Blissburg's main drag where she now lived. The old farmhouse was tucked in a rambling garden shaded by a giant magnolia tree behind the tiny Victorian cottage Julie used as her office. Her new home had six rooms – a living room, kitchen, two small bedrooms, and two new baths. Plenty of space Emma had thought when she agreed to move in. For Emma. For her four-year old grandson if he stayed overnight. For a long weekend visit from one of her San Francisco friends. Except now that Mary was gone, her best friend wouldn't be visiting.

Emma pulled in front of the house and took out her keys, climbing three steps to the old fashioned wrap-around front porch. Then she let herself into the tiny front hall, tossing her bag onto one of the enormous easy chairs in the living room that she'd had specially covered in hand woven fabrics Mary bought from a coop in Mexico. Everything else in the house she'd brought from the San Francisco condo she sold. The handmade Moroccan rugs in natural-but-colorful colors. The wooden farmhouse dining table. The painted dressers. Julie called it her mother's hippy look; but Emma thought that really wasn't fair.

She sighed as she climbed the stairs to her second floor bedroom. Much as she loved her new home, she was Julie and Piers' tenant now. Never in her wildest dreams had Emma ever thought it would come to that. She was proud of being independent all those years, raising Julie as a single working mom.

But now she was successful, she reminded herself. And happy, right? The yellow farmhouse was one of the oldest buildings in Blissburg, having once belonged to a legendary Wild West mountain man. All of which appealed to Emma. To her love of California, her love of history. Making her feel unique despite her just-like-any-other-divorced-single-mother-trying-to-get-by life story.

Upstairs in her bedroom, Emma eyed the second hand designer skirt that Julie had nixed the day before as too flowery for a City Opera fundraiser. It was vintage Ungaro, for heaven's sake. How, Emma wondered, had she raised a daughter whose closet had the color palate of a UPS store?

"Neutral. When in doubt, go neutral," was Julie's advice. Everything Julie owned was gray, putty or black. Like the woman Emma hated in that TV show, *House of Cards*.

Emma pulled out her black wool slacks and glanced longingly at the thrift store Missoni sweater in orange, purple, black and gold. That definitely would not pass the Julie fashion police. Instead, dropping her sweat pants and T onto the floor, she chose a beige silk pullover that Julie and Piers had given her for Christmas the year before. Surely the fashion police would not complain about that. Then she grabbed the ancient Hermes scarf that Andy, Julie's father, gave her for their third anniversary. It had come as a romantic surprise. Now she smiled when she remembered wearing it, and nothing else, to bed the night he gave it to her.

It was only later that she recognized the guilt gift for what it was. But that was water long under the bridge. Or was it tears? Where had all those tears gone, anyway, Emma asked herself? She was so much happier now without him. Why hadn't she just collected all those tears in vats to water the roses? At least they'd have gone to good use.

Once dressed, Emma looked at herself in the full-length bathroom mirror. Lately, she found herself avoiding mirrors. That evening, she was pleasantly surprised.

Those big Hermes scarves really didn't go out of style, she noted. Nor did the Tods pumps, thank goodness. They'd cost a fortune, even on sale, but boy were they comfortable if you had a bunion. Since she'd cut her gray hair short, she had no worries in the coiffure department. Her hair always looked the same. She dug an old cosmetic case out of a drawer under the bathroom sink and dabbed on some mascara and eye shadow to highlight her pale blue eyes.

She examined the full effect for a few seconds. Jewelry. She realized that with the opera crowd she needed to wear jewelry. Her plain gold button earrings would do. The ones she bought on the Ponte Vecchio in Florence on the Italy vacation she took to research the cookbook. And the big apple green jade graduation gift ring, from one of her father's Chinese immigrant clients, was perfect. She rarely had the occasion to wear it. ("Wouldn't it make more sense to charge them a reasonable fee, dear, so they could skip the gifts?" her mother had asked when the ring arrived. Her father had hated to charge his trouble-ridden clients.)

The ring matched the scarf perfectly. For the first time in months, Emma stopped to study herself critically in the mirror. To her surprise, she looked fine. Maybe Julie was right. At her age, simple was better. As for her identity? She shrugged. If she didn't have one by now, she figured she never would.

2
____

FRIDAY NIGHT – DINING WITH THE STARS

Cocktails for Opera in the Vineyard began promptly at 6:30. Emma arrived five minutes early and stationed herself at her post behind a copy of her book.

In fact, Emma was not a natural when it came to cocktail parties – a trait her ex husband had rarely failed to point out during their marriage. Small talk eluded her. She wanted sagas, life stories. And who in the noise and crush of a cocktail party had time for that?

Of course, she had learned years ago to answer "great" to the question "How are you?" And "fabulous" to all queries about her daughter. But really, what was the point of saying "great" when you weren't? Except that no one but your best friends really wanted to hear about it. Now, it seemed things really were great, except for the Big D, and who wanted to talk about that? In fact, Emma suspected that one of the reasons cocktail parties were popular was so older people like her could forget about the Big D for a while.

Seconds after she arrived at her post, Piers stopped by to give her a hug. Underneath all his bravado and bluster he really was the perfect son-in-law. He was six feet tall, impeccably dressed, with a face, though Julie denied it, vaguely reminiscent of Leonardo di Caprio. What was not to like?

Sure, he was a spoiled only child who liked to be waited on hand and foot. And sure, he had a quick bratty temper when he didn't get his way. But Julie managed to handle that. Particularly when, as the only son of a Midwestern grocery chain multi-millionaire, he had an impressive trust fund in addition to his own highly successful law practice. He worked hard. He could afford to be waited on hand and foot. And not by Julie.

Shortly after Piers, Julie stopped by to thank Emma for lining up Carmen. "Lexie Buchanon is thrilled. Good going, Mom. And by the way, you look great tonight. Piers said he didn't recognize you when you walked in."

Next Puss Carleton, a transplanted Bostonian who owned the chicest of the thirty odd antique stores in Blissburg, sauntered up to the silent auction table and began to leaf through *Dining with the Stars*. Julie was one of Puss in Boots' best customers; Emma often accompanied her daughter on her trips to Puss in Boots in search of the perfect two hundred year old Provencal country farmhouse kitchen table, or the not too ornate American Chippendale dining room chairs. Julie was a wonk when it came to antiques. And Emma often stood in line with Puss at Little Pete's gourmet grocery where Puss never recognized her. Now, leafing through the cookbook, Puss noticed the photo of Emma on the back cover leaf and glanced at Emma seated behind the table.

"You work for Julie Larkin, don't you? You're her secretary, right?" Puss asked.

Emma felt her chest constrict. Since moving to Blissburg, she admitted that, despite her success with the cookbook, she spent way too much time tagging along with her busy daughter. Or helping out with her grandson, Harry.

"No," she finally replied. Then added with a smirk, "I'm the au pair."

"Au pair," Puss thought for a moment. "My daughter in Boston has been looking all over for someone just like you. Older, responsible, someone she doesn't have to care for like a third child. What agency are you with?"

Emma paused for a moment. "Catholic Charities." With any luck that would be way off Puss's map.

Puss grimaced. Then she looked down her upturned WASP nose and asked, "Do you have to be Catholic? I mean to use the service?"

"I'm afraid so," Emma nodded, looking appropriately apologetic.

"Too bad," Puss sucked in her bottom lip.

"I know," Emma agreed.

Puss was still holding the copy of the cookbook she'd picked up. "You must be quite a cook. Lucky Larkin family. *Dining with the Stars*," she repeated the title out loud. "Whatever gave you the idea to write this?" she asked.

"Actually," Emma began, "my grandmother was an opera singer who came to San Francisco from Bologna at the turn of the century to perform with the Opera. There was almost no northern Italian cooking in San Francisco at the time, just southern red sauce joints. She was such a good cook that when she stopped singing, she opened a restaurant that was mostly patronized by the opera stars when they came to town. You know, Gigli, Pinza, Chaliapin. And composers like..."

Too late Emma realized that she'd lost Puss Carleton to their hostess, Mrs. Lexie Buchanon, who was walking by.

When Emma abruptly stopped talking Puss called over her shoulder, "Love your vintage Hermes."

"TMI" Emma muttered under her breath, vowing to stick to yes, no, great and fabulous from then on. She quickly changed her plan when she realized that Mrs. Lexie Buchanon, all 98 pounds of trapped energy and raked blond hair, was making a bee line past Puss to her table.

"Hi, I'm Lexie Buchanon," she introduced herself. "And you're Julie's mom." She stared at the cookbook sitting in front of Emma on the silent auction table. "So that's your yummy spaghetti sauce Sergio serves at his restaurant."

Emma nodded.

"Wow." She grabbed the electronic bidding device by Emma's cookbook. "Let's get this silent auction started. What's the minimum?"

"$1000," Emma blushed. It was an absurd amount for dinner for six people cooked by an amateur. "But I don't think…"

"Nonsense," Lexie interrupted. "I'll start it at $3000." She hit the enter button. "That sauce of yours is worth its weight in gold! By the way, the gypsy Julie hired? I haven't met her but one of my friends who just had her cards done says she's fabulous."

"I'm so glad," Emma replied.

"Vera Vasiliev at the Honorage Spa suggested the idea to me a couple of days ago," Lexie explained. "You know, because of that gypsy in the opera. Anyway, Vera knows a lot about opera 'cause her twin sister is Natasha Vasiliev. That soprano everyone thinks is sooo gorgeous."

Lexie wrinkled her nose when she spoke, implying that she did not agree.

"My husband, Barry, salivates every time he sees her," she continued with a shrug. "Personally, I think she looks unhealthy, don't you? Kind of like a sack of flour with buck teeth. But you know as well as I do. Whatever it takes to get men to the opera. Anyway, thanks to you we got Carmen." The young woman rolled her eyes and smirked. "Is that really her name?" Then she added, "My friend said that Carmen told her everything about herself, past, present and future. Things not even her best friends knew. After that, about ten people took Carmen's card. I'd have had her read mine. Except I know too many people here. It would be uncomfortable, if you know what I mean."

While Lexie spoke, Emma caught sight of a short, thin, dark skinned woman circulating among the guests gathered in the garden where the silent auction was in progress. It was Carmen. She was dressed in a long black skirt and white peasant blouse with a multi-colored shawl. Her long black hair was combed back into a tight bun secured at the nape of her neck by a large tortoise shell comb. She held a basket decorated with red and green silk ribbons in one hand. With the other she waved to Emma who waved back. Then Emma motioned to Carmen to meet Mrs. Buchanon.

"Mrs. Buchanon," Emma began.

"It's Lexie, please," the young woman smiled.

"I want you to meet Carmen. Carmen, Mrs. Buchanon. I mean Lexie," Emma corrected herself. "Lexie heard you did a fabulous job reading cards just now for one of her friends."

As they spoke, a young woman approached them holding a small plate.

"A Beluga blini from Barry. They're yummy," the woman added handing the plate to Lexie."

Lexie took the plate. "Beluga. My favorite."

Lexie then introduced the young woman to Carmen and Emma. It was Vera Vasiliev, a masseuse at the nearby Honorage Spa. The same spa where, according to all the gossip, Lexie was employed when she met Barry Buchanon.

"Vera suggested the fortune teller," Lexie explained to Carmen. "She's Natasha Vasiliev's twin sister. But of course, you already knew that. You're a psychic," she laughed. "And I guess you already know that Natasha Vasiliev is singing *Trattoria* on Opening Night."

"*Trovatore*," Vera corrected her. "The opera about the gypsy who tries to avenge her mother's murder by kidnapping the Count's infant son and throwing him into her mother's funeral pyre. Except that in her excitement she throws her own infant son into the fire instead." Vera sighed dramatically and shook her head, visibly moved. "Such a tragedy!"

Carmen grimaced. "What happens to the gypsy?"

"She raises the noble infant as her own son," Vera replied. "He becomes the troubadour, translated into Italian as *Il Trovatore* – the title of the opera. Later, the troubadour and his real brother vie for the love of the same woman, Leonora. Of course, they don't know they are brothers." The young woman's face grew sad. "Naturally, the two real lovers, Leonora and the troubadour, die in the end."

At that, everyone listening nodded gravely. It was Grand Opera, after all.

Vera's face suddenly brightened and she continued. "It's Natasha's debut with City Opera as Leonora. She's been rehearsing for months." She leaned forward as though to impart a secret. "Massimo, the conductor, has her sing that difficult garden aria lying on her back. That will be a first," she laughed. "Or will it? Anyway, Natasha's singing the aria tonight, right after dinner. Standing up, of course."

At that very moment, Natasha Vasiliev, herself, appeared along with Chiara Bruno, her understudy for the lead role of Leonora. The dazzling blond Natasha had dished herself up lavishly that night in a tight green silk tube dress that matched her eyes and fit her curves like the sheath of a scimitar. The dress's neckline, held at the shoulders by two brilliant diamond clasps, plunged in a generous V all the way to her navel, exposing the two half moons of her breasts.

"Did I hear someone say Beluga?" Natasha licked her full glossy lips.

She and her twin sister, Vera, exchanged a warm hug.

There was no doubt Natasha and Vera were twins, Emma noted. Both possessed regal posture and voluptuous figures. Both were green-eyed blonds. But somewhere the resemblance cruelly disintegrated. Where Natasha had the fragile beauty of a fawn, Vera's only slightly thicker features reminded one more of a dray horse. Her neck was just enough thicker and her long nose cascaded just too far over her perpetually downturned mouth for her ever to be considered beautiful. And to think, Emma observed, Natasha got the voice of an angel as well. Sometimes life really wasn't fair.

Natasha turned to Chiara, "I don't know why I always get the flutters before these donor concerts. I never get them on stage."

As if on cue, the famous Russian bass, Alexis Kuragin, joined them. He carried a bottle of vodka in each fist. He was scheduled to sing during dinner, so Emma was surprised to note that he was already roaring drunk. He elbowed his way next to Natasha, emptying the last of one of the bottles of vodka into Natasha's sparkling water, and bumping Lexie who spilled her glass of red wine all over her dress.

"Russian courage for my little Russian song bird," the famous singer winked, unaware of the mess he had made.

Lexie dropped her plate of caviar blinis and the gorgeous clutch she was carrying onto a nearby table, and grabbed a cocktail napkin to wipe off her dress. Emma noted that Lexie's clutch was made of vivid burgundy leather encrusted with multi-colored jewels. The perfect complement to her elegant, if skimpy, mother of pearl silk dress. The ex-masseuse had certainly acquired exquisite taste, Emma noted.

Lexie glared at the bass singer. "I'll never get these stains out!" When she leaned over to grab her purse off the table, she whispered in Emma's ear, "Russian boors!" Then she stormed off in the direction of the house.

The Russian bass was too engrossed in Natasha to notice. "I know you get nervous singing for donors, Natasha. At least you don't have to sing this one on your back!" he said.

Natasha covered her mouth with her hand and gasped. "Shame on you!"

Chiara giggled. "He's right. It's hard singing lying down. I'm just hoping you don't get sick. I'm not sure I could do it."

The bass singer laughed. "Why Chiara, you'd kill for that job. Bottoms up, as they say," he added sloshing a finger of vodka from the second bottle into Chiara's glass before weaving unsteadily through the crowd filling glasses and knocking over chairs as he passed.

Natasha and Vera exchanged worried glances. Then Natasha hurriedly emptied her glass before asking her sister to bring her some water.

Emma looked around for more Beluga caviar. But as far as she could tell, the Russians had scarfed it all up. The only waiters she saw carried water chestnuts wrapped in bacon. The plate Lexie left was empty.

Emma turned her attention back to the soprano and her understudy, who vied to see whose cards Carmen would read first.

"Natasha, you go," Chiara insisted.

"No, you." Natasha waved her hand theatrically at Chiara. Emma couldn't help noticing the ring on Natasha's finger. The emerald, the size of a robin's egg, was exactly the color of Natasha's eyes. It was set in a nest of pave diamonds.

Chiara relented. She turned to Carmen, took a deep breath and closed her eyes. "OK. This better be good!"

Emma watched to see what Carmen would do.

First she took Chiara's hand for a moment and held it with her eyes closed. Then she began arranging the cards on the nearby auction table.

When she had laid them out to her satisfaction, she started to read.

"See this card," she said, pointing to a card bearing the picture of a sun. "It stands for growth. For you, it means your hard work will pay off. I see a big opportunity in your future. A big, how do you say, break. And this card means there is a mentor somewhere who will help you. But this," she pointed to a card with the image of a falling tower. "This means you will lose something that you are afraid to lose." She pointed to a fourth card. "But, strangely, you won't mind."

Natasha erupted in hoots of laughter. "You are going to sing at Carnegie Hall. I'm sure of it," she cried. "I'm so excited for you,

Chiara. Your debut will be a huge success, just like mine. Carnegie Hall was the best night of my life."

Chiara became excited as well. Her cheeks flushed a ravishing red that lit up her olive complexion and made her black eyes sparkle. Then she hugged her slightly overweight self. "Maybe what I'll lose is some weight," she giggled. "But I'm always afraid I'll lose my voice along with it, like they say Maria Callas did when she lost all that weight."

Chiara motioned to Natasha to go next. "I want to know about your secret admirer, Natasha. The one who sends you roses every night."

Natasha turned to Emma and Carmen, "Who says it's an admirer, not admirers?"

Carmen, in the meantime, began shuffling the deck. Once. Twice. Three times. Then she dealt the cards and took Natasha's hand. That's when all the color drained from her face.

"What is it?" Emma asked. She had been watching Carmen's performance with interest.

Carmen's whole frame seemed to shudder. Her forehead broke out in a sweat. "All good. All good. But I'm afraid I'm feeling faint," she said, setting her basket down on the table so she could fan her face with her hands. "Don't mind me. It happens often. I just need some air." They were standing outside. "I mean I need some water."

Emma caught Carmen by the elbow. "I'll get you some," she said.

"No, never mind. I'll get it myself. Besides," she looked at her watch, "it's almost 8:00. Dinner will be starting. I gotta go."

Carmen practically ran back towards the house. But Emma noticed that she did not stop at the table where white coated bartenders served San Pellegrino on ice. Instead, she slipped into the crowd of partygoers and disappeared from their view.

"What was that all about?" Natasha shrugged. "I hope she's all right."

Emma shook her head. "I'm sure she's fine." But in fact Emma wasn't sure.

A few minutes later, when the time for the silent auction bidding ended, Barry Buchanon picked up a microphone and announced that dinner was served.

Emma checked to see who had won her catered dinner. To her surprise, someone named Jack Russo had actually paid $5000 for it. Poor guy, Emma thought to herself, making her way to the table her daughter had assigned her to for dinner.

The sit down dinner for the fundraiser was served in the middle of a meadow between the Buchanons' main house and the Buchanons' vineyards. The meadow was nestled under an overhang of enormous flood lit ancient oak trees providing a canopy for thirty picnic tables covered in white linen and strewn with white roses. Leave it to Julie, Emma thought. The perfect spot.

Emma found her seat at the table, locating her name on a hand painted place card created by a local artist in keeping with the fundraiser's *Trovatore* theme. She glanced at the name printed on the card to her left. To her extreme annoyance she saw that it was Andy Bodreau, her ex husband! What on earth was he doing there, she wondered? At a $500 a plate fundraiser? She, at least, had donated services for her ticket. What could Andy do? Besides, she asked herself, wasn't he under house arrest?

At that moment Emma saw Julie running towards her across the lawn.

"Mom," Julie whispered grabbing the back of Emma's chair to catch her breath. "I forgot to tell you something. There was too much going on with the Russians wanting more vodka, and the microphone not working, and the florist arriving late. It's been a madhouse. So, please forgive me. I just plain forgot. It's Dad. He's coming. I had to put him at your table. There was nowhere else I could squeeze him in. Please, please don't be upset."

Upset? Emma thought. Why should she be upset? Andy Bodreau

was only the man who left her with a small child named Julie to run off with one of the secretaries at his law firm. Emma later learned he'd been bonking every secretary in sight before quitting the firm and going solo so he conveniently had no money to pay alimony. Most recently, he'd been disbarred and then convicted of misappropriating hundreds of thousands of dollars in connection with a joint real estate venture with one of his clients. Emma wasn't surprised. Andy had never been well organized.

Andy, of course, claimed that he was framed. By the client. So, according to Andy, everyone should feel sorry for him. That was her ex-husband, Andy Bodreau. So why on earth should she be upset about sitting next to him at a dinner party?

Julie caught the look on her mother's face. "You're the one who married him, Mom."

Emma sighed. Julie's was right. It wasn't her daughter's fault that Andy Bodreau was her father.

"He was cute, smart and fun in bed," she replied. "I was twenty. How was I to know that wasn't enough for a lifetime?"

Julie covered her ears with her hands. "TMI, Mom. Way TMI."

"Besides, how can he come?" Emma added. "I thought he was under house arrest."

"That's just it," Julie pleaded. "He *is* under house arrest, but he has one of those ankle thingies, like in *The Wolf of Wall Street*, and he can go out for a few hours now and then. So he said he'd heard about the party from Piers and he wanted to come. It's like his way to celebrate getting out of the house. And he adores Natasha Vasiliev. He claims that listening to her CDs saves his life when he's cooped up in his apartment."

Emma rolled her eyes. This was the man she introduced to opera. It was embarrassing. With a father like that, no wonder Julie turned out to be little-miss-perfect-with-an-iron-rod-jammed-up-her-back. At least for her sake, thanks to *The Wolf of Wall Street*, ankle thingies were now trendy.

"Mom, you know how Dad guilt trips me."

Emma nodded. "I know. And I know how you always cave. Don't worry. I'll be nice. No scenes."

"And nothing about the money he owes you. Not tonight."

"Not tonight, honey," Emma replied. "By the way, how is he paying for his ticket?"

"He offered to help you with the dinner you donated. The heavy lifting. All the stuff you complained you were too old to do. I thought you'd be happy."

Just then, Emma felt a hand on her shoulder and a dry kiss on her cheek. "Well, hello there," Andy greeted her in his jaunty voice, taking his seat next to hers. "My, don't you look pretty tonight, Emma. And the cookbook. I saw it on the auction table. I remember when your Mom used to make Nonnie's delicious recipes. The veal with prosciutto. The roast pork. I haven't tasted that stuff in years. When do I get my autographed copy of the book?"

"You can order one on line," Emma answered.

Then she saw the look on Julie's face and quickly revised her reply. "Just kidding. I'll send you one. You're looking good yourself," she added on a friendlier note.

Indeed, Emma thought, he looked remarkably good for someone under house arrest. He was tan. He'd lost weight. He had a great haircut and he wore a suit that fit. Had she just been convicted of a federal crime, she'd look like a cadaver. Having stabbed herself in the heart like Madam Butterfly.

"Thank you," he grinned, for a second recapturing the young Paul Newman good looks that she had once found so attractive. "And look at our daughter. My! Isn't she beautiful?"

Just then, the waiter served the first course, plates of steaming fresh *tagliatelle* covered in Emma's sauce.

Andy put a forkful in his mouth. "Oh my gosh. It's Nonnie's famous *salsa di pomodoro*. I haven't tasted this in years."

"Excuse me," a voice to Emma's left interrupted. "Are you the cookbook lady – Emma Corsi?"

Emma turned to look at the man who had taken the other seat next to hers. With his full head of graying hair, prominent Roman nose, dark eyes and swarthy complexion, he reminded her of someone out of Goodfellas.

"Yes," Emma replied.

Suddenly Andy reached his hand across Emma's plate to shake Mr. Goodfella's hand. "Hi. I'm Andy."

"Jack Russo," the man introduced himself. "Nice to meet you."

Emma froze. It was the man who'd just paid $5000 for her dinner.

"I've heard of you," Andy replied. "You're a VC, right? JJR Cap. Your company was involved in getting Groboticks off the ground. Complicated stuff."

Jack shrugged. "Yeah." His voice was deep and gruff. "I like complicated." Then he turned back to Emma. "Forgive me. I saw a copy of your cookbook over on the auction table. The recipes all looked so good, I bid on that dinner you donated."

"And won," Emma winced, wracking her brain to define VC. All she could think of was Viet Cong, but she knew that wasn't right.

Jack nodded. "We'll need to talk about that." His eyes shifted from Emma to Andy, "Tell me something. From the book flap, I assumed you were single, but from the way you two are," he feinted left and right like a boxer, "I figure you two must be married, right? Partners?" He grinned. "Or else he's your brother."

"He's not my brother, he's my former husband," Emma replied; but before either of them could say more, Barry Buchanon picked up the microphone to announce the evening's entertainment.

The first person he introduced was Natasha Vasiliev, the world renowned Russian soprano who would sing the famous first act aria from the City Opera season opener, Verdi's *Il Trovatore*. Emma couldn't help noticing the predatory once-over Barry gave the star when he handed her the mic. Like a lion appraising an antelope grazing too far from the pack.

Natasha took the mic and walked to the center of the stage. Emma perceived a sudden stillness as hundreds of males stopped breathing. On the dais, Emma noticed that the young diva looked two, three times her actual size. Then she began to sing, and the voice of an angel erupted from the goddess' form.

Emma, along with most of the audience, didn't understand a word of the aria. But she knew it was about love and longing. There was a moment of silence when the young women stopped singing. Then men everywhere jumped to their feet in an explosion of applause.

"What a voice," Jack whispered.

"What a chest," Andy said.

Natasha exited the stage to a warm embrace by Barry Buchanon. But the exquisite performance had clearly exhausted the artist. By the time her feet touched ground, Emma noticed she looked flushed and pale.

Barry next introduced Chiara Bruno.

"Chiara Bruno," Jack leaned over to murmur in Emma's ear. "Light Dark. That's a funny name."

"You speak Italian?" Emma asked. "I tried to learn a little to research my cookbook."

"Trying to learn. I hired a tutor," Jack replied. "He's terrific. I'll give you his number..."

The music started, interrupting him.

Chiara, too, looked bigger on stage. Though the change was not as dramatic as it was with Natasha. She sang *O Mio Babbino Caro* by Puccini, a perennial crowd pleaser in which an ingénue daughter pleads with her father to let her marry a disfavored suitor. It was a charming vehicle to show off Ms. Bruno's considerable acting skills as she pouted her full red lips and batted her eyes to the delight of every father in the audience.

The only jarring moment in the flawless performance was when a beeper went off, seemingly from somewhere right under Emma's feet, causing Chiara, momentarily, to break character in consternation.

Forty pairs of accusing eyes turned on Emma from nearby tables. Then Andy abruptly stood up to leave.

"It's this infernal beeper," he whispered to the table. "I can't turn it off. There must be something wrong with the timer. I was sure I had another twenty minutes."

Emma rolled her eyes. As if it were the ankle thingie's fault!

Andy checked his watch. "Nope. I was wrong. I gotta scoot." But he took the time to wave jauntily at Julie as he wormed his way between the tables.

By then, the aria was over. There was another big round of applause.

"So, your ex is what? A doctor? On call or something?" Jack asked above the noise of the crowd.

"He was a lawyer," Emma answered. "And yes, he's on call." Then so as to avoid further conversation on that topic, she added. "So, are you really an opera lover, Jack?"

"What?" he squinted his eyes at her mistrustfully. "I don't look like an opera lover? Too what? Too blue collar for the Opera House?"

"No," Emma protested, embarrassed by her *faux pas*. Though, in fact, she thought he did look a little too rough around the edges for an opera lover. "Not at all. I take it from your name that you are of Italian descent. Opera takes you back to your roots, I guess," Emma replied.

"Sicilian," Jack made the distinction. "No opera in my roots. But my daughter took me to one of those Opera in the Ballpark benefits in San Francisco, and ya know what? I loved it!"

Before Emma could respond, Barry introduced the final singer.

Jack put his finger to his lips and winked.

"Our final number tonight," Barry announced, "is the devil's song from Gounod's Faust, sung by the devil himself, Alexis Kuragin."

Something in Barry's joke made Emma think there was no love lost between the two men. In a way, Emma could see why. Alexis Kuragin was a good twenty years younger than Barry. His full mane of blond hair provided a striking contrast to Barry's thinning white tonsure. According to Julie, Kuragin was a lady killer.

Well, at least he sang like one. And from the looks on the ladies' faces in the audience, most of them were ready to follow him all the way to hell. To Emma's surprise, despite the vodka, he sang flawlessly, tripping only slightly as he stepped down from the dais to a big round of applause.

By then the *tagliatelle alla salsa di pomodoro* had been cleared. Emma watched Kuragin take his seat beside Natasha at the Russian table in front of a plate of Sergio's signature *saltimbocca* (veal scallops literally translated as jumping into your mouth). But Kuragin, who had grabbed a glass of vodka as he left the stage, didn't look pleased. He scowled at the veal before whispering something in Natasha's ear.

"Bad boy, Sacha," Emma heard Natasha reply.

"More vodka," Kuragin called to a passing waiter. "More vodka if you want me to eat this Italian slop and sing this French drivel."

Emma saw Natasha press her hand to her forehead and cast a pleading eye at a young Russian seated across the table. He picked up on her distress. "No more vodka. No more vodka for Sacha," he shouted to the waiter.

The next thing Emma knew, Sacha threw his empty glass at the shouting Russian. It shattered against his wooden chair. The shouter tossed his plate of veal across the table at Kuragin like a Frisbee.

Before anyone could stop them, the Russians were hurtling glasses, bread sticks and little veal rollups, shouting, "No more Italian slop! Where's the caviar?"

That's when Sacha turned to Natasha and forced a sloppy stage kiss on her lips. Then, with a dramatic cackle worthy of the devil, he rolled an olive down the mostly missing front of the soprano's dress and chased it with his tongue.

Well, apparently that was too much for Barry Buchanon. Emma watched him storm out of his seat below the dais and make his way to the Russian table. When he got to Sacha, he grabbed a big clump of his blond hair and yanked his face off Natasha's chest. "Get off of her, you pig," he shouted.

Emma saw Natasha grab the bass singer's arm before he could throw a punch. Then a dozen men from nearby tables intervened obscuring her view.

At that point many of the guests started to leave their seats and head for the parking lot, even though it was barely 9:00 and the waiters hadn't served dessert.

Emma wasn't sure what happened next, but a few minutes later when she looked at the Russian table again, Barry was gone, Natasha's seat was empty and Vera, her sister, sat next to Sacha trying, in Russian, to talk him down.

"Which opera was that scene from?" Jack leaned over to ask.

"One I've never seen," Emma replied, too preoccupied with the embarrassment this fiasco would cause her daughter to think of a witty reply.

Jack stood up. "I'm outta here. Do you need a ride somewhere?"

Emma shook her head. "It's OK. I have my car."

"You want me to walk you to the parking lot? It's kinda dark out there," he added.

Emma shrugged. "No. I should stay here in case my daughter needs moral support. She's the PR person for this mess."

Jack nodded. He started to walk away from the table, then stopped and turned back. "About that dinner I bid on...," he hesitated. "Should I call you to discuss it? I think your number's on my receipt."

"Sure," Emma answered, only half listening. "Whenever," she

added over her shoulder as he turned around and headed for the parking lot. She was too preoccupied now with all the damage to Julie's perfect party, to worry about her dinner donation.

On their way to their cars, a few people stopped to complement Emma on her sauce; but under the circumstances, she wasn't sure the publicity that night would do her any good. The fundraiser was a shambles. She sat at her empty table, watched the wait staff clear the tables of broken dishes, splintered glass and untouched desserts, and wondered how the press would deal with the disaster.

She'd fretted for almost an hour about how to help Julie with damage control when Vera Vasiliev unexpectedly grabbed the mic and made her way to the stage.

"Natasha!" she called. "Has anybody seen my sister, Natasha? I think she's missing."

At the sound of her voice, the few remaining guests and cleanup crew stopped what they were doing and looked around.

"Natasha? Are you out there?" Vera shouted into the darkness surrounding the dimly lit meadow.

Nobody answered.

"Has anyone seen my sister, Natasha?" Vera repeated. Now her voice sounded worried.

It was Barry Buchanon who organized a party to look for the missing soprano. It was Barry who led the search. It was also Barry who found the body. And Barry whose screams everyone heard pierce the darkness that fateful night.

"Oh my god! Oh my god! Natasha. My darling Natasha!" Each cry was punctuated by a heart-wrenching sob. It was Barry who carried the body back to the meadow and laid it on the stage where it now looked small and lifeless as a doll. It was Barry who uttered the words that Emma would never forget.

"It's over. She's dead. My darling songbird is dead!"

3

FRIDAY LATE NIGHT – QUESTIONS

The police and an ambulance arrived twenty minutes later, their sirens shattering the midnight silence surrounding the vineyard. Two lieutenants led the investigation, Lieutenant O'Hara and Lieutenant Bates. O'Hara's first order was that no one leave the meadow until everyone had been questioned and the police had IDed them and obtained their contact information.

After an hour of questioning, it appeared that the last person to see Natasha alive was a waiter who had gone out to the vineyard to look at the moon. His English was poor, but it sounded like he saw someone he thought might have been the singer stumbling through the vineyard about an hour before Vera raised the alarm. He thought she was drunk. She entered the vineyard from the direction of the women's port-a-potty. Later, when he went out for a smoke, he saw someone wearing a long dark skirt leave the garden where the auction was held. He didn't get a good enough look at that person to identify her.

Prior to that, a female guest said she thought she saw Natasha leaving the port-a-potties; but she only saw the woman from behind, and in the dark could not be absolutely sure.

Emma observed the officer's questioning carefully in the hope of gleaning something helpful for Julie. It was Barry Buchanon's story that caught her attention. She was grateful her hearing was still good. The officers had cleared a space around the witnesses. Apparently they didn't realize the faceless senior, seated at a table on the perimeter of the meadow staring into the darkness, could hear everything that was said.

"Where was the body when you found it, Mr. Buchanon?" Lieutenant O'Hara asked.

Emma noted that, unlike the Mexican waiter, Barry Buchanon was handled by the police with kid gloves.

"At the north edge of the vineyard, under an olive...," was all Barry could get out before breaking down in sobs.

"What was the position of the body, Mr. Buchanon?" Lieutenant Bates added.

"Face down. That beautiful face in the dirt. Her arms splayed out on either side." Barry broke down again.

"Was there any sign of violence, a struggle? Anything at all that you noticed?" O'Hara asked.

"Well," Barry hesitated, "not violence. She'd thrown up a little. And it was on her face. That gorgeous face."

Officer Bates gestured towards the corpse that the medical examiner's team was preparing to load onto a gurney. "There was no sign of vomit on the victim's face when you laid her on the stage, was there?"

"Oh," Barry dismissed the officer's statement. "Of course, I cleaned it off. I had my napkin still in my hand. So I wiped her face. She wouldn't have wanted people to see her like that, poor darling. I wiped that beautiful face and wiped up some of the vomit that was on the ground. Thank goodness nothing got on her dress. She'd have hated that."

"And what did you do with the napkin sir? Can you show it to us?" Bates asked.

Barry shrugged. He looked dazed. "Oh that. No. I rinsed it in the irrigation ditch when I was done. Before I picked up her body. As a sign of respect. You know. Then I threw the napkin back in the water."

He looked at the officers, imploringly. "You won't say anything about the vomit, will you? It just sounds so...so vulgar, demeaning. Like poor Mamma Cass choking on a ham sandwich. Or Lenny Bruce dying on the can. Who needs to know? It's embarrassing. Who wants to remember someone that way? Especially Natasha. She was an angel. That's how her fans should remember her. Pure as an angel." He looked at the policemen. "You won't mention the vomit. You promise me. You *must* promise me."

When the officers didn't answer, he continued in an angry voice. "I should have known not to tell you. It was so little anyway. Natasha ate like a bird. It was red. The vomit was red. You know. From that sauce. That garlicky red sauce on the spaghetti. Why did Sergio serve that anyway? Wouldn't a salad have been better? I guess they thought they had to serve Italian food because of the opera. Now my little songbird is dead!" He broke down completely in uncontrollable sobs.

The speech sent tidal waves of panic through Emma's body. Had she heard that right? Was Barry Buchanon blaming Natasha Vasiliev's death on her *salsa di pomodoro*? In an instant Emma's world collapsed.

She couldn't dwell on her personal tragedy for long, however. Seconds later, Vera Vasiliev threw herself at the policemen screaming something about a ring. It was only when she calmed down a little that Emma understood what she was saying.

"Officer, I need to show you something. Before you put my sister's body away. Come here quickly." Vera grabbed Officer O'Hara's hand and dragged him to the gurney that the medical examiner's staff was wheeling towards a van.

"Look." She unceremoniously tore the cover off her sister's body. "The ring. Where's the ring?"

The medical examiner quickly stepped forward. "I'm sorry Miss?"

"Vasiliev," Vera answered. "I'm the twin sister. Natasha was wearing an emerald ring tonight that matched her eyes. It was here on this finger." She grabbed the dead woman's right hand and showed them the empty fourth finger. "Now the ring is gone."

"Look Ma'am," the medical examiner answered, glancing at his staff for corroboration. "When we first examined the body, there was no ring."

The staff members nodded. No one remembered a ring.

By then, Vera had attracted a small crowd of listeners, including Lexie Buchanon who materialized out of the shadows. She stood near Vera listening intently.

"I didn't see any ring on the body," Officer Bates concurred.

O'Hara nodded in agreement. "Will you describe it please?" he said.

"It was big, a big brilliant emerald, almost exactly the color of her – of our eyes. Four carats. The shape of a robin's egg. And it was set in what looked like a nest of pavé diamonds. It was one of a kind. Custom," Vera added.

"You mean like this?" Lexie Buchanon stepped forward, raising her right hand to display a sapphire ring, the huge stone roughly shaped like an egg sitting in a nest of pave diamonds. The sapphire blue appeared to match the blue of Lexie's eyes.

Vera stared at the ring. Surprise flickered for just a second in her eyes before she said calmly, "Yes, it looked like that. Only green. Natasha's had an emerald in it."

Emma watched Lexie direct a glance at her husband sharp as a dagger. He turned away.

"Ms. Vasiliev, are you sure your sister was wearing the ring tonight?" Bates asked.

"Yes. I am absolutely sure," Vera replied.

"Anyone else see the ring on the victim's finger tonight?"

A few people raised their hands.

Then Chiara Bruno stepped forward. "I definitely saw it," she stated. "I saw the ring on her finger when we were having our tarot cards read. Then I noticed it again when she sang her aria. She wore it on stage."

"Tarot cards?" O'Hara repeated. "You had tarot cards read tonight? Who read them? Was one of those gypsies here? We've had trouble..."

He stopped talking, seeming to think better about revealing too much.

SHORTLY AFTER VERA'S discovery of the missing ring, the questioning resumed in the Buchanon's kitchen. As Emma feared, based on Barry Buchanon's narrative, the police focused their attention on the red sauce.

After identifying himself as the chief caterer and owner of one of Blissburg's top restaurants, Sergio took the brunt of the interrogation. Unfortunately, neither of the officers seemed aware of Sergio's stellar reputation in culinary circles. They focused on the kitchen, eventually finding a large box of rat poison stuffed in a broom closet. "Use this a lot?" Bates asked Sergio.

"No," came his terse reply. "My kitchens are always *impeccabile*."

O'Hara shook his head. "What does that mean?"

"Clean*issimo*," Sergio explained.

"So nothing made you get out the rat poison tonight, right? You might as well tell us the truth. We'll check the box for fingerprints."

"Never touch the stuff. Never need to," Sergio explained. "Everything in my kitchen is pure, clean." He glanced pointedly at Emma, as if to say it was all her fault for dropping that spoon. "I have never had a sanitation violation in my life. You can check with the health department. Besides," he added. It was nothing more than Emma expected. "She made the pasta sauce, not me." He pointed to Emma.

"Did you use any rat poison tonight, Ms.?"

"Corsi," Emma answered. She was sweating bullets and she knew everyone saw them. "I didn't use any poison of any kind. Why would I?" she asked.

Out of the corner of her eye, she saw Julie standing at the back of the kitchen giving her the hatchet sign. Cut it.

What? Was she being too defensive?

"I was trying to sell my cookbook not sabotage it," Emma explained. "The recipe is in the book. Tomatoes, garlic, parsley, onion, butter and olive oil. No poison."

"But an extraordinary young woman is dead," Barry Buchanon shouted from the back of the room. "Dead after eating your sauce!"

4

SATURDAY EARLY MORNING – DOUBTS

After the policemen dismissed them, Julie and Piers walked Emma back to her car. Emma had hoped for support from her daughter and son-in-law after Barry Buchanon's shameful outburst. She got silence instead. Were they blaming her sauce for the disaster, too? She wondered but couldn't bring herself to ask.

Piers opened her car door for her. "Are you sure you're OK to drive home? We can drop you off and pick up your car here later. Come to think of it, Emma, why don't you just spend the night with us? I'm pretty creeped out by what happened."

Emma shook her head. "Don't worry. I'll be fine."

Julie was more practical. "Mom's right, Piers. Let's not exaggerate. I'm sure there's a good explanation for what happened to poor Natasha. Maybe she had an undetected heart defect. Maybe she fell and hit her head. Maybe she had an allergic reaction."

To my sauce, Emma felt like adding, but didn't.

"There is no reason, yet, to jump to creepy conclusions," Julie said.

"What about the ring?" Piers asked. "The stolen ring?"

"The ring is probably lying in vomit in the vineyard where she fell," Julie replied. "I bet it turns up tomorrow."

Emma marveled at Julie's ability to rationalize things. At least no one mentioned her tomato sauce. But as Julie and Piers walked away, deep in conversation with each other, Emma worried that they were thinking about it. Along with most of Blissburg.

Nonetheless, after checking the locks on the front and back doors, and locking all the windows, Emma put on her nightgown, went to bed, and quickly fell asleep. She was exhausted after the long day's work. But four hours later, in the middle of the night, she awoke to the full comprehension of all that was now at stake.

To begin with, one of the brightest rising stars in the world of opera was dead after eating her *salsa di pomodoro*. Forget book sales. Face it, Emma told herself, no matter what happened next, her career as a food writer was over.

And it struck her full force that *that* was the very least of what had happened that night. More importantly, that poor young woman was *dead*. Her twin had lost her sister. Perhaps, though no one spoke of it, somewhere in Russia a father and mother mourned the loss of their child. Undoubtedly, others had lost a lover. Fans had lost a diva. The world had lost a voice that uplifted the hearts of millions of people.

Was it possible, Emma wondered? Was there any way at all that she, Emma Corsi, had caused the woman's death? Was there something on the counter, something in the tomatoes? She knew she should have used canned, but her grandmother always said to use fresh if they were in season. Something in the olive oil? Something in the pan?

Unfortunately, in the middle of the night, at the very heart of her own inner darkness, Emma believed that maybe there was. That maybe she was responsible for the tragedy because she, like Icarus, had presumed to fly too high. What was she thinking writing a cookbook anyway? Puss Carleton was right. What was someone like *her* doing writing a cookbook like *that*?

Emma pulled the covers over her head and started to weep. And just when she thought she couldn't sink lower, another catastrophic thought entered her brain, and another. And finally a third. The worst one of all.

First of all, what about Julie? Would *her* business ever recover from such a fiasco? Buchanon Vineyards was her best customer. Forget that. What other winery in Sonoma County, in all of California for that matter, would hire Julie to do PR now?

Then the second thought hit her. What about Piers? Would *his* clients leave because his mother-in-law managed to ruin Buchanon Vineyards and send a promising young star to her grave? What would Julie's family live on if Piers' practice went belly up? Thank goodness for that trust fund, Emma thought.

That's when she realized that even the trust fund wasn't safe. What if Natasha's family sued her? Or someone else got sick and sued? Legal bills would eat up all her savings and perhaps even Piers' trust fund, too. Oh why, she wondered as the clock struck four, why had she ever presumed to write a cookbook?

Emma must have finally drifted back to sleep. When she woke up, the Blissburg sun was shining. She got up, put on her fleece muumuu, went downstairs and shuffled into the kitchen to make coffee. What happened to Natasha was terribly tragic, but by light of day, like Julie, Emma was sure there was a good explanation. One that had nothing whatever to do with her pasta sauce. One that wouldn't destroy her daughter and bankrupt her son-in-law.

Then she opened her front door to pick up the Blissburg Herald, and the two-inch headline brought her crashing back to earth.

"FAMED SOPRANO DIES AFTER DINING WITH THE STARS."

The article didn't even mention Emma's cookbook, but the allusion to its title in the headline was impossible for anyone to miss.

At lunchtime, Julie called to make sure her mother was all right. Emma, who'd gone back to bed, decided not to answer her cell phone. That only brought Julie knocking on her door. Julie's office, after all, was in Emma's front yard. She brought roast pork sandwiches with onion conserve from their favorite bakery, Claud's.

Julie took one look at her mother standing in her muumuu at the front door, and went on a rampage.

"Mom, you're not even dressed. You look defeated. Why aren't you doing something? You know perfectly well that nothing in your wonderful pasta sauce killed Natasha Vasiliev." She paused a moment for a reply. "Well, don't you?"

"Of course it didn't." Emma had been through it a thousand times in her head. "Everyone at the party ate the pasta and no one else got sick." She too paused a moment. "Did they?"

"Of course not, Mom. We all ate it. We're fine."

"So," Emma continued, motioning to Julie to follow her into the kitchen, "she must have died of natural causes. An undetected illness or allergy. Like you said last night."

"Yeah," Julie nodded, "except Piers called the coroner this morning. They know each other from the Chatham Club. Based on the preliminary results of the autopsy, it does *not* appear that Natasha died of a heart attack, or a blow to the head, or some weird allergy. The toxicology report will take about ten days. It probably won't be ready until next Tuesday. But as of now it looks like she died from some kind of poison."

They had sat down to eat on two kitchen stools, facing each other across the butcher-block counter of Emma's remodeled-to-look-like-an-old-farmhouse-kitchen.

"You mean...," Emma hesitated. "Let me get this right. You mean the coroner thinks she was murdered?"

Julie nodded. "Probably by someone at the party. The problem is, the coroner can't prove that for a couple of weeks. In the meantime every day that passes will give this town more time to mess with your story. People will joke about it. You're a sitting duck. 'Soprano Dies after Dining with the Stars.' Mom, it's just too good to pass up. I mean, I might have had fun with it myself. If I weren't your daughter. And in the meantime, because of you – and I don't mean that I think it's your fault, Mom – but because of you my customers are calling to cancel their accounts. Piers has already lost a client. Granted, it's a Buchanon relative who was at the fundraiser, but the valley is crawling with them."

"Piers has already lost a client?" Emma cringed.

"Yes! The media is having a field day. I hate to say this, but the embarrassment with Dad's arrest didn't begin to affect us this much. Some people even thought the arrest was kind of sexy."

"Julie," Emma was too angry to cry. "I can't believe you would dare to make that comparison. *I* am the victim here."

"Funny, that's just what Dad said."

Emma felt like someone had punched her in the stomach. She hugged herself like she was about to fly apart. Then she said. "OK. What exactly am I supposed to do about it?"

"Simple," Julie answered. "Find the killer."

"Find the killer? Me? You're joking," Emma scoffed.

"I'm dead serious, Mom. Piers and I are willing to jump in to help you. But you need to track down the murderer before that toxicology report comes out. Because by the time it does, your career, my career and Piers' will be down the tubes."

Emma took a deep breath. It was not the way she had envisioned beginning her so-called retirement. It seemed, however, that she had no choice. She rolled her eyes. "Right. I'll find the killer. How do we begin?"

To Emma's surprise, Julie and Piers had already thought this through.

"We make a list," Julie began. "A list of anyone we can think of who could be the murderer. Then we divide up the list and, one by one, we start checking them out."

"OK," Emma replied. "Who are your suspects? Off the top of my head I can think of two: Lexie Buchanon the jealous wife, and Chiara Bruno the understudy. Both of them had something to gain by Natasha's death. And if poison *was* the murder weapon, I'll bet a woman did it."

"Oh, come on Mom." It was Julie's turn to scoff. "That's sooo Italian of you. Anyway, of course we thought of Chiara. She had the most to gain from the death. She's the understudy. She just got her first big break. Singing opening night in *Trovatore*. But why Lexie Buchanon?"

"Because of the ring," Emma exclaimed. "Didn't you catch all that stuff about the ring?"

"No, I missed it. I could see Lexie was mad about something, but what?" Julie asked.

Emma explained. "When Vera described the supposedly custom emerald ring missing from Natasha's finger, Lexie raised her hand to show off the identical ring with a sapphire to match the color of *her* eyes. Who do you suppose gave it to her? Her husband, Barry, duh. So who must have given the same ring to Natasha? Lexie's husband, Barry! But that little four carat bauble isn't just a thank you for a great night at the Opera, honey. That is a thank you for singing naked on your back in someone's - Barry Buchanon's - bed!"

"Stop!!!" Julie cringed, covering her ears with her hands. "Stop it Mom. The visuals. I can't take it. Not out of your mouth. You have to stop talking like that!"

"Don't you see?"

"Mom! Again. Stop! I see. Lexie is definitely on the list. Her husband was probably cheating on her and she was jealous."

"So who did you come up with?" Emma asked.

"Well, based on what you just said, why not Barry Buchanon?" Julie replied.

"Barry? No way!!!" Emma shook her head. "He was heartbroken. Didn't you see him? Distraught. Sobbing. I don't think so."

Julie rolled her eyes. "Neither do the police. Did you see how careful they were with him? All the more reason he could have done it. He knows the police will stay off his back."

"But why?" Emma asked.

"Because Natasha must have had other lovers," Julie answered. "Like Sacha. He was all over her at the dinner table. So Barry was jealous and killed her. Who knows how? Maybe he did one of those Kevorkian injections. Something that looks like a heart attack. He's rich. He could get hold of anything. And then he cleaned up the evidence. You heard him say he wiped off Natasha's face and then rinsed his napkin before throwing it away. Afterwards, of course he was distraught. Who wouldn't be, killing your favorite songbird. Personally, I think Barry did it, but Piers won't agree."

"Who does Piers think did it?" Emma asked.

"Piers is putting his money on the gypsy, Mom."

"Roma."

"Right. The Roma," Julie corrected herself.

"Well, that's preposterous. And Piers is a bigot if he thinks so," Emma added. "The Roma are peaceful people who have been unfairly targeted due to prejudice and ignorance. Which are more or less the same thing, by the way."

"Mom, Piers is not a bigot. But he works in the justice system. And he happens to know that the Roma, as you call them, cause a lot of trouble in the vineyards. Camping out. Stealing stuff. Their dogs run wild and attack people."

"Hardly murder, Julie," Emma replied. "And besides, most of that stuff is never proved against them. It just sticks because people want it to. Roma are scapegoats, plain and simple. Always have been. Just read Sir Walter Scott."

Julie looked exasperated. "Forget Sir Whatever, Mom. And believe me, I don't want to know. The point is, the Roma don't play by our rules. OK? They never have. That's why people don't trust them. They have their own rules and we don't know what those rules are. Anyway, that's a good list of suspects for now. Unless you want to add anyone else."

Emma thought for a moment. "Yeah. Let's add the lady killer." Emma smiled at her pun but it whooshed right over Julie's head.

"Who?"

"Sacha, the bass. He has a temper. He was drunk. And from what I could see last night, he doesn't play by our rules either. He was pawing Natasha, and if he was jealous of Barry, which I think he was, there's no telling what he might do."

"OK," Julie agreed, "add Sacha, the Russian bass. *But* if it was poison, the killer had to premeditate the murder. Get the poison. Bring it to the dinner. And put it in the food. Unless there wasn't poison and someone bonked her on the head. But so far there was no sign of that."

"Don't forget that Kevorkian needle," Emma reminded her.

"Bear with me, Mom," Julie continued. "If it was poison, Sacha, the Russian bass, being drunk at the party doesn't really prove anything. But I agree. If he was jealous, he's still a suspect."

"Anyone else?" Emma asked.

"What about Vera? The twin," Julie suggested.

Emma sighed and shook her head. "She was so broken up. And what was her motive? Jealousy? I don't think so. She seemed genuinely proud of her sister. And what did she have to gain? From all accounts, Natasha was incredibly generous with her once she got famous. But sure. Add Vera Vasiliev to the list. With sisters, you never know."

Julie did a recap on her fingers: "Lexie Buchanon, the jealous wife; Barry Buchanon, the jealous husband; Chiara Bruno, the understudy; Carmen, the Roma; Sacha, the Russian bass; and Vera Vasiliev, the twin. That's six."

"What about Sergio, the celebrity chef?" Emma asked. She was still smarting from her treatment by him in the kitchen. "Maybe he has Mafia connections."

Julie waved her finger at her mother. "Wow. There's a surprise. Now look who's a bigot. Come on, Mom. Sergio's from Bologna. He may be a communist, but he's not *Sicilian*. He's not even southern Italian."

"So?"

"So, Sergio has no Mafia connections. He hates the Mafia and he's not involved in this. But OK, if you want him on the list, you can check him out along with Carmen and the Russian bass. However, don't expect Sergio to push your book anymore."

"Believe me," Emma answered. "I'm not expecting *anyone* even to *read* my book now."

5

———

SATURDAY AFTERNOON – SLEUTH

After lunch with Julie, Emma spent the rest of the day in bed not answering the phone. Granted, not many people called. Those who did were clearly off limits. Sergio called. Probably to tell her to pick up the twenty copies of her book that he'd been selling at his restaurant. He didn't say that in his message; but Emma guessed that was the point of his call.

The local gourmet grocery store's manager also called. Something about carrying too many frozen pasta sauces. Little Pete's needed to rethink stocking a new brand.

Then there were three messages from the Blissburg Herald and one from the Santa Rosa Messenger. Until she found Natasha's killer, she had nothing to say to *those* scandal mongers.

The truth is, she really didn't believe Natasha was murdered. Murders took place in the movies, mystery novels, and crime shows. Not in Blissburg. Not among *her* acquaintances. Not in *her* everyday life! And if there were a murderer in her midst, Emma Corsi would be the last person to find him, or her.

As Julie pointed out, however, murder was the only cause of Natasha's death that completely let Emma and her family off the hook. Even if Natasha did have a heart or allergy attack, people would still believe that, somehow, Emma's sauce triggered it.

It was that realization that finally got Emma out of bed. At 2:00 pm. She'd already blown off most of the Saturday free legal clinic that she volunteered for every other week. But it was open three more hours. If she pushed herself, she could get her hands on Carmen's file before the clinic closed, and begin to check out her first suspect.

Emma noticed there was one last unopened message on her phone. It turned out to be from Jack Russo, her other dinner partner and winner of her home cooked dinner for six.

"Ciao bella. OK to say that in Italian, right? No offense. Saw the headline in the Herald. Just calling to say that *I loved* your sauce. I'm alive and well. Had a great night's sleep. And bought a copy of your cookbook on line this morning. Also want to mention that there's an Ormon Society Rising Young Stars concert at the Opera House in San Francisco Tuesday night. It's the concert for people who donate money to support young opera singers. Would you care to join me? Maybe over a glass of wine we could discuss that dinner I bid on at the auction. No pressure. I'm going anyway. Just thought we could kill two birds, so to speak, if you're interested. Ciao. By the way, it's Jack."

Jack the Sicilian, Emma thought, then caught herself. Julie was right. Maybe *she* was the one who was prejudiced? But as her grandmother said, there is no one an Italian mistrusts more than another Italian. And when one Italian is from the north and the other is Sicilian, the mistrust runs deep.

Emma weighed the invitation. On the one hand, Mr. Goodfella definitely was not her type. But so what if the guy looked like a Hollywood hit man? She was only going to a concert with him. And sooner or later they'd have to discuss that dinner he bid on. Not to mention the fact that he was Piers' client. No need to offend.

Emma picked up the phone and hit Jack's call back number. The line went straight into voice mail. "Hi. Jack. Leave a message."

"Hi Jack." Emma tried to sound jaunty. "I'd love to go to the Ormon Concert with you on Tuesday and discuss that dinner you bought. Talk soon. Emma."

The minute she hung up the phone, Emma panicked. What if this East Coast transplant was really part of a gangland witness protection relocation program? What had she just done?

The Blissburg Free Legal Services Clinic was located a few miles north on 101 in an all but abandoned shopping mall outside of town. The four large storefronts surrounding the empty two acre central parking lot bore faded signs for Borders Books, The Liberty Store, the Hat Box and One of a Kind. Businesses that had either closed their doors for good or moved away. A couple of smaller storefronts bore signs for Luigi's Pizza and Jack's bail bonds shop. Emma wondered if these were some of JJR Capital's investments. Then she mentally slapped her hand. Still, there was something about Jack Russo's tough guy accent that reminded her of gangsters and red sauce.

Fortunately, parking was always easy in the half-abandoned place. Emma pulled her Prius into a spot in front of the clinic, exited her car and entered the building through the sliding electric double doors.

Barbara, the receptionist, shot her a sympathetic smile. Obviously, she read the Herald. Barbara had been one of the first recipients of a free signed copy of Emma's cookbook.

"Well look who's here. I thought you might skip today, honey, given the bad news." Barbara shrugged. "That headline was so unfair. I've used your tomato sauce recipe twice now, and *never* been sick. Anyway, don't worry about being late. It's been slow. Mrs. Hunt is in with Steve discussing another eviction notice. He may need some help later."

Emma nodded. "Thanks."

She made her way to her cubicle at the back of the vast, open retail box that now served as a free legal clinic. It was staffed by one paid lawyer named Steve and an ever-changing stable of volunteers.

Emma's cubicle was formed by three plastic partitions that barely afforded the privacy she needed for the client intake interviews she conducted as part of her job. It was a far cry from the carpeted cherry paneled private room she'd occupied at Foley, Dunn & Munster from the time Andy left until just a few months ago. And so was the work. Fighting insurance companies for health benefits or property damage coverage on behalf of Sonoma County's disenfranchised poor was nothing at all like fighting over defense coverage for directors and officers of multi-national billion dollar corporations who had screwed their shareholders. Let me see, Emma reminded herself for the umpteenth time as she sank into the definitely non-ergonomic computer chair in front of a battered third-hand metal desk. Which is more satisfying? Bingo! At least if the cookbook failed, the Free Legal Services Clinic still needed her.

First Emma checked her email. Nothing pressing. Still plenty of time to reinvent herself as a – sleuth? Preposterous, she thought. Then she remembered Julie's unkind jab. That her father's conviction was sexy compared to her mother's tomato sauce fiasco. She decided to get to work.

Based on her discussion with Julie, she had three suspects to investigate: Carmen, Sacha Kuragin the Russian bass, and Sergio the celebrity chef. Emma had already decided to begin with Carmen. First because Piers thought Carmen killed Natasha. Second, because Emma was determined to prove that Carmen had *not*.

Emma grimaced. She'd watched too many Inspector Lynley episodes on Public Television not to know that was the *wrong* approach.

Emma could hear the aristocratic detective lecturing his frumpy sidekick. "You must begin with an open mind, Havers. If you lose your professional objectivity, you don't belong on this job." Or something to that effect.

OK. She'd admit it. She didn't have any professional objectivity. The Roma was innocent and she was out to prove it.

Emma removed Carmen's intake file from a cabinet behind her desk and reviewed what little she knew about the suspect.

According to her file, Carmen was born in New Jersey under the name of Sylvia Louisamaria Stella Reboso-Moreno. She was thirty-eight years old, except her driver's license had her listed as Carmen Havlek aged forty-two. The age discrepancy due, Carmen said, to a clerical error.

Carmen lived with a man named Tonio Havlek, but was actually married to a man named Louis who was in jail for a theft which, according to Carmen, he didn't do. She and Louis were divorced, and she and Tonio married, under Roma law not recognized by the State of California.

Carmen was listed in the public school files as having three children in the Santa Rosa public school system. But on further investigation, one of the children had turned out to be her cousin's daughter who had assumed the name of Carmen's grown daughter by Louis whom Tonio had adopted under Roma law but who currently lived in Mexico.

Emma exhaled slowly. That had all sounded perfectly logical two months ago when she and Steve applied for, and *got*, coverage for the whole family under Covered California. Why, she wondered, did it suddenly sound so *sketchy*?

She was trying to recreate their winning Covered California argument when her phone rang.

She picked up the receiver. "Hello, Blissburg Free Legal Services. Emma Corsi speaking."

"Hi." The voice on the line was husky and hushed. "Emma. It's

Carmen. Are you at the clinic? Can we talk?"

Wherever she was calling from must have been nearby. Carmen walked into Emma's cubicle a few minutes later.

Unlike the night of the City Opera fundraiser, Carmen's dark, petite frame was covered in an Indian print summer skirt and a pink tunic top, her black hair pulled back in a long ponytail. She wore plastic flip-flops and carried a large Peruvian woven sac slung over her shoulder.

"I can't stay long, Emma," Carmen explained. "Tonio is watching the kids, but he leaves for work in about an hour." Though Emma didn't ask, Carmen volunteered, "He plays Flamenco guitar at a restaurant in Guerneville on Saturday nights."

"What's up?" was all Emma managed to reply.

"Well, I heard about that headline in the Herald this morning," Carmen answered lowering her voice to barely above a whisper. "By the way, I can't believe what they're doing to you, Emma. I mean, the cookbook. It's terrible. And you, completely innocent. I mean, that opera singer? She didn't die of no bad cooking."

"How do you *know*?" Emma interrupted. "I mean, the toxicology report won't come out till a week from Tuesday. Yes, I agree that she didn't die from *my* cooking. But so far, no one knows how she died, Carmen."

Carmen shook her head. "Emma. I know. Believe me, I know how she died. I *know*."

Emma felt a shiver run down her spine. "What are you talking about, Carmen? How could you possibly know what happened to her?"

Carmen threw her hands up and stared at Emma as if to say, isn't it obvious? Then she lowered her arms, sank down into the chair facing Emma's across her desk – up to then she had been standing – and leaned forward to speak in a voice even lower than before.

"I read her cards," she said. "Remember? First I read the little dark fat one's."

"Chiara's," Emma nodded. "The understudy. Yes."

"Then everybody got very excited and the little fat one said something about losing weight. Right?"

"Right." Emma remembered the scene quite vividly.

"Then, I read the blond's cards. Or started to. Not the ugly twin. The pretty blond," Carmen said.

Emma nodded. "Yes. And then you felt faint, or something. And you didn't finish reading the cards because you weren't feeling well. That's when you left."

Carmen shook her head. "No." Her voice trembled. "No. I...I was feeling fine. Physically fine."

Emma didn't buy it. "Carmen, I saw you. You turned pale as a ghost. Remember? You felt ill. You looked ill."

"I wasn't sick. It was the cards, Emma. It was what the cards said that made me look sick. I read the cards. Before I left, I read the blond lady's cards. And the cards said MURDER. Loud and clear. The cards said the blond was going to get murdered. Soon. Very soon. Like, it was in the cards. She just disappeared from view. And it was bad. Very bad. Emma, I never seen cards that bad before. What could I do?"

Emma nodded. "Under the circumstances, it would be hard to know what to do."

"I couldn't tell her," Carmen answered her own question. "You don't tell someone whose cards you're reading something like that. What if you're wrong? You could kill them with such news. Or they could kill you. Or sue you. I mean, if I said something like that about the Buchanons, they could have me put away. I was scared. That's why I said I was sick and got out of there as fast as I could."

"I guess I understand," Emma agreed.

"But all night, I felt so bad," Carmen continued. "What if I was right? What if the pretty blond twin really was getting murdered that night? I should have warned her. Right? It was my duty to warn her, right? That's why I was given these powers."

Emma shrugged. "Honestly Carmen, I don't know what to say."

Carmen resumed her story. "So, later I snuck back into the vineyard. That's when I heard someone screaming that Natasha – that was her name, right? The woman whose fortune I was supposed to tell? I heard this guy screaming that Natasha was dead. And I saw him. I saw him leaning over the pretty blond's body, doing something to her. I couldn't see what. I felt so bad, Emma. Then I ran. Because you know how things go. If anybody saw me, they'd blame it on the gypsy. Just like it happened to Louis. And I have three little children to take care of, Emma. I can't let that happen. You understand? You have to help me *not* let that happen. You're a lawyer, right? You can help me."

Carmen was shaking so badly, Emma reached across the desk to grab her arm.

"First of all," Emma said, "I'm not a lawyer, Carmen."

Carmen's face fell.

"But I *will* try to help you," Emma added. "Listen, when you read the cards, did they tell you who the murderer was? Did you see anything that might give us a clue?"

Carmen shook her head. "Honestly Emma, I was so freaked out when I first saw the cards, I just shuffled them up and put them away. Now I wish I had never gone back to that party. If anyone saw me. I know. They'll blame the gypsy."

Emma didn't want to tell her that some people already were blaming the gypsy. She thought for a minute. If Carmen saw Barry Buchanon with Natasha right after she died, Carmen probably had a duty to go to the police. The bigger question was, if Carmen wouldn't go, did Emma have to go to the police herself? If Emma were an attorney, the answer would be simple. Anything Carmen told her would be confidential. But Emma wasn't an attorney. The problem was, Carmen had come to her thinking she *was*.

Emma made a quick decision. "Carmen, I think you should go to the police and tell them what you saw. Go now. They are going to question you anyway. Someone at the party told one of the policemen that you were there last night. He took that information down. Sooner or later they are going to call you. Better that you volunteer the information, before they come looking for you."

Carmen started shaking again. "I can't do that, Emma."

"Well, you *should*. Now. Think about it." Emma paused. "By the way, I'm curious. What have you heard today about the death? Have you talked to anyone? Has anyone called you?"

Carmen nodded. "Yeah. Someone called. I thought it was the police, so I hung up."

Emma cringed.

"Oh, I almost forgot. The dead lady's ugly twin. She came by my trailer this morning. She was frantic. She's afraid whoever killed the sister will go after her too."

"Why?" Emma asked. "Did she say there was some connection?"

"Just, I don't know, like that they're twins. And if someone wanted to kill one twin, they would want to kill the other one too. She wanted me to read her cards to reassure her that she wasn't going to die. I don't know how she found me. She was shaking and crying. She said her sister was the best person in the world. And that if anyone was going to die it should be her, the ugly twin. Then she begged me to do her cards. But at the last minute, she said she felt sick and ran out the door."

"So you never did the cards?" Emma asked.

"No. She left."

Poor Vera, Emma thought.

Carmen was still shaking when she rose abruptly from her seat. "I gotta go, Emma," she said. "Tonio's waiting for me. You won't tell anyone about our conversation, will you?"

Emma didn't answer. Instead, she eyed Carmen sternly. "Carmen, I mean it. Go to the police now. Before they come to you."

Carmen hurried out of Emma's office without a reply.

6

SATURDAY NIGHT – FAVOR

Emma left the Blissburg Free Legal Services Clinic shortly after. She spoke to no one about her conversation with Carmen, still unsure whether it was confidential – or whether she should report what she heard to the police.

She headed straight for her daughter's house. Saturday was Piers and Julie's date night. When she moved to Blissburg, Emma volunteered to babysit for them, her schedule permitting. She hadn't missed a Saturday night with her grandson, Harrington, yet.

Before Julie and Piers left to catch a movie, Julie served a delicious take out meal from Sergio's.

"Sergio's was empty, Mom," Julie replied when Emma commented that the pizza she'd bought smelled delicious. "Completely empty. Natasha Vasiliev's death has ruined his business. Kind of shoots your theory about him being a suspect."

Piers strolled into the kitchen with a glass of wine. "By the way, Emma, I saw you talking to my client, Jack Russo, at the fundraiser. What did you think of him?"

"You mean the Goodfella?" Emma replied.

Piers shook his head. "Why does everybody say that? Who is the Goodfella?"

Emma sighed. Where Piers came from, Goodfellas were the guys who drove ice cream trucks.

"Sorry to be so predictable." She thought about Jack Russo for a moment. "He seemed nice, Piers. What?" she joked. "Are you trying to fix me up with him? Don't you want to keep my Saturday nights free?"

Julie looked up from the steaming thin crust pizza topped with figs, prosciutto and gorgonzola cheese she was serving on her hand painted Deruta ceramic dinnerware. "Fix Mom up? Whose idea is that? Mom's fine the way she is." She looked at Harrington. "Right?"

"Yeah, Nonnie's fine the way she is," Harry replied. "Don't change. Can we play Concentration after dinner?"

"Sure, honey." Emma loved her grandson's loyalty. "But you always win. I can't seem to remember anything, these days." Emma turned back to Julie and laughed, "I think Piers is trying to fix me up with some Goodfella business client of his. That's sort of sweet."

"With Russo?" Julie grimaced. "You're kidding, right? They have absolutely nothing in common, Piers. Besides, when he talks he just doesn't sound, I don't know, smart."

Piers shrugged. "Smart enough to have made a bundle of money as a VC. Enough to need *my* services."

"And enough to bid $5000 for my dinner for six," Emma added still wondering what a VC was.

Julie's jaw dropped. "Five thousand? For Mom's dinner?"

Piers put down his wine glass and raised his hands, palms up. "Look Julie, all I know is that he moved here from the East Coast a few months ago and hired us to do some estate planning work. Then I saw him thumbing through your mother's book at the fundraiser and I mentioned that the author was my mother-in-law and a great cook. He said he loves to cook and that he's an opera fan. Made some joke about how all those loud female voices fill the void since his wife died. I think the guy's lonely."

Piers glanced at Emma. "I hope you were nice. He's a really, really good client. How good, of course, is totally confidential."

"I'm always nice," Emma answered. "Speaking of confidential, Piers. What if I get a client at the clinic who tells me something that is confidential because he thinks I'm a lawyer when I'm not. Is it still confidential?"

Piers shrugged. "I don't know for sure, but if someone at my firm mistook a paralegal for a lawyer, I'd keep the information confidential. Because the client holds the confidentiality privilege and the client intended the information to be confidential. It's an interesting question though." He grinned. "So what, exactly, did you hear?"

By then Julie had brought all the food to the dining room. They sat down to eat. For the moment, Harry was busy with pizza and milk.

Julie began. "So, what do we have to report about our suspects? I'll go first. I poked around today about Lexie and Vera Vasiliev, Natasha's twin sister."

"Lexie D?" Harry interrupted. "Are you talking about Lexie D from my school?"

"No, honey," Julie answered. "Lexie Buchanon. Different Lexie." Then, realizing the four year old was listening to everything they said, she made him an offer. "Hey, wanna watch *Cars*? You can eat in front of the TV as a special treat tonight. Then you and Nonnie can finish watching the movie before you go to bed."

A few minutes later, Julie had settled Harry in front of the TV in the breakfast room, and was back at the dining table. She lowered her voice. "Anyway, our theory for Lexie Buchanon is that Barry Buchanon was having an affair with Natasha, and Lexie was jealous enough to kill her. That would give Lexie a motive and the opportunity to swing by Natasha's table and slip something into the food on her plate. So while I was at the restaurant, I asked Sergio if Lexie spent any time in the kitchen. You know, before the food was served."

"What did he say?" Piers asked.

Julie raised her eyebrows. "Get this. He said that Lexie spent half an hour in the kitchen flirting with him while the guests were arriving. In fact, she specifically asked to taste your pasta sauce, Mom, because she told Sergio that she adores it. Apparently she calls it Italian comfort food."

More like discomfort food now, Emma thought to herself.

"The other thing is," Julie continued, "apparently while they were talking, Lexie made a little plate of hors d'oeuvres that she said she was taking out to Barry, along with a glass of wine. She said the wine they were serving wasn't good enough for Barry. He wouldn't drink it. So she opened a *special* bottle and took a glass of it along with the hors d'oeuvres out to the garden. I'd say, motive *and* opportunity."

"For what?" Piers interjected. "She's already married to one of the richest men in California. Even if Barry dumped her for the songstress, Lexie'll get enough money to refinance the bachelor of her choice. Why risk all that for a life sentence in the women's correctional facility?"

"Jealousy, passion," Julie replied. "Look, if you gave a four carat emerald ring to some starlet, I'd be so jealous I'd rip her to shreds. With my bare hands. Forget the alimony. I want *you* Piers."

Piers looked at his wife skeptically. "You're kidding, right?"

Julie nodded. "Yes, I'm kidding. I'd rip *you* to shreds, honey. Not the floozy."

Piers smiled. He appeared to have taken that as a compliment.

But Julie was getting impatient. "This is serious guys. There's more. According to Oleg, my masseur at the spa."

"Oleg?" Piers interrupted. "I didn't know you were getting all those massages from a guy!"

"Who's under investigation here?" Julie shot back.

"Yeah," Emma agreed. "Oleg gives a great massage."

"Enough from you about massages, Mom," Julie shuddered.

"Anyway, Oleg was full of gossip today about the death last night. He said all his appointments this morning were talking about it. Apparently the debacle was *good* for *his* business, unlike mine. Well, Oleg heard that, a few years ago, when Natasha was an Ormon Rising Young Star Fellow at the City Opera, Vera, who was Barry Buchanon's masseuse, introduced him to her twin sister. That was before Lexie started doing him."

Julie glanced into the breakfast room at Harry. He was engrossed in the film.

"Literally," she added. "Anyway, way back then, when Vera introduced him to Natasha, her twin sister, Barry fell head over heels in love with her. But Natasha wouldn't let him touch her. Apparently that turned him on more. Then Natasha moved to New York and Barry married Lexie, his new masseuse. But a few months ago, when Natasha returned to San Francisco to sing *Trovatore*, Barry basically crawled back to her on his knees. The more she rejected him, the more he craved her. Well, at least that's one version. The other is that Natasha was doing Barry all along, *and* Sacha Kuragin, *and* every other bass, tenor, alto in the business."

"So what does Oleg think?" Emma asked.

"Oleg worships Natasha. He thinks she's pure as the driven snow."

"Is that it?" Piers asked.

"I think that's a lot for one day's work," Julie replied.

"What about Vera?" Emma asked.

"Nothing. Adoring twin sister. Natasha shared everything with her."

"Except enough money to quit being a masseuse," Emma added.

Julie shook her head. "The word is Vera was planning to retire once Natasha made it big. I asked about the money. It seems Natasha shared *everything* with Vera. Oleg said he thought Natasha felt guilty because she got both the voice *and* the looks."

Emma nodded sympathetically.

"Problem was," Julie continued, "there wasn't much to share in the beginning. Natasha's recordings have just started to pay off. Both girls had taken out enormous loans for Natasha's lessons: voice, acting, English, Italian, colors, wardrobe, you name it. But this morning, one of Oleg's B of A executive type clients said that someone had just paid off all those loans. Like last week. Of course, Oleg wouldn't tell me who that was. But I'll bet I can guess."

"Who?" Piers asked.

Julie turned to Piers. "Barry Buchanon, duh. So what did *you* find out?"

"More than you," he began.

Why, Emma thought, did the busiest person always seem to get the most done?

"I checked out Barry and Chiara, the understudy," he continued. "Since I really don't think Barry did it, I started with Chiara. First I called Clare Blumberg."

"Madame City Opera Director," Emma interjected.

"Mom," Harry called in from the adjoining breakfast room where he was watching the video. "It's the scary part. Turn it off. I don't like it." He ran into the dining room and jumped into his mother's lap.

"Honey, there *is* no scary part in Cars, remember?" Julie said.

"Mom, it's the mean trucks at night. The Peterbuilt truck."

Emma interjected, "I can sit with him, Julie. I can hear Piers from the breakfast room. Besides, I need a snuggle."

Julie gave Harry a hug. "Don't worry. I'll protect you from those Nonnie Snuggles. You can stay here until the scary part is over, but then you need to go back to the movie. Mommy and Daddy are having a boring grown up talk with Nonnie."

Harry squirmed off his mother's lap. "OK."

Emma grabbed him on his way back to the breakfast room and gave him a kiss.

Piers continued, "I'll cut to the chase. Otherwise, we'll be late for the movie. Clare knew exactly why I was calling. She was at the fundraiser. She no more wants a killer wandering around backstage at City Opera than we want one here in Blissburg. The police have already contacted Chiara, the understudy. Clearly she had the most to gain from Natasha's death. Singing on Opening Night will be the biggest break of her career."

"I'll say," Emma nodded, thinking about Sacha Kuragin's comment that Chiara would kill to perform Natasha's role.

"Chiara's freaked out because she knows the police are investigating her," Piers added. "But according to Clare, underneath her bubbly exterior, Chiara would stop at nothing to claw her way to the top. She's been carrying on with Massimo, the conductor, who is besotted with her. By the way, according to Clare, Massimo has a temper that could catapult *him* to the top of the suspect list. She's heard Massimo blow up at the musicians. The union even got on his back. Last year he threatened to dismember the French horn player during a *Gotterdammerung* rehearsal."

"Did Clare say anything to the police?" Emma asked.

"No," Piers answered. "She says she's used to that kind of behavior. It's Grand Opera, for goodness sake. Everyone acts that way. But as far as Chiara is concerned, Clare said she wouldn't put murder past her. There's a rumor that during the Ormon Rising Young Star auditions, *Chiara* was the one who tainted the picnic lunch so that half the candidates had the runs the day of the competition. No one knows who started the rumor. Maybe it was just a sour grapes loser. But every other Ormon Fellow believed it. And by then, they all knew Chiara pretty well."

"Why didn't someone report *that* to the police?" Julie asked.

"Someone did," Piers replied. "But no one could prove it."

That's when Emma repeated Sacha Kuragin's jab at Chiara the night before. That she'd kill to sing the first act aria on her back. Emma wondered what more Sacha knew. And if he'd tell.

"Anyway," Piers continued, "according to Clare, the police are already milking this angle. Personally, I think it's a little too obvious. But Chiara isn't the sharpest tack. As for Barry, first of all, he's a client. I know the guy. He just wouldn't do it. But for what it's worth, Clare is convinced that Natasha never gave in to him."

"Piers, hogwash," Julie replied. "She took the ring, didn't she?"

"Yeah, but Clare doesn't think he got past third base. And she would know. Clare and Barry had a thing going themselves. Pre-Lexie during Mrs. Buchanon II's reign. Now Barry confides in Clare. She said he's devastated about Natasha. But according to Clare, she took the ring and never delivered the goods."

"And that wouldn't be enough to drive him into a jealous rage?" Julie asked.

"Not according to Clare. And not based on anything I've ever seen in the guy's temperament. He's a depressive. He mopes. He whines. But he's not a killer." Piers shook his head. "I also talked to Chief Tompkins. In fact, I had coffee with him today at the Plaza Café. By the way, the apricot galettes this morning were *amazing*. Anyway, the police are getting a subpoena to search the gypsy's..."

"Roma," Emma interrupted.

"The Roma's," Piers continued, "trailer. Somebody made off with that ring, and based on something Vera told him, Tompkins thinks the gypsy, I mean the Roma, got it. Oh, get this. Barry reported a few stolen articles from his house last night. Some silver and a couple of Japanese netsuke miniature ivory sculptures from the living room. Guess where they turned up this morning? In a garbage can near Tonio's and Carmen's trailer. When the police tried to contact Tonio about it, no one could find him. Which brings us to you, Emma. What did *you* find out about Carmen today?"

Emma froze. Stolen silver at Tonio and Carmen's trailer? If Carmen knew the police had found it, why hadn't she mentioned it earlier that afternoon, Emma wondered. All of a sudden, her mouth went dry. She'd started out trying to prove Carmen was innocent. Now she wasn't so sure. She looked from Julie to Piers.

"Nothing," she shrugged. "I didn't find out anything yet. Sorry. I... I spent most of the day in bed."

"Mom!" Julie and Piers exchanged worried glances.

Emma looked at her watch. "Shouldn't you two be leaving soon?" She got up and joined Harry on the couch in front of the TV.

WHEN JULIE and Piers returned a few hours later Emma and Harry were still on the couch. Both of them fast asleep.

"Mom," Julie accosted her before she was fully awake. "I can't believe you let Harry fall asleep on the couch. Even worse, you fell asleep with him. What kind of a babysitter does that? You're deteriorating, Mom. Letting things slip. Piers and I ran into Barbara at the movies. *She's* worried about you, too. She said you didn't show up for your volunteer job at the clinic till almost 3:00."

"Traitor," Emma muttered, still only half awake.

"She also told us the gypsy showed up," Julie continued. "And that you talked to her. You lied to us about that, Mom. What's going on?"

"Nothing. I'm fine," Emma replied grabbing her coat and heading for the door. "We'll talk tomorrow."

7

SUNDAY MORNING – STROLL

Sunday morning, Emma decided to leave her self-imposed house arrest bright and early, and join the weekly Blissburg Historical Society's Sunday Stroll. Julie's criticism the night before hurt. So Emma left her house at 8:30, before Julie phoned, or worse, showed up. The Sunday Stroll would surely be better than more of the Julie treatment.

Besides, Emma liked the Historical Society's Sunday Stroll. After six months she had barely scratched the surface of Blissburg's history. So far, she had learned that the town plaza, bordered on all four sides by well preserved buildings dating back to the turn of the last century, comprised the heart of the old Molino land grant. Five hundred thousand plus acres of rolling hills, open pastures and fertile soil that the king of Spain deeded to Alfonso Molino over 200 years before.

Molino managed to maintain control of his holding after Mexico won its independence from Spain; only to have it lost by his n'er do well grandson in a game of monte in Yerba Buena (aka San Francisco). The new owner was Eliazer Bliss, an eighteen year old gold seeker who was murdered a year later in a dispute regarding a prostitute at a nearby hot springs. Eliazer's six brothers and sisters in

Utica, New York, who inherited the property when Eliazer died, sold the land off to Moses Stearns on the condition that it include the picturesque town plaza now shaded by maples, sequoias and redwoods, and that it be renamed Blissburg in honor of the family.

No, Emma thought when she heard the story of the town's founding at her first Blissburg Historical Society Sunday Stroll, Blissburg didn't boast the illustrious history of a Concord, Massachusetts, home of the shot heard round the world, where her son-in-law's family originally put down roots after coming to America in the 1600s; or even Pittsburgh or the back breaking quarries of Stonington, Maine where Piers' family summered on nearby Blue Hill. But it sure was the quintessential history of the California where Emma was born. A place made famous by fortune hunters, crooks, gamblers and quacks. By people perpetually reinventing themselves.

Now, waiting for the rest of the strollers to show up, Emma sat on a park bench next to the plaza's decorative fountain. With a coffee and a still-warm apricot galette in her hand that she'd bought from the Plaza Cafe, she surveyed the surrounding hills dotted with twenty-five million dollar mansions attached to rolling vineyards protected by electric fences and remote controlled gates. And thought that things hadn't changed much in a hundred and fifty years. People still came to California to seek their fortunes and reinvent themselves.

Julie and Piers, bless them, lived in a house resembling a Walt Disney French chateau. And what about her Tuesday night date? Where had Jack, the tough guy turned VC, made all his money? Emma took another bite of the galette and wondered whatever happened to plain old, honest, hard work. The kind that trendy, modern-day Blissburg *wasn't* built on? The kind that meant showing up on the factory line or at the office nine hours a day for forty years. Till the Big D rewarded you with one long endless nap.

Stop that! Emma slapped her hand. She was happy, right? And at sixty-five who wanted to worry about a French faux chateau? A hermit's bowl and a tent looked more appealing. Apparently Emma's thoughts betrayed her.

"It's a beautiful day. You're alive. These galettes melt in your mouth. Why are you scowling?"

Emma looked up to see the Goodfella, aka Jack, staring down at her, the identical warm apricot galette in his hand. In the Sunday morning sunlight, he looked short and stocky. Compact but not fat. Or maybe it was the well fitting loden-green corduroys, definitely not GAP, and the (did that tiny logo say Paul & Shark, she wondered) tight weave midnight blue sweater with the canvas elbow patches, that made him look so fit.

Before she could answer, Jack added, "You know how to make one of these?" Except in Jack speak the "these" sounded more like "dees."

Emma squinted her eyes at him mistrustfully.

"Oh boy! Sorry," he said.

Was that a blush? No, Emma thought, his complexion was too swarthy for a blush. Or was it?

"Now you think I'm one of those chow diggers who's after you for your cooking." Jack covered his face with his hands and peeked out at her through his fat fingers. "Really, no offense intended. I been tryin' ta make these things at home, but I can't figure out the, you know. What do they call it? Pat brisay?"

Pate brisée? What planet was this guy from, Emma thought. "That's because these galettes are made with a *mille feuille* pastry," she explained. "Not *pate brisée*. *Mille feuille* uses a lot more butter."

Jack threw his hands out in front of him palms up.

There was another thing she didn't like. He used his hands too much when he talked.

"See," Jack winked again, "I knew you'd know."

Just then, Carter from the Historical Society strolled up to the fountain along with three or four Sunday Stroll regulars.

Jack waved at them. Then he turned back to her and asked, "You here for the stroll? Carter mentioned it to me at the bocce tournament over at da Paolo's restaurant, the one that has the bocce court. It's my first stroll, but I figured it was a good way for me to burn off one of these galettes. I'm addicted to them."

It had been exactly Emma's rationale. Why, she wondered, did this guy always seem to be reading her mind?

Emma nodded and smiled. Then she stood up and approached the fountain where the stroll was getting underway.

That day, Carter's short introductory lecture was about the olive industry that long ago had formed the backbone of Blissburg's agricultural heritage. It seemed that Don Alfonso Molino had planted some of the first olive trees brought to California from Spain. They thrived in California's warm climate. Eventually, at the turn of the last century, a young entrepreneur from Tuscany bought a subdivision of the land to start an olive oil business. He brought with him dozens of poor relatives from Tuscany to pick the olives.

According to Carter, there were still old residents of Blissburg who remembered hearing them sing what Carter jokingly referred to as Tuscan rap. One group of olive pickers spontaneously calling out couplets and another inventing refrains. During the olive harvest, this form of entertainment went on for hours.

Eventually, the land where the original trees grew had been subdivided into the nearby popular Molino Mall. The trees were all cut down. But some historically minded descendant had transplanted a small grove of the original Spanish olive trees onto his property at the outskirts of town and turned it into a public park. The park was the destination of the morning's stroll.

Emma glanced at her companions. She already knew a few by sight. Most of the Blissburg women's walking group, the Walkie-Talkies, were there: Annemarie who owned the local bookstore; Babs the celebrity hairdresser at Cutters the chic downtown Blissburg hair salon; Lila who owned the gourmet culinary shop; and

Trish the local realtor. Along with a couple of other women and two men whom Emma did not recognize.

A few of them waved in her direction, but Emma eventually realized that they were waving at Jack who apparently already knew half of the people there. The other half clearly couldn't wait to be introduced to him. Emma quickly found herself jostled to the back of the pack, Walkie-Talkies elbowing their way past her to stand by Jack in what looked like a round of Women's Senior Roller Derby.

The few that did recognize Emma gave her passing sympathetic smiles. Some of them murmured things like "what a pity" or "used to love that sauce," before putting as much distance as they could between her and them.

Eventually, she found herself walking slowly beside a white haired man with a cane whose elbow she had grabbed when he stumbled at the crosswalk curb.

"Hi, I'm Emma," she introduced herself hoping to ease the awkwardness of her intervention that prevented a nasty fall.

"Tom Fitzpatrick," he answered, then added, "I'm a native here in Blissburg. In the garbage business since 1948, when I came back from the war. My father owned the land used for the town dump. I turned it into a business. Did pretty well, too, if I do say so myself. Of course, my son Ronnie runs it now."

Tom stopped talking for a moment, looked sharply at Emma, and then continued.

"'Course I still worked every day, even after I sold the business to Ronnie for a song (don't tell the IRS that), until the surgery that is. Last March. Open heart. Had me splayed out like a corpse on the table. Come to think of it, I *was* a corpse. They cut me open from my sternum down to my belly button, stopped my breathing, took my heart clean out of my chest, and put me on one of those heart and lung machines so they could replace a valve. Want to see my scar?"

Before Emma could refuse, Tom unzipped his North Face windbreaker and unbuttoned the top four buttons of his plaid Woolrich flannel shirt. Emma tried to look away, but not before she clearly saw what looked like a giant red worm crawling in a straight line down his chest.

Emma cringed. Talk about TMI!

Tom caught her look. "Nope. Pretty it ain't. But my doctor assured me that come summer, this will fade into such a thin line no one will even see it when the chest hair grows back. Nothing to scare off the ladies," he assured her with a wink. "If you get my drift. Quite something for an old geezer like me. Dead on the table and still kicking. My son calls me Lazarus. Course I think he and his wife were betting I'd kick the bucket and leave them the family jewels. Sure fooled them, didn't I?" He added with a laugh, "Little do they know. There'll be nothing left once my three exs get through with me."

Eeeew! Emma tried to keep a poker face. Double TMI! And why did it seem like all people talked about these days was the Big D?

Emma changed the subject. "So, was that your, I mean your son's, company that found the stolen items from the Buchanon Vineyards this morning?" Emma had no idea how many trash companies serviced the area; but it seemed like a good guess.

"You heard about that already?" Tom replied. "Thought the police were trying to keep it hush."

Whoops! Emma didn't remember Piers saying that it was hush. She shrugged, "Word gets around."

"Well," Tom continued, "I guess there's no harm in telling you. Our guys found the stuff, all right. 'Course, once it lands in the truck, who knows whose can it really came from? But they do know *for sure* it was the can nearest to that gypsy's trailer. Or it was the cans servicing the dry cleaner and the Goodwill store. Or that Mexican grocery on the outskirts of town."

"Wait," Emma's head was spinning. "I heard it was in Tonio's trash can. No one said anything about the drycleaner, or the Goodwill, or the Mexican grocery store."

Tom squinted at her. "I don't know anything about a Tonio. Is he that gypsy? The one whose wife tells fortunes? I hear he plays Flamenco guitar sometimes at that Mexican bar in Guerneville."

Emma nodded. Clearly Tom got around. Then she backed off. "Really, I'm not sure. I just heard someone say the name, Tonio. It sounded sort of foreign, so I took note."

Tom appeared to relax. She could almost see his foreign sympathizer antennae retreating behind his ears. Hopefully he'd tell her more.

"Look, obviously the stuff was in the gypsy's trash can. Right?" Tom continued. "With the lid on. He was hiding it there. Unless it was in the Mexicans' can, but they work for us. They don't cause trouble anymore."

Hiding stolen goods in a trash can on trash day really didn't make sense. But Emma nodded anyway. "So, of course," she added, "your son didn't even mention that the trash might have come from anywhere else. Why should he? We all know the gypsy stole it. Right?"

"Exactly!" Tom nodded, clearly pleased with her analysis. "Why complicate things? Why throw the police off the track? Get that Tonio, or whatever his name is, behind bars. Along with his wife, or whatever she is. I don't think those gypsies even believe in marriage."

Unlike you, Emma thought to herself. All three of them!

Tom stopped walking and looked at Emma again. They had reached the park and Carter had started lecturing about the old olive trees. Tom leaned on his cane and waved the noise of the lecture away with his free hand.

"Listen, Emma," he said. "I know more about this place than Carter and that whole gosh darned Historical Society put together. I came here for the company. Not the speeches. So I'm gonna level with you. I recognized you this morning. You're the lady who wrote that silly cookbook, *Dining with the Stars*. I mean, first of all, who'd want to dine with the gosh darned stars anyway? What stars? I leafed through the book at Annemarie's shop and I didn't recognize a one of those names in it. What do I care what a bunch of Eyetalians ate a hundred years ago? But frankly, I like a woman who can cook and I liked your picture on the cover. You're kind of a fatter, senior version of that lady on the television, Jade."

"Giada," Emma corrected him wondering if she should take that as a compliment.

Tom laughed. "Eyetalian name. Like yours if I remember correctly. Anyway, all day yesterday I heard the jokes on the news. About the title of the cookbook and the poor Russian singer who died. Pretty girl from the look of the picture in the paper. And I remembered your photograph; and well, being the sentimental kind of guy that I am, I felt sorry for you."

Emma nodded, encouraging him.

"'Course even though the police *know* that the gypsies killed her, till that toxicology report comes out, they can't rule out your spaghetti sauce for sure," Tom continued. "I figured, the sooner they pin it on the gypsy, the sooner a nice little lady like you can get back to business. So when my son found that trash and told the police it was in the gypsy's can, I was glad. Figured it would speed things up. Then I recognized you here today, and thought I'd find out what you were like. Well, you know what?"

Emma shook her head. "What?"

"You made a good impression. Now, is that worth a home cooked dinner for an old softie?" Tom winked. "Unless you know something that I don't, and I'm taking my life in my hands."

Emma forced a laugh. "I'll check my calendar as soon as I get home." She made a mental note to turn off her phone. "So, Tom," she added, "you're absolutely sure your son isn't going to tell the police there is any doubt about where the Buchanons' stuff was found?"

"You have my solemn promise about that, young lady," Tom grinned.

Emma hesitated. "But what about the guys who actually found

the stuff? The trash men. Your employees. If the police question them, won't they tell the truth?"

"The Mexicans?" Tom shook his head. "Nah. They'll say whatever Ronnie tells them to. Besides, the Mexicans hate the gypsies as much as we do." He winked again. "Kind of like us Irish and you Eyetalians in the old days, right? You hate whoever's the next rung down on the ladder."

By then, Carter had finished his lecture. The stroll was starting to break up. Some people headed back to their homes; some back to the plaza.

Emma noticed Jack watching her out of the corner of his eye as she waved goodbye to Tom. Then he excused himself from a gaggle of adoring female fans.

"Emma, wait up," he called, pulling off his sweater in the midmorning Blissburg heat. "If you're going that way, I'll walk with you back to town."

Emma nodded. "OK." It was hard not to enjoy the disappointed looks on the faces of his admirers.

"See you soon, Jack," Babs called after him. "Don't forget to come in for that complimentary manicure."

Jack didn't answer. He was already sprinting towards Emma. She noticed that his sprint wasn't half bad.

"Do you have time to grab another coffee with me at Claud's?" He asked. "Maybe we could discuss that dinner I bought."

Emma laughed. "Sure. But how do you manage to hit every good bakery in town and still stay so fit?"

"I like Claud's multigrain sourdough," Jack explained, smiling at the compliment. "They only bake it on Sundays. And, by the way, we gotta make tracks. They sell out by noon."

Jack meant what he said. They walked so fast down Blissburg's tree shaded lanes, past hundred year old gingerbread Victorians, the local high school, at least six churches and finally across the old plaza, that by the time they joined the multigrain sourdough line at Claud's Emma was out of breath and sweating.

"So, was that another ex husband, boyfriend, brother you were talking to on the stroll?" Jack asked. He had purchased the sourdough and two lattes, and found a table in a corner of the café. "Forgive me for noticing," he said, pulling her chair out for her to sit down, "but he's a little old for a boyfriend. Frankly Emma," he winked, "you can do better. But who am I to judge? Just tell me, is it the cane? Do you have a thing for canes?"

Was he flirting, Emma wondered? Or did he kid everyone this way? Emma was beginning to believe the latter. She liked it.

She shook her head. "He runs the dump. Actually, he told me some very interesting things about the death Saturday night. As you can imagine, I have something of a personal stake in solving this thing quickly. In proving that it was murder. Not food poisoning."

Jack blew out his breath. "Yeah. I get it. I gather your daughter's feeling the fallout too. I ran into Buchanon at the Chatham Club yesterday..."

Jack stopped talking and gave Emma a dirty look. He shook his finger at her. "I know what you're thinking," he said. "I don't know either why the son of a Sicilian bricklayer from Providence, Rhode Island would ever join a snooty country club called The Chatham. When I moved here, my son-in-law thought it would be a place to meet people. To hang out. It was a mistake. Anyway, to get back to my story, Barry was pretty hard on your daughter. Said he'd never hire her again. Funny thing, I remember seeing him at the club with Natasha. I didn't recognize the singer though. She just looked like another blond. Bigger teeth than an American blond. I figured she was foreign."

The news that Barry publicly blamed Julie for the tragedy gave Emma a jolt. "He really said that about Julie?" she asked.

Jack nodded. "He blamed your tomato sauce too. Bottom line,

he's convinced there was no foul play. That Natasha's constitution was just too delicate for your robust red sauce."

At that, Jack started laughing in spite of himself. Emma could tell that laughter came easily to this man. When he finally stopped, he continued.

"Emma, look, I didn't want to bug the guy. He was hurting. And let me tell you, I know when a guy is hurting. But finally, I just had to say something. I said, Barry, be reasonable. I know you don't want to think that anyone would murder that angel."

Jack stopped talking again and glanced sideways at Emma. "Don't get me wrong. I don't know if she was an angel. The word at the Club is that she took Barry's cash and delivered the goods elsewhere. Be that as it may, to make him feel better, I told Barry that I didn't think an angel like Natasha Vasiliev could be mixed up in a murder. But realistically, I said, Barry, it wasn't the sauce. You can't blame the *salsa di pomodoro*."

Wow, Emma thought. He even pronounced it correctly.

Jack continued, "I told him. I'm Sicilian. I eat red sauce. And that sauce they served at the fundraiser was delicious. I ate it. Barry, I said, you ate it. A couple hundred people at the party ate it. And we are all alive to tell the tale. So I said, look Barry, the sauce didn't kill Natasha. Now maybe someone *put* something in the sauce that killed Natasha. And maybe they didn't. But the sauce didn't kill Natasha and we gotta stop murdering that poor woman who made the sauce!"

Emma was impressed. "Thanks. What'd he say?"

"He nodded. He even said he'd try to repair some of the damage he'd done to your reputation. But unfortunately, he also said that whatever you did, or didn't do, didn't get Julie off the hook. As far as he's concerned, that fundraiser ruined his reputation, and the reputation of his vineyard. He said he's never hiring Julie again."

Emma's heart sank. "Jack. I *have* to figure out who killed Natasha. Fast. I don't think she died of natural causes."

"Who's on *your* list of suspects?" Jack asked. "The Furies hounding me on the stroll talked of nothing else."

"Did they come up with anything interesting?" Emma asked, shaking her head at Jack's name for the Walkie-Talkies.

"Most are convinced it was a gypsy who killed her," Jack replied. "By the way, who's the gypsy?"

"Roma," Emma corrected him. "They prefer to be called Roma."

"Sorry. Who's the Roma?"

"She was telling fortunes at the party," Emma answered. "Like the character in the opera, *Il Trovatore*. I know the woman, Jack. I'm sure she didn't do it."

Jack shrugged. "I don't know. According to the Furies, the evidence points to the gypsy, I mean Roma. Babs from the hair salon said the police chief's wife came in for a blow job. That's a funny name for a hairdo."

"Blow dry, Jack," Emma corrected him.

"Ooohhh!" he laughed again. "Of course. Anyway, she said the chief is hoping to make an arrest today. They found some of Buchanon's things hidden in a trash can on the gypsy's, I mean Roma's property."

Emma related to Jack what she'd heard that morning from Tom on the stroll.

Jack let out a slow whistle. "Oh boy," he sighed. "Whatta ya do with that information? Your word against Ronnie Fitzpatrick's denying he ever heard such a thing? And his employees agreeing with him. I don't think so."

"Right," Emma said. "You do nothing with the information. You find the real killer."

"OK," Jack shrugged. "Here's something. Annemarie was the only one on the walk who disagreed with the rest of the Greek Chorus. She said Sergio, the chef who catered the fundraiser, came into the bookstore a couple of weeks ago to ask whether she carried any books on poisons. Kitchen poisons. He said it was for rats, kitchen rats, so maybe it's legit. He asked her to order one particular book and hold it for him on the QT. He picked the book up a few days later. Annemarie didn't think much of it until now. Anyone owning a fancy restaurant would want to keep his rat infestation quiet. Right?"

"Right," Emma answered. "Except Sergio swore Friday night at the fundraiser that he had *never seen* a rodent in his kitchen. It was clean*issimo*."

Jack raised his eyebrows at that. "The stories don't exactly jibe. Maybe there's more there than we think. When I first got here, I visited the casino. Bear Creek up on the hill."

Emma rolled her eyes.

"Don't get me wrong," Jack shrugged. "Hard as it may be for you to believe, I am not a gambler. My Dad was. And he got into a," he hesitated, "a jam when I was young. It's a bad habit I never acquired. But as you know, I *am* a finance guy and Bear Creek is the local poster child for financial disaster. It's got a ten thousand car garage built next to a pre-fab casino that only holds 5,000 people. Max. And it's an accident waiting to happen."

Emma shook her head. "What do you mean?"

"The whole structure would blow down in a fifty mile an hour wind," Jack explained. "I visited it one day. Purely out of curiosity. And you know who I saw at the craps table, excuse my language. None other than Sergio. And he wasn't checking out the kitchen. He was losing money. Big time. When he recognized me from the Blissburg bocce ball tournament, I swear, the guy looked like he wanted the floor to swallow him."

"Very interesting," Emma replied. "Think you could find out more?"

"I got friends. I can try."

"Speaking of recognizing someone." Emma peeked over Jack's shoulder. "Look behind you."

Seated a few tables over in the middle of the room, dressed in a

Prada jumpsuit and Vuitton silk scarf, was Trish, the realtor. She stared at them, her lasered eyelids lowered menacingly at half mast.

Jack turned, saw the look, and waved at Trish. Then he picked up his loaf of bread and stood up.

"Thanks for coming here with me, Emma," he said. "I'm meeting my daughter in Calistoga. I gotta run. Maybe we can discuss that dinner I won at the auction some other time."

He was about to leave when he stopped and started laughing again. "One thing puzzles me, Emma. Why do people around here make me feel like I'm ruining my reputation hanging out with you?" He shrugged his shoulders in that fatalistic Italian way. "It's a new feeling for an East Coast Sicilian." Then he added, "You're still on, right? The Ormon Concert. I'll pick you up. Five o'clock, Tuesday? Dinner in the City first. OK?"

Emma nodded hesitantly. Still unsure.

"Meanwhile, I'll make a few inquiries. About Sergio," he added.

"Thanks," Emma answered wondering where all this might lead.

8

MONDAY MORNING - WALKIE-TALKIE

Emma's doorbell rang early Monday morning. She was still in her favorite Vermont Country Store green fleece muumuu. Never a cold night in *that* she assured herself. And she still clutched her oversized mug of coffee. The mug Harry had decorated with monsters for Christmas. Aside from still being suspected of Poisoning the Stars with her famous *salsa di pomodoro*, life was good, she told herself.

Apparently Julie didn't think so. When Emma called out "who's there" and then opened the door, her daughter stared at her and shook her head.

"This is the second time you've answered the door in that muumuu thing, Mom," she said. "I say this lovingly, but it's weird. It's the kind of thing people wear in the dead of winter in nursing homes in northern Minnesota. When the electricity fails."

"I think it's cute," Emma defended herself. "Mary gave it to me and it's comfortable." She shook away her annoyance. No use arguing with Julie. Besides, how many of her friends' daughters bothered to check up on their mothers at 8:00 a.m.? Most of her friends' children lived thousands of miles away.

"Obviously," Emma continued in a more conciliatory tone, "I

only opened the door dressed like this because I knew it was you. Besides," she added, trying to be funny, "I'm half way to the nursing home already."

Julie sucked her breath in quickly. "Mom, you've got to stop talking that way," she replied. "Harry said you told him the LED bulb in his Elmo lamp will live longer than you will. It's *not* funny. You don't say that to a four-year old."

Emma winced. Julie was right. She was out of control.

"Look," Julie's tone softened, "I care about you. You're too young to just drop out, to use one of your generation's phrases. All I'm trying to tell you is that you could still look good if you tried."

"But I don't want to try," Emma leveled with her. "I don't care *how* I look anymore. And frankly, it's a blessing. At the office, I had to, you know, look professional all the time. Now who cares?"

"That's another thing," Julie continued. "What's going on with you and that Russo guy? Trish told Piers' secretary that she saw you two at Claud's having breakfast early Sunday morning. You aren't...," she stopped. "No. I can't even say it! This is a small town, Mom, and rumors fly. I don't know *what* Piers was thinking encouraging you two. Russo! I mean he's out of central casting. And that Jersey Shore accent. Where does *that* come from?"

Emma found herself defending Jack. "He's from Providence, Rhode Island. His father was a bricklayer. What? That makes him a gangster?"

Julie shrugged. "Who knows? The look, the voice, the accent. He's just not like *us*. You see that, don't you? If you're trying to find your roots, I think you've picked the wrong tree."

"At least he's not wearing an ankle thingie," Emma shot back.

She immediately knew she had gone too far. Julie's face started to crumple, but she quickly gained control.

"Mom, what you just said stinks. First of all, he's my father. Second, my whole career is going down the tubes and you're jumping into bed with some bozo."

"Julie, I'm not jumping into bed with him. I ran into him on the Blissburg Historical Society's Sunday Stroll. Trish was the one throwing herself at him. He asked me to grab a coffee with him while he picked up some of Claud's multigrain sourdough. By the way, they only make it on Sunday. I hear it's delicious."

"I know."

"Anyway," Emma continued, "Trish was all over Jack on the stroll. And then she saw us at Claud's. We were discussing the murder, for goodness sake. Jack had some very helpful information for me. I think Trish was jealous. So she started a nasty rumor. But honestly, honey, at my age who cares? And by the way, he invited me to the Ormon Fellow concert on Tuesday night. And I accepted."

"You're kidding." Julie sighed. She waved her hand dismissively at her mother. "I guess there's no accounting for taste. I just didn't realize you were so desperate, Mom. I thought you were happy here with *us.* Anyway, what was the interesting information?"

Emma stretched the truth a little. "Well, for one thing, he knows Barry and tried to talk him out of blackballing us. He also told me that Sergio bought a book from Annemarie on common poisons two weeks ago, *and* that he may have a gambling problem."

Julie raised her eyebrows at this.

"Finally, he confirmed that Chief Tompkins is hoping to make an arrest this morning in the murder. Tonio." Emma then proceeded to explain everything Tom Fitzpatrick from the garbage company had told her about the stolen items in the trash can.

"That's terrible, Mom!" Julie exclaimed. "We can't allow Ronnie Fitzpatrick to get away with lying like that. I'm calling Piers right now to see what he thinks we can do."

Julie started down the front stairs of the old yellow farmhouse. Half way, she turned back. "Mom, get dressed in something nice and see what you can find out in town today. Go to the Honorage. Get a massage. Put it on my account. But whatever you do, *don't* hole up at home all day in that muumuu."

Emma finished her coffee, climbed the staircase to her bedroom, showered, and dressed in black jeans and the Liberty print blouse Julie gave her for her birthday. The blouse was a concession on Julie's part. Julie wouldn't be caught dead in a Liberty print herself. But she knew her mother loved them.

Emma sat down on her bed and slipped on her black and purple Nikes, something comfortable for a long walk; followed by her fuchsia ultra lite parka to beat the early morning chill. At least she wouldn't embarrass anyone dressed like that. And a walk into town sounded like just what the doctor ordered. In fact, she mused, it *was* just what the doctor had ordered: at least forty minutes of heart thumping exercise every day, along with numerous blood pressure pills, cholesterol pills and vitamins to keep the Big D at bay.

Emma began to insert the ear buds for her iPhone into her ears. Then she decided against it. How was she going to hear any gossip with music piped into her head?

Emma started down her driveway at a brisk pace, making sure to peek into the window of her daughter's office across the driveway from her front porch. She caught Julie's eye and waved so Julie would get off her case. Then she turned right on Blissburg Avenue past the fire station, and headed down Third Street towards the footpath that ran along the creek. It was a popular route for the Walkie-Talkies and other ladies' walking groups in Blissburg.

At first, the part of the path between the creek and the old train tracks was deserted; and, except for the gurgling stream and twittering birds, completely quiet. Emma realized that plugged into Spotify, she'd almost forgotten how relaxing those sounds were. She walked along, past the overgrown blackberry shrubs, savoring the whisper of the wind in the leaves of the tall poplar trees, the chirping of crickets and the birdcalls, till she came upon the Walkie-Talkies: Trish, Annemarie and Lilah, walking with Maureen Tompkins, the police chief's wife. In the morning stillness, their voices carried around a bend in the path. So Emma knew exactly what they were talking about even before she saw them. She stopped to listen.

"So they got them. Thank goodness!" she heard Lilah's voice exclaim.

"I'm sooooo relieved!" That was Trish. "Please thank the Chief for all of us, Maureen. He acted so quickly."

"Yes. I'm very proud," Maureen replied. "They were on the bus. Headed for Vancouver, Canada! Thank goodness Ronnie came up with all that evidence when he did. About the stolen statues and the silver. A few hours delay, and the Chief says they might have made it across the border."

Ronnie, Emma thought. That liar. She rounded the bend at a fast clip. The Walkie-Talkies burst into view. Emma confronted them, barely able to control her anger.

"They arrested both of them?" she demanded. "Tonio and Carmen?" Then, realizing that the Walkie-Talkies were staring at her, she tried to plaster a smile on her face.

"Hi," she began again. "I couldn't help overhearing the great news." She took a deep breath. "By the way, how did they implicate Carmen? I mean, she didn't necessarily know what her husband had done. The theft of a couple of netsuke by one's partner doesn't exactly a murderess make. Or does it? I mean, how do they tie Carmen to the murder?"

Apparently, Emma wasn't so good at disguising her true sentiments. The Walkie-Talkies' raised eyebrows said, whose side is she on?

Emma tried to recover, "Forgive me. I've worked for years in a law office. I just *pray* the case is tight. You know, Maureen. No holes. We don't want them to beat the rap."

Maureen looked around at her friends and nodded. "Emma's got a good point. She hasn't hung around those tricky lawyers for nothing. She's right. Just on the basis of the stolen goods, they *couldn't* have tied both the gypsies to the murder." She paused. "But there was more." She lowered her voice. "A lot more."

Everyone sucked in their breath at once.

Maureen hesitated a moment.

They waited.

"I probably shouldn't tell you this until the Chief," Maureen always referred to her husband as the Chief, "makes the official announcement." She paused again. This time for dramatic effect. Then she shook her head. "No. I better not."

Trish broke first. "Please Maureen. Please tell us. Please, please, please. Pretty please? We won't breathe a word until the Chief announces it. We promise. Don't we?" She glanced from Lilah to Annemarie.

Everybody nodded, except Emma who waited skeptically to hear the next lie. She braced herself, her hands folded belligerently across her chest.

"Girls, you really have to promise," Maureen cautioned. "My reputation is at stake. If the Chief knew I told you, he'd never tell me anything again."

"We promise," the women all assured her. Even Emma this time.

Maureen took a deep breath. "Here goes. I swear, it gives me chills just to think of it." She placed her finger tips to her temples and exhaled slowly, as though to calm herself. "Last night the chief got a search warrant for Tonio's trailer. The judge issued it after they found the stuff in the trash can."

Everyone nodded.

"Well..." She paused to drag the suspense out a little longer. "They searched Tonio and Carmen's trailer early this morning. Of course the suspects weren't there. They were already on the bus to Canada when the state police arrested them. But guess what they found in the trailer? Buried in the bottom of Carmen's tarot card basket. You know, the one she uses when she reads the cards, or reads your palm. The one with those red and green silk ribbons?"

Everyone nodded again. Emma clearly remembered the basket from the Opera fundraiser. But why, she wondered, did the Walkie-Talkies recognize it? Had they all had their fortunes read? By Carmen?

Maureen dragged the suspense out with a few more seconds of silence. Then she dropped the bomb.

"They found the ring!" she whispered. "Natasha Vasiliev's four carat emerald and diamond ring! The one missing from the body the night Natasha died. Susie at The Jewel Box says its gotta be worth at least fifty grand. The ring was buried at the bottom of the gypsy's basket. I guess *that* ties Carmen to the dead woman. And gives her a motive, opportunity and means." She stared at Emma, waiting for her legal authority to agree.

Emma had been trying all morning to remember the third requirement for a murder suspect. Motive. Opportunity. That was it. The means.

She looked at Maureen and nodded. "Right. Yeah. I see motive and opportunity. But what about means? Did Carmen carry a vial of poison around her neck all the time looking for victims with four carat emerald rings?"

"Well yeah. Duh," Trish shot back. "At a fundraiser like that? She knew darned well someone would wear something worth stealing. She probably cased the party while telling people's fortunes. Then, once Natasha was dead. Just thinking about it makes me shiver. She stole the ring from her dead finger."

Lilah agreed. "After all, Emma, she stole the other stuff too. For all we know, she'd seen Natasha wear the ring before."

Everyone else nodded agreement.

Even Emma had trouble scraping her chin off the floor. The evidence that Carmen was involved in Natasha's death seemed almost insurmountable now. With Natasha's ring buried in Carmen's basket, it was getting hard for Emma to believe she wasn't involved.

9

MONDAY AFTERNOON – BETRAYAL

Emma continued along the footpath with the Walkie-Talkies all the way to Little Pete's Gourmet Grocery, hoping somehow to clear the doubts gnawing at her heart. She'd worked with Carmen. Thought she knew her. Trusted her. Could she really have been that wrong? Maybe Carmen was just the victim of a bad relationship. Tonio was the killer. But Carmen, not Tonio was at the fundraiser. The ring was in Carmen's not Tonio's things. It sounded more like Carmen had set up Tonio, than the other way around.

Still, some things didn't add up. Carmen only learned of the gig the afternoon of the fundraiser. She didn't have time to concoct an elaborate plan to kill Natasha and steal her ring. Or did she? And if Carmen was the killer, why had she admitted to Emma that later that night, she'd returned to the scene of the crime? It didn't make sense. Or was Carmen cleverly covering her tracks?

To make things worse, everything the Walkie-Talkies said hammered more nails in Carmen's coffin. According to Lilah, one of her customers swore that just days before the murder she saw Carmen in Santa Rosa at a shop for the occult buying potions. Babs said that one of her best customers – she couldn't say who – reported that recently, after reading her palm, Carmen predicted that they would never see each other again."

"She knew she was leaving town!" Annemarie from the bookstore gasped.

Rumors. All rumors. But what if they were true?

At the intersection where the footpath veered left into the wild life preserve, Emma bade the Walkie-Talkies goodbye saying she needed to buy milk at Little Pete's. Really, she just wanted to get away. She was starting to sweat. September in Blissburg, she sighed, wiping her forehead. Indian Summer. What did she expect? Every breath of cool morning air had already been sucked through a furnace. By noon the temperature would have climbed into the nineties. She took off the ultra lite parka and tied it around her waist before directing a limp wave to her companions.

"Bye darlin'," Maureen waved back. She patted her hand over her heart. "You must be soooo relieved. One of the first things I thought when the Chief told me about the arrests was thank goodness for Emma's sake. She's been through hell, what with people making fun of her and saying her famous spaghetti sauce killed the soprano. I heard you made that Jon Stewart comedy news show." She nodded her head. "Now honey, *that* kind of publicity ain't half bad."

Jon Stewart? Emma didn't believe it. Surely Julie would have told her if Jon Stewart made fun of her. "No. I don't think so," she shook her head.

"Anyway," Maureen replied, "all of us are just glad that this cloud of suspicion hanging over your head has been lifted. You can get on with your life." She wagged her finger at Emma, "Maybe you won't want to write cookbooks anymore. But there's lots of other things you can do."

"You're right," Emma answered. "It's a huge relief to have this resolved." She turned into Little Pete's parking lot.

The truth was, she didn't feel relieved. And why, *really*, did any of them ever think that her pasta sauce actually killed someone? Cloud of suspicion! Emma barreled into Pete's, grabbed the milk, glowered at the checkout lady, paid for the milk and began to power walk home.

Suddenly, the quaint town plaza shaded by redwood trees, bordered by nineteenth century stucco buildings now housing clothes boutiques, wine tasting bars and three star restaurants, felt claustrophobic. Thank goodness she was going back to cold, foggy San Francisco Tuesday night for that concert. Tomorrow couldn't come soon enough. It was the first time, since she moved to Blissburg, that Emma had felt that way.

She walked up main street past Claud's. Inside, she caught sight of Jack. What *was* that he was reading? The New York Times? Who read the actual newspaper anymore? Even Piers read four papers on line. But she was tired of running into someone every time she turned around. She didn't stop to say hi. Instead she practically ran all the way home.

And she didn't take Julie's advice and go to the Honorage Spa. Instead, without even stopping at the house, she got into her car. If Carmen really had been arrested because of the ring, someone at the legal clinic would know about it. Maybe Carmen had even called.

As she suspected, when she got to the clinic it was buzzing with news about the arrests. Cameramen milled around the parking lot. Inside, a handful of volunteers discussed the murder at the reception desk.

Barbara greeted her. "You heard, right?"

Emma nodded.

"Steve wants to see you," Barbara jerked her head in the direction of the glass-enclosed office of the clinic's only full time attorney. "He's mad about something. I'm warning you."

Emma's stomach started to churn. She tapped on Steve's door.

"Come in." Steve's usually carefree, for an attorney, voice sounded unusually strained that day.

In the midmorning heat, the young man was dressed in his usual Giants T-shirt and shorts. He said he identified better with his clients that way. Maybe he did, Emma thought. She wasn't one to judge. But dressed in baggy shorts and a rumpled T-shirt, with his oval face, blue-eyed regular guy features and scraggly hair pulled back into an untidy ponytail, he reminded Emma of the Dude in *The Big Lebowsky*. A far cry from Piers' tailored lawyer Zegna look. And to think, he and Piers were classmates at Boalt Hall, the prestigious law school at Cal.

"It's you," Steve said glancing up from his computer screen. "Glad you decided to show up."

"I don't usually come in on Monday," Emma started to explain.

"I know," he answered, his tone more unfriendly than before. "That's why I said I'm glad you decided to show up. I didn't want to have to track you down. You know, our client, Carmen Havlek, has been arrested for grand theft and murder, right? Along with her husband, or whatever he is."

Emma nodded.

"Now let me just say," Steve continued, his voice still gruff, "I heard some things from Barbara that could make me worry. But I'm hoping, after I talk to you, I don't have to."

Emma felt her shoulders cringe. "Can I ask you something?" Emma began.

Steve nodded.

"Did Carmen contact us? I mean since her arrest?"

Steve nodded again. "Yes, she did. This morning from the police station. The police let her call us because we were her attorneys of record in the Covered California health insurance proceeding. But here's the funny thing, Emma, that I want you to explain. She didn't ask for me. She asked for you."

Emma shook her head. "I...I don't know."

"Don't give me that." Steve was starting to look angry. "Barbara told me Carmen came in Saturday and talked to you. To *you*. That's the part that has me worried. You wanna tell me exactly what you two talked about? And why you didn't tell *me* on Saturday?"

Emma felt another involuntary cringe. In fact, she explained, after Carmen left on Saturday, she had peeked into Steve's office. And he wasn't there.

That wasn't exactly true. On her way out, Saturday, Emma noticed Steve wasn't in his office and was glad. Carmen had asked her not to tell anyone about their conversation. She wasn't sure what to do. That's why she didn't bother to look around the office for Steve before she left. Instead, as she now told Steve, she assumed he was gone for the weekend and decided not to bother him on Sunday at home.

"*Nothing*," she stressed the word, "*nothing* Carmen told me couldn't wait until this morning. At least, that was my best judgment at the time. It *is* Monday morning, Steve. I'm here, and it's not my regularly scheduled volunteer day. But I came in anyway, as soon as I could, to tell you what I know."

"Go ahead," was all Steve said.

"First of all," she began, "you need to know what happened Friday night." With that, she told him about Lexie Buchanon's request to hire a Roma to read fortunes at the fundraiser, about her call to Carmen, about Carmen's attendance at the party, including her strange behavior while reading Natasha's cards.

Steve interrupted. "Natasha? You mean the victim? The Russian opera singer? I'm not an opera fan. So set me straight."

"Yes." Emma nodded. "Natasha Vasiliev's the opera singer who was found dead at the party."

"Right. And then, according to Barbara, there were all those jokes," Steve added. "About you, right? About your book. I didn't know you wrote a cookbook, Emma. I love Italian cooking. Did you know that? My lasagna's incredible. Just ask my wife. I even make the dough."

"The pasta."

"Yeah, the pasta dough."

Emma wondered where this was leading. She interrupted him. "To get back to my story, Steve. Just as Carmen started to read Natasha's cards, Carmen turned white as a sheet. First she said she was sick. Then she kind of slipped away and I didn't see her again. Until Saturday."

That's when Emma told Steve *everything*. What Carmen had said about seeing the murder in the tarot cards, about rushing home, worrying, and then returning to the party to see a distraught Barry Buchanon holding Natasha's head in his arms. Emma even explained to Steve that Carmen had told her all this because she thought that Emma was an attorney. That Emma had told Carmen she was *not* an attorney. That Emma advised Carmen to go to the police with her story. And that Emma had *not*, despite Carmen's urging, promised to keep Carmen's story a secret.

Emma concluded, "When I told her she *must* go to the police, she ran out the door and disappeared. I ran after her. That's when I looked for you, but didn't see you in your office." Emma knew she was stretching the truth a little. "But she was gone. Frankly Steve, I was confused. I mean about whether what she told me was confidential, attorney-client stuff. Without researching it, I figured that it *was* because," Emma tried to remember Piers' rationale, "because she, the client, intended it to be."

Steve rubbed his eyes. "It's a reasonable argument, at least. But you should have told me. That kind of thing was worth a call at home."

"From hindsight, I completely agree with you," Emma nodded. "But honestly, at the time, it didn't even occur to me that Carmen committed the murder. Nothing she said made me think so. I told her what she should do, and thought the rest could wait until Monday. I never dreamed she stole the ring."

"Did she?" Steve asked.

"It was in her basket," Emma shrugged.

"Maybe someone put it there. Tonio?" Steve suggested.

Emma threw up her hands. "The garbage men lied about finding those netsukes in Tonio's trash," she explained, describing her conversation with Tom Fitzpatrick. "But the theory that someone planted the ring in her tarot basket is a little farfetched, Steve."

He laughed. "No more farfetched than killing someone to steal a ring, taking a bus to Canada to escape being caught, and leaving the ring in your trailer."

"*Hiding* the ring in your trailer," Emma corrected him. "Maybe there was an accomplice planning to pick up the ring and meet them in Vancouver."

"And maybe the real killer put the ring there to frame her. Happens all the time, Emma. I say we visit Carmen in jail and hear her side. Just one more thing. If you told her you aren't an attorney, how come Carmen asked for you on the phone today and not me?"

Emma shook her head. "I don't know, Steve. Because she likes me. Because I'm nice."

It took Emma and Steve about fifteen minutes to drive to the jail where Carmen was being held on $1,000,000 bail. By the time they arrived, the jail was full of reporters from newspapers and stations all over California, all over the world.

Steve identified himself as Ms. Havlek's attorney, and Emma as his paralegal from a prior representation of the accused in an unrelated matter. That got them into a holding area consisting of a bare room with two entries, one from the jail and one from the hall. It was furnished with a table and three chairs. After a short wait, two armed sergeants ushered Carmen into the room. From the hall, Emma heard the hum of reporters who had gathered there.

The minute Carmen entered, Emma's heart sank. The bird-like woman looked ten years older than she had at the fundraiser. She sat down, resignedly, looked at Steve and said, "Thank you for coming."

When she caught sight of Emma, however, she glared.

Then to Emma's surprise, pointing a thin shaky finger at her, Carmen began to scream. "You. The traitor. I curse you. You're to blame for this. You got me that rotten gig. You had me read those cards. You incriminated me. You told the police that I returned to the party later that night and saw the dead girl with the old man. This is all your fault. You framed me. I'll bet you even planted the ring. You pretended to be my friend. That you were on my side. But you turned me in. I called you this morning only because I wanted to tell you this. Now get out. I never want to see you again!"

Emma turned white. "Carmen, no! I didn't turn you in."

"You're the only one who knew," screamed the Roma. "You're the one I told, in secret, about what I saw. I told you because I trusted you. You with all your Roma bullshit. Acting so PC." Carmen broke down in sobs. Then she turned to the two armed guards. "Get her out of here. Please, get her out. *She* is the curse."

The guards opened the door to the room as Carmen finished speaking.

When one of the guards ushered Emma into the hall, at least a dozen reporters heard Carmen yell, "Traitor!" before he shut the door.

That was when a hundred tiny lights flashed in front of Emma's eyes.

10

TUESDAY MORNING - TEARS AND TURNAROUND

Julie rang the doorbell ten minutes after she saw her mother on the early morning news. They sat down to talk in Emma's kitchen.

"Mom," Julie began, "they had the killer. You were off the hook. Couldn't you just leave well enough alone? Why did you have to visit Carmen in jail? She crucified you on that video! Did you see the ticker on the bottom of the screen? 'Star-crossed foodie accused in jailhouse betrayal.'"

Thank goodness, Emma thought, Julie at least had the kindness to bring two lattes and warm cinnamon buns from Claud's. After seeing herself on the late night news, Emma hadn't slept a wink. She'd forgotten the milk for her coffee in the car, but didn't want to brave the reporters lurking in her driveway to go get it. She pointed to the coffee with a weak smile and nodded, barely holding back her tears.

Julie's voice softened. She gave her mother a hug. "Poor Mom. I figured you might need a little comfort food. Look, Piers and I understand that you mean well. That you were only trying to help Carmen. But we both agree. You are way, way too trusting." Bitterness crept back into her voice. "You and your Roma PC."

Emma bit into the warm bun. All the butter and cinnamon melted in her mouth. Thank goodness, she thought. At least she still had her taste buds. When those went, she would *really* get depressed.

"Funny, that's what Carmen said," she mumbled through a mouthful of bun."

"What?"

"Nothing," Emma sighed. She'd been trying all morning to recall the name of that movie she hated. Now it popped into her head. *No Country for Old Men*. Maybe this was *No Country for Old Women*. Maybe this was the sign that it was time to move on. She wondered if that was what the Big D was all about. Realizing it was time to move on.

"Honey, thanks for the cinnamon bun," she added. "Sometimes I think they're too sweet, but this morning it really hits the spot." Emma took another sip of the hot coffee and tried to put things in perspective. "I mean, why am I sooo upset about this? No one's dead."

Julie gave her a funny look. "Mom, Natasha Vasiliev's dead."

Emma covered her face with her hands. "Right. You're right. Of course. Someone's dead. I think what I meant is, I'm not dead. You're not dead. Piers isn't dead and Harry's not dead. That's what I meant. At least, *we're* not dead."

Julie shook her head. "That sounds really selfish, Mom. Don't say stuff like that. I mean, there are reporters crawling all over the place." She stared at her mother. "Are you OK? I mean, do you need…"

Emma sat back in her chair, bit into the cinnamon bun, took a deep breath and laughed. "Honey, I'm fine. Just fine. But would you do me a favor? Would you call that Jack Russo fellow and tell him… tell him that under the circumstances, I really don't feel like going anywhere tonight. Or seeing anybody. He'll probably be relieved."

"You really want *me* to call?" Julie asked. "Isn't that kind of personal?" She noted the look on her mother's face, and relented. "All right, give me your cell phone. What's his number?"

Julie dialed. After a short pause she said a little gruffly, "Hello? Is this Jack Russo?"

Emma winced. "Don't sound so unfriendly," she whispered as Julie waved her quiet.

"This is Julie, Emma's daughter."

Pause.

"Yeah, hi. Well, you know, Mom's not feeling that well. And she asked me to call you to say that she's not gonna to be able to make it to the Ormon thing tonight. I'm sure you understand."

Another pause.

"Yes. No. Wait." Julie covered the receiver with her hand and whispered. "What do I do? He wants to talk to you. He knows you're here."

"No!" Emma whispered. "Tell him I'm not."

Julie uncovered the receiver. "No she's not here, Mr. Russo."

Pause.

"Right, *Jack*. She's not here, *Jack*."

Another short pause.

Julie covered the receiver with her hand again. "He says he heard you. And that you should stop acting childishly and talk to him."

Emma grabbed the receiver out of Julie's hand. "I think that's ridiculous, Jack. Saying I'm being childish. I've had a very, very bad couple of days in case you didn't know."

Pause.

"OK. So you did. Well. Never mind. I just don't want to go. Anywhere. With anyone. It's not about you. So don't feel sorry for yourself."

Pause.

"OK. Right. Maybe another time."

Pause.

"No. I'm not changing my mind, but thanks anyway. Now bye." Emma hung up the phone.

"Wow," Julie rolled her eyes. "He's a persistent little so-and-so, isn't he? Anyway, Mom. It just occurred to me. Since you're not going out, would you mind babysitting for Harry tonight? It turns out Piers and I have to go to the Ormon thing ourselves. It was kind of last minute and we don't have anyone lined up yet."

"Sure, I'd love to," Emma immediately agreed. She looked forward to being with Harry any time she could. But why, she wondered, did she suddenly feel used? "Why do you and Piers have to go to the Ormon thing?" she asked.

"Because after the concert, Clare, Madame Director, wants to talk to Piers and me about a Russian Opera Endowment that Barry Buchanon is making to City Opera in Natasha's memory. Clare's having a little post thingie dinner at Jardin. Barry will be there with Lexie. Under duress I heard from my hairdresser. Along with Massimo the conductor, Vera Vasiliev and Sacha Kuragin the bass. Barry's gift is huge. Clare has hired *me* for all the publicity. It's kind of a fence mending now that everybody agrees that the gypsy killed Natasha and we had nothing to do with her death. Or with the disaster at the party. Barry has assigned Lexie full responsibility for *that* since hiring the gypsy was *her* idea. If you remember, I was completely against it."

"Roma," Emma interrupted, then giggled.

"Mom, are you drunk?" Julie asked.

Emma shook her head. "No. It's just...." She sat up a little straighter in her chair and looked her daughter in the eye. "Julie, I just understood something. I mean, just now, when you were talking about the Roma and the endowment, and all those Opera people coming to dinner. Something has suddenly become very clear."

"What are you talking about, Mom?"

"Don't you see?" Emma answered. "Julie, it finally makes sense. What I'm talking about is this. Carmen did *not* kill Natasha. I'm sure of it." Emma's troubled expression had cleared. She looked determined, like someone on a mission.

"Mom, now you're acting crazy. Carmen was arrested because they found Natasha's ring among her things. She tried to flee. What's more, she just turned on you, her friend, like a viper."

"No!" Emma answered. "That's what I just understood. Carmen didn't turn on me like a viper. She turned on me like someone who is *innocent*. Someone who thought she'd been betrayed. Like every other Roma who's been framed. Carmen did *not* kill Natasha. I'd bet my life on it. Someone else did. And that someone may be sitting with you at dinner after the Ormon thing."

Emma's eyes narrowed. She was thinking. "Get Jack Russo on the phone," she added. "I'm going tonight."

"What?" Julie shook her head. "You're not babysitting?"

"No," Emma replied. "I said, call Jack. I'm going to the concert. With *him*. And I'm going to that dinner with *you* after the show. I'm going to clear Carmen and find out, once and for all, who killed Natasha Vasiliev!"

Julie raised her hands, palms facing forward. "That's it. I give up, Mom. It's your life. Do what you want. But *I* am *not* calling Jack Russo again. That is a call you will have to make yourself!"

11

TUESDAY EVENING - TEAM SPORTS

For the first time in years, dressing for a night with Julie was not a problem. At 4:30 Emma pulled her ancient black velvet pants out of the closet along with her even more ancient orange, pink, purple and gold Missoni sweater. Who cared if she looked like a retro designer hippy? She loved these clothes. And forget heels. She was wearing her comfortable old black loafers. If Jack was looking for a date in stiletto heels who towered six inches above his head, he shouldn't have invited her.

Speaking of Jack, Emma thought to herself, replaying their last conversation in her head. While he seemed a little surprised at her abrupt change of heart, his voice, at the other end of the line when she phoned, had sounded pleased.

"You're on," he'd replied. "I'll pick you up. Five-thirty sharp. It'll take an hour to drive to the City. That still leaves plenty of time for dinner."

"Appetizers," Emma had corrected him. "We're only having appetizers and some good wine. I have a plan for dinner after the show."

"*You* have a plan," Jack repeated, suddenly sounding wary.

"Emma, I gotta warn you. I'm a man who doesn't like surprises. I like to be in control."

Emma smiled to herself. Yes! She'd finally found his weak spot. "Don't be so uptight, Jack. You're gonna love this. See you at 5:30." She hung up the phone.

At 5:30 sharp she was seated by the front door in her classic, fitted, double-breasted black cashmere overcoat from Costco. She peeked out the window. The morning's news hounds had left her front door, lured by juicier scandals. She had just finished buttoning her coat when she saw headlights turn into her driveway.

The porch light was on. In its glow, a glittering dark blue car seemed to glide down the path like a kinetic sculpture before stopping at the end of her driveway. Emma had expected Jack to pull up in one of those stuffy Mercedes, or a BMW; but she didn't recognize *this* car. She opened the door and walked onto the porch. Aside from the crunch of the vehicle's wheels on the gravel, she didn't hear a sound. A high end Prius? *Was* there such a thing, she wondered?

"Love your car," Emma called over her shoulder while she closed her front door.

Jack had gotten out of the driver's seat and walked to the passenger side to open her door.

She walked towards him, squinting her eyes in the glare of the headlamps. As she passed the hood, she leaned forward to stare at the insignia.

"A Tesla!" She couldn't mask her surprise. "You gotta be kidding, Jack." Lately, Piers talked of nothing but how long the wait list was for the car. "Isn't this is a little over the top?"

The pride on the short square man's face as he opened her door was unmistakable.

Without answering her question, he shut the door and returned to the driver's seat, settling himself comfortably into the incredibly luxurious leather interior.

"You know, Emma," he finally said, not looking at her as he

turned on the car, "I've had some good fortune; and I've also had some rough times. When my wife died, I decided to treat myself to something special. This is the only car I have ever truly *desired*."

He said "desire" like a man who knew what that word meant.

They drove in silence for a while. It was Jack who broke it.

"So Emma," he began, "I got a dinner reservation at Jardin. I hope that's OK. I know the maitre d'. He fit me in on short notice. And what's this about appetizers? I was looking forward to a good meal."

Emma didn't bother to mask her enthusiasm. "Jardin? Perfect! You couldn't have made a better choice, Jack. And you know the maitre d'? That will come in handy."

"Handy for what?" Jack took his eyes off the road to stare at Emma. They had just hit the two lane construction stretch of highway around Petaluma. "I told you I don't like surprises."

"Watch your driving," Emma ordered before continuing. "OK. Listen carefully. Here's what we're doing. I said appetizers because you and I are having dinner *after* the performance at Jardin as guests of Clare Blumberg, the Director of City Opera."

Jack looked at her again.

She pointed her finger back at the road.

"Why?" he asked. "Is she hitting me up for another donation? Are you two in cahoots? I mean, sure I like opera. But it isn't exactly a cure for cancer, if you know what I mean."

Emma nodded. After Mary's sudden death, she knew exactly what he meant. She shook her head. "No. Don't worry. No donations." She paused. "But there *is* one problem. Clare Blumberg hasn't exactly invited us to her little dinner party. I know about it because my daughter and son-in-law will be there."

Then she explained about Carmen's arrest, that she believed Carmen was innocent, and that she intended to be at the party to help her figure out who really committed the murder.

"So," she concluded, "what I'm asking you to do is to accompany me somewhere we don't exactly belong."

Jack's answer wasn't what Emma expected. He shrugged. "OK. I'm used to being places I don't belong. I been doin' *that* all my life!"

They were past the Sir Francis Drake exit nearing the Golden Gate Bridge, when Jack turned to her again. He was driving 80. Once again Emma waved his eyes back to the road. "Don't you know how dangerous that is?"

Jack turned back to the road and laughed. "You sounded just like my wife when you said that."

Emma noted, however, that the joking comparison was tinged with longing. There was no bitterness in his voice or anger or even regret.

A few seconds later, this time *not* taking his eyes off the road, Jack addressed her again. He began as if he were making an announcement. "You know, Emma. There's something about you that's different tonight." He hurriedly added. "Not about your looks. Of course, you look great. You always look great. That's not it. But there *is* something different. I heard it in your voice this morning when you called me back. Did something happen?"

Emma thought about what he'd said. The truth is, he was right. Something *had* happened. She *did* feel different.

"I don't know," she answered. "Am I really different?" She paused. "Maybe. Maybe I *do* feel a little more sure of myself." That was it. "In control."

Jack agreed. "Yeah. That's right. You got more confidence all of a sudden. Before, I don't know. It was like you were apologizing for yourself all the time. Walking on eggshells. I notice a lot of women your age have that problem." He squinted at her. "I got a theory about it. Ever play team sports?"

Emma snorted. "No. *Team* sports. What would I play?" She thought a moment. "OK. Dodge ball. I played dodge ball in the fifth grade."

"That's all?" he laughed.

"Yeah. So what about you?" she replied.

"Me? I played ice hockey. Forward."

"Ice hockey?" Emma couldn't imagine where this was going. "Oh, right. You grew up on the East Coast. Like in high school?"

"Yeah," he answered. "High school. College."

"Ice hockey's not much of a college sport out here," Emma replied. "Where'd you go? UMass? Boston College? They're big hockey schools, aren't they?"

"Actually, I played for Harvard." Jack replied. There was a hint of defensiveness in his voice. "We had a pretty good team. A few of us went to the Olympics."

Ouch! Why, Emma wondered, had she automatically assumed UMass? Suddenly she felt like Henry Higgins in drag.

"Blue collar profiling aside," Jack continued, "my theory is that team sports teach confidence. You learn to take a shot. And to take the consequences. Sometimes your shot scores a goal. Most of the time, it doesn't. But you gotta take the shot. If you don't play team sports, you don't learn that. And a lot of women your age never played team sports. So you lack confidence. That's my theory. OK, not exactly *my* theory. I read it in the Wall Street Journal."

Emma nodded. "It's a good theory." Then she tried to back pedal. "About the U.Mass comment, Jack. I don't know. I guess I just don't automatically think everyone from the East Coast went to Harvard."

"Especially people who talk like me," he added. Then he took his eyes off the road again to look at Emma. "Let me tell you something. When I left my friends in Providence, Rhode Island and went to Harvard on a scholarship, and then to the Harvard Business School on financial aid, I vowed never to lose my accent. It's who I am." He took his right hand off the wheel and shook a thick hairy finger at her. "Never forget where you came from, Emma."

This time she didn't complain about his driving. Instead, after a moment of silence she said, "But isn't that the point, Jack?"

"Of what?" he asked.

"Of moving to California," she replied.

As they sped through the FasTrak lane into San Francisco, he turned to her again. "You know what I like about you Emma?" He didn't wait for a reply. "You're a smart lady. But what's more, you're nice. Me, I'm a VC. I can't afford to be nice. But the older I get, the more I think there's a lot to be said for nice."

Emma still didn't know what a VC was; but, that night, she decided not to ask.

12

TUESDAY NIGHT – IMPROV

Ten minutes later they stepped through the front door of Jardin where the maitre d' greeted Jack with a friendly clap on the back.

"Great game the other night, Jack. You still pass like an Olympian. You haven't lost your touch."

"An assist, Vince. You scored the goal." Jack winked at Emma. "Not too shabby for the Old Guys' Hockey League. Emma, you know Vince Gagliardo? He's a part owner here."

Jack quickly added in a lowered voice, "Hey Vince, Clare Blumberg asked me to tell you I'm joining her party after the Ormon Concert. Is that OK? Can you squeeze the two of us in? It's some kind of a fundraiser, I guess. I told her I'd help her out."

"No problem, Jack. No problem at all."

"So Emma and I will just be having appetizers and a bottle of wine for now, OK?"

"Of course. Anything you like, Jack. Anything at all. I'll tell your waiter."

Emma couldn't have been more impressed. When they were seated at their table she exclaimed, "Wow! That was easy. But what if Clare objects?"

Jack laughed. "She won't. It would be too embarrassing. What's she gonna do, say who invited you, Mr. Platinum Circle Director's Chair Club?" He shook his head. "Ain't gonna happen. She's hoping I'll leave City Opera something in my will. Sure, she'll look a little bit surprised to see me. Then she'll figure her secretary screwed up and say 'so glad you could make it, Jack.' Trust me. I know. That's how it goes."

The waiter had handed Jack the wine list.

"Emma, red OK with you?" he asked. "I feel like red tonight, even though I'm ordering oysters." He turned to the waiter. "We'll have the *Nuits Saint Georges.*"

The waiter beamed. "Excellent Mr. Russo. I'll be back to take your order momentarily."

They were enjoying an appetizer of Golden Mantle oysters when Jack turned the conversation back to the murder.

"By the way," he began. "For what it's worth, I did some more checking on Sergio. Contrary to what he told you at the party, the city's been on his back for almost a year. Maybe not about rats. There are no health department complaints."

"That shoots the obvious excuse for why he ordered that book on poison from Annemarie's store," Emma added.

"In some ways his problem's more serious," Jack explained. "The city's demanding major renovations to bring his old building up to code. He owns the place. The location's great. Right on the plaza. But according to my banker friends, he hasn't been able to get loans."

Emma shook her head. "Why? He runs one of the most successful restaurants in Sonoma Country."

Jack winced. "He's a good cook. That doesn't make him a good businessman. The restaurant's in debt up to its ears. And if Sergio doesn't make the improvements, the city has already threatened to shut him down. That's totally confidential, of course."

Emma nodded. "Of course. But none of that implicates him in Natasha's death."

"Here's what could," Jack continued. "Sergio, it seems, owes a truckload of money to at least one of his purveyors, Nesson Wholesale Liquors. I know Nesson. He's a billionaire who also owns an estate near Bodega Bay. He and Sergio got to be friends. They socialize. You know. Both of them bachelors. Well, guess who Natasha was singing for, all those years while Buchanon came up cold?"

"Sergio?" Emma asked.

Jack nodded.

She considered this for a moment. Sergio was definitely a handsome young devil. Way better looking than Buchanon. Who could blame her? "So maybe Sergio killed Natasha in a jealous rage."

Jack nodded. "According to Nesson, it was passion at first sight. They met at a party and rendezvoused in his guest house on the Bodega Bay estate. But," Jack continued, "Natasha insisted on hushing it up because she never wanted to let the wealthy Buchanon completely off the hook."

"Enough to drive any hot blooded Italian wild," Emma mused. "But murder? Now? That all must have happened years ago."

Jack shrugged. "Here's another hook," he added. "A few months ago, the city started breathing hard down Sergio's back. According to Nesson, that's when Sergio started gambling at the place up on the hill, hoping his luck would turn. Instead, of course, things only got worse. Soon, he owed the casino so much money, the Sicilian Mafia, my relatives..."

Emma gasped.

Jack rolled his eyes. "Emma, I'm *joking*. My father was a poor bricklayer, not a Mafia Don. Anyway the Mafia, who own a chunk of that debt ridden sorry excuse for Las Vegas, told him to pay or else someone else would."

"Like who?" Emma asked, her voice still husky from the Mafia scare.

"That's the point," Jack replied. "What could they do to him?

Sergio has no family. No wife. No kids. His business is deep under-water. No assets. They could either kill him…"

"Or someone he loved." Emma ended Jack's sentence for him.

Jack nodded. "So, according to my friend Nesson, when Natasha was murdered Sergio convinced himself that his Mafia brethren administered the poison to Natasha in order to punish him. Nesson says Sergio's been holed up in his office at the restaurant ever since. He's sure the Mafia will come after him next."

"Why doesn't he go to the police?" Emma asked.

"Cause he's overstayed his visa, for one thing," Jack explained. "And he's scared."

"Do you believe all this?" Emma asked. "That the Mafia killed Natasha because of Sergio's debts? It sounds far-fetched. Like a smokescreen. Like something Sergio invented because he has more to hide."

"Sweetheart," Jack replied, looking at his watch and motioning the waiter to bring them their check, "I'm just repeating what I heard. I don't know what happened. But I do know that, no matter who you are, if someone analyzes the soles of your shoes, they are sure to find some dirt."

By then, he had signed the check and was helping Emma on with her coat. "Of course," he added, "there's a cruder way to say that, but I thought I'd spare a nice lady like you."

By the time they'd found their seats for the Ormon Society's thank you concert for major donors, Emma's thoughts were in a whirl. Sergio the jealous lover was one thing. But the Mafia? *That*, Emma shivered, was way out of her league.

Since she didn't take the time to review the thick program distributed by the ushers when they took their seats, Emma really couldn't follow much of the Ormon Fellowship program. It consisted of one after another of the Ormon Rising Young Star Fellows singing a favorite aria in thanks for the donations that supported their training.

Just before the intermission, however, Chiara Bruno, the prior year's winner of the Ormon Rising Young Star award, stepped on to the stage. She sang an old favorite, *Un Bel Di* from *Madam Butterfly*. The song where the jilted geisha declares her faith that her callous American lover will one day return. It was a song that almost everyone in the audience knew by heart.

Halfway through Chiara's exquisite performance, the audience's own sniffling chorus began. Anyone caught without a hanky better at least have had a sleeve. When Emma couldn't control her tears and reached for her purse, Jack handed her his starched white monogrammed pocket handkerchief instead.

The first half of the program ended in an explosion of enthusiastic applause.

"Champagne at the Allegro?" Jack suggested.

The Allegro was a plush private lounge where the really big donors relaxed among their own. Emma loved it. She had been there once with Julie and Piers whose law firm made a large annual donation to the Opera.

"Sure," Emma replied. "I'll probably see Julie there. That way I can warn her. So she won't act surprised when we show up at dinner."

In fact, Julie was standing in front of them in the line waiting to be recognized by the elegant bouncer stationed at the entrance to the lounge.

Emma introduced Julie to Jack.

Julie nodded coolly. "I think we've met. At one of my husband's firm's parties. You'd just moved from the East Coast."

Jack squinted at Julie like he was trying to size her up. Then shook her hand.

Emma just had time to whisper in Julie's ear before they entered the lounge, "Everything's set. We're coming to the dinner. Don't act surprised."

Julie did a double take. "What?" she answered a little too loud. "You're kidding! Right?"

Emma couldn't hide the frustration in her voice. "See? That's exactly what I *don't* want you to do at the restaurant!"

By then, Clare, the Director of City Opera, was waving to Julie to join her at a small table near the back of the lounge. When she saw Jack standing behind Julie, she blew him a kiss and mouthed "Ciao Bello" before motioning him to come too. Soon, champagne glasses in hand, Julie, Piers, Jack, Clare and Emma squeezed together around a tiny glass table surrounded by a crush of major donors. Emma only recognized a few, including her old boss, Trent Dunn, from the law firm where she'd worked as a paralegal all those years.

"Emma," he greeted her. "Fancy meeting you here. I didn't know you were an opera fan. How are you finding the work up there in Blissburg? I remember your saying you were afraid it would be boring compared to the City. Anything but! I saw you on the news."

Emma cringed and introduced him to Jack. Trent did a double take. "I know this guy. Hockey. Harvard. Hell of a team. Didn't know you were out here."

"Yeah. Just moved." Jack nodded and turned away.

Emma watched Julie watch Jack. Her daughter's success meter recalibrating his score.

Then Julie turned to address the director. "Chiara was fabulous, Clare. I had no idea she was such an actress in addition to having a wonderful voice."

Instead of accepting the compliment to her new hot diva, Clare frowned.

"Just between us," she whispered, "that girl is a royal pain in the backside. Acting? I'll say she can act. She just threw a hissy fit before she went on stage. She's threatening not to sing opening night unless we redraft her contract and give her more money." Clare looked at Piers. "Of course, she knows she has us over a barrel. She'll call in sick. Strained vocal chords or something. And we'll be up a creek. *Her* understudy isn't half prepared. We'd have to call in Smetnova from New York for opening night. Which would cost us a fortune and Chiara knows it. It's extortion, Piers! And Massimo, my besotted conductor, is taking her side. Don't even get me started on *him*. Grrrr."

By the time Clare's little tirade was over, the lights flashed signaling that the second half of the program was about to begin. Emma and Jack hurried back downstairs to their orchestra seats.

As they sat down and the curtain rose, Emma whispered into Jack's ear, "I think we just found another pair of dirty shoes."

13

—————

TUESDAY LATE NIGHT – DRAMA

Emma was so worried about her subterfuge at Jardin that, the minute the singing stopped, she insisted she and Jack leave the Opera House. She wanted to beat the rest of Clare's guests to Jardin, the chic restaurant located just kitty corner to the Opera House.

"I thought about it all through the second half of the concert," she informed Jack as she urged him into the aisle while the performers were still taking their bows. "I figure Clare will be the last one to arrive at the restaurant. Julie tells me the Director's Box, where she sits, is way at the end of the mezzanine. I've watched her glad hand everyone from the foyer to the carriage entrance. And from what she said at the intermission, she'll probably have a few words with the conductor too. So if we're in the private room at Jardin before the other guests arrive, I think this thing may work. Julie and Piers know not to say anything. The Buchanons, the bass and Vera Vasiliev, Natasha's twin sister, have no idea we were never invited. The conductor, if he comes, will assume he misunderstood something. Then, if what you said is true, Clare will breeze in late and blame the mistake on her secretary. You and I will be home free."

Jack had grabbed Emma's elbow and maneuvered her out of the Opera House and across the street. "Wow," he exclaimed. "That's some plan. Did you happen to hear anything they sang for the past forty-five minutes? Does that brain of yours ever shut down? I don't think I've thought *that* hard about something in fifty years."

"Fifty years? What was it you thought so hard about then?" Emma asked.

Jack smiled. "How to get my future wife to break up with her boyfriend so I could take her to my senior prom. I wracked my brains for weeks over that one."

"What did you finally do?' Emma asked.

Jack smiled. "I simply asked her to the prom. She dropped the poor sucker like a hot potato. Done. And the rest is history."

Emma wondered about that. She had a very strong feeling that, whatever the rest was, it wasn't history.

Indeed, all Emma's planning paid off. She and Jack were the first to arrive at the private dining room. Vera Vasiliev, the dead singer's twin, was second, dressed in an expensive looking black sequin evening dress. Emma couldn't help wondering if it had belonged to her sister. She immediately noticed that Vera looked distraught. Her green eyes, outlined in mascara, were red from crying. Even the thick layer of foundation that Vera had smeared on her face couldn't hide the dark circles around them.

Emma introduced herself and Jack, reminding Vera that they had met the night of the fundraising party. But the very mention of that fateful night seemed to plunge the poor girl deeper in gloom.

Only the sight of Sacha Kuragin making his entrance noticeably lifted the partnerless twin's spirits. Emma watched her rush to embrace him, as though the poor girl thought she might interrupt the bass singer's self-absorption. She didn't. He ignored her, along with everyone else in the room, occasionally casting a desperate glance left or right like a great trapped blond bear. When the waiter entered with a tray of champagne, Emma heard him order vodka. Then he took out his cell phone and looked like he was texting.

The Buchanons arrived minutes later. Covered in his and her layers of frost, Emma noted. Dressed in a revealing silver tube, Lexie looked unsteady and disheveled. Even if their angry voices in the hall hadn't been clearly audible through the closed door to the private room, it was obvious to everyone that they had been arguing.

Vera Vasiliev did not greet the Buchanons when they entered. Emma saw Barry Buchanon avert his eyes as though Vera's near miss looks were too strong a reminder of all he had lost in her twin sister.

When Barry caught sight of Jack, however, he greeted him with a slap on the back. "Clare didn't tell me you'd be here," he said.

"It was kind of last minute," Jack replied. "Her secretary called me this morning. Someone must have told her I like Russian opera," he added with a laugh.

"Really?" Lexie stared so brazenly at Jack, Emma deduced she was drunk. "Does anybody?" she added.

"Does anybody what?" Jack replied.

"Like Russian opera," Lexie answered with a laugh. Then she looked Jack up and down and added, "Personally, I like hot blooded Italian."

Jack winked at her. "So do I."

Just then Julie and Piers appeared, saving all of them from the awkward moment. Emma couldn't have been more relieved. Finally, someone to talk to.

But Emma didn't have time to greet her daughter. Clare, the Director, and Massimo, the City Opera's conductor, followed them through the door. Clare still looked annoyed. In spite of herself, Emma froze, afraid that her ruse to crash the Director's party was about to fall apart.

Clare surveyed the small room. "Are we all here?" she asked.

When her gaze rested on Emma and Jack, her face expressed but a moment's surprise. Then her brow furrowed, as if she were trying to remember something. She glanced at each guest, mentally taking a tally. And seemed to count the chairs at the round table set in the middle of the room. Ten and ten, the numbers matched. Her face relaxed. She walked up to Jack, her hand extended.

"Jack, so glad you could come," was all she said.

Moments later, her guests took their places at the table. But before anyone ordered, Clare announced the point of the meeting.

"As all of you *may* know," she looked pointedly at Jack, "the Buchanons, today, made a profoundly generous donation to City Opera." She added, "Probably one of the biggest opera donations of its kind. The donation was made in the memory of our beloved friend and colleague, Natasha Vasiliev."

"Waida minute," Lexie interjected. Her voice had begun to slur. By then, the spaghetti straps of her platinum trash tube had fallen to half mast and one of her dangling earrings was caught in her hair.

"I wanna get one thing straight," she announced. "This isn't my gift. Unnastand? The gift isn't from," she made quotation marks with her fingers, "the Buchanons. See, I'm," she pointed to her chest, "one of the Buchanons. An I don't give a rat's you know what about opera. If it were up to me," she paused, "which it isn't." She wagged the forefinger of the hand bearing *the* sapphire ring. "I'd give the money to some poor little sick kids."

She stood up, cracked her neck a couple of times, and took a deep breath to better address her audience, most of whom sat perfectly still watching. Only Sacha the Russian bass, Emma noted, seemed to enjoy Lexie's performance. Lust was written all over his face.

"Becau-ause," Lexie continued in a singsong voice, "I don't unna-stand why a handful of jerks, like my husband Barry here, should be allowed to squander their money on a bunch of people screaming at each other up on a stage." She paused to giggle. "Except maybe to get his hands up the soprano's you know what. So please don't say

Buchanons in the plural, M'dam director. Cause Lexie Buchanon ain't givin' one red penny to honor that Russian whore! In fa-act," she paused. "I'm glad she's dead." Lexie stared at Clare and curtsied. "I hope my remarks have been duly noted, M'dam director." She sat back down.

At the end of Lexie's performance, Sacha erupted in such enthusiastic whistling, howling and applause that, for a second, Emma wondered if the entire act had been planned. But, if so, which opera was it from? She reconsidered. No. That theatrical number was strictly impromptu.

Emma didn't have much time to consider all the possibilities, because at that moment, Vera, the dead soprano's sister, sprang from her seat, raced around the table and grabbed Lexie by the throat.

"How dare you?" she cried. "How dare you talk that way about my sister? It's all your fault she's dead!"

For a moment, no one had the presence of mind to pry Vera's hands off Lexie's neck. Jack was seated too far away. Sacha, to Lexie's left, was laughing too hard to intervene. Piers to her right, froze as Vera lifted Lexie by the neck out of her chair and pushed her down onto the table. Barry, Lexie's husband, who should have sprung to her defense, had his head buried in his hands, sobbing at the far end of the table. Finally it was Julie who intervened. In the nick of time. By then Lexie was choking and turning blue.

It took some time for Julie to pry Vera's hands loose and wrestle her to the ground. Nobody helped. The men all looked stunned.

When Lexie flopped back on the table gasping for breath, however, it was Piers who cried, "Water. Give her some water." He grabbed a full glass, but was so flustered he dumped it on Lexie's chest instead of splashing it on her face.

Lexie sat up, suddenly sober. She looked at her sopping wet dress and burst into tears. Before anyone could stop her, she ran out of the room.

No one ran after her. Instead, Clare stood up from the table.

"I think we need to resume this discussion of Barry Buchanon's generous gift another time," she said, clearly having registered the point of Lexie's speech.

Then she and Massimo high-tailed it out of the room. But not before Clare bent over to whisper something in Piers' ear. Emma was seated close enough to him to hear.

"Thank goodness I've already deposited Barry's check," was what she said.

Emma and Jack said little in the car on the way back to Blissburg. Half way across the Golden Gate Bridge, Jack turned on the radio to catch a replay of the last innings of the baseball game. When they pulled up in front of Emma's house, Jack got out to open her door and escort her up the stairs.

"Sorry about that dinner," Emma apologized. "Are you hungry? I could make you some eggs."

"I'd better go," Jack replied.

While Emma searched her purse for her keys, he folded his arms across his chest defensively, nervously drumming his fingers on his coat sleeve. "And please don't apologize," he added. "For what it's worth, the dinner was *unforgettable*. But," he paused for a second and his fingers stopped drumming, "did it help? I mean, are you any closer?"

"Closer to what?" Emma asked.

"To figuring it out. To knowing who the murderer is."

Emma shook her head. "No. If anything, I more confused now than ever."

14

WEDNESDAY MORNING - WHO DONE IT?

The next morning, Emma awoke to the phone ringing. It was Jack.

"Hi," he greeted her. "It's me."

As if there were only one "me," Emma thought. That was another thing she didn't like. People who didn't identify themselves on the phone.

"In all that drama last night," he continued. "I forgot to ask you something."

Emma waited.

"I have two tickets to Opening Night on Friday. Wanna come?"

"Opening night?" The first thing Emma thought was that she had nothing to wear. She sighed. "Fancy, right?"

"Yeah," he replied. He must have heard the sigh. "I'll probably get dressed up. Have to amortize the expensive tux my daughter made me buy for her wedding. But frankly, Emma, you can wear sweat pants for all I care. I go for the music."

"O-K," Emma replied tentatively, put off by the sweat pants joke. Is that how she looked now, she wondered? Like a woman who wore sweats to the Opera? Had it come to that? "I can probably do a little better than sweats," she added.

"Your call." He hung up.

Later that morning, Emma didn't wait for Julie to knock on her door. The minute she heard her daughter's BMW turn into the driveway, she dressed, grabbed her full coffee mug, ran out of her house and knocked on Julie's office door.

Julie gave her a hug. Then she waved her into her elegantly remodeled, glass, cherry and chrome office where they sat down to talk.

"What was that all about last night?" Julie asked. "If the police hadn't already nailed the two gypsies, I'd be tempted to believe that *Lexie* knocked Natasha off. And what about Vera Vasiliev? That girl is strong. I'm in pretty good shape, but I didn't think I could pry her hands off Lexie's neck in time. Not that anybody helped me!"

"I had exactly the same thought," Emma agreed. "If Barry was inclined to give Natasha fancy jewelry and who knows what else, Lexie certainly had a motive to kill her. Last night, she proved she had malice as well."

Julie shook her head. "Personally, Mom, I still think the police already have the killers. But if it'll make you feel better, I'll see what else Oleg at the Honorage can tell me about Lexie. He'll love hearing a firsthand account of her performance last night. He's never been her biggest fan. Maybe he'll be interested in an info exchange. I got the feeling he hasn't told me *everything* about Lexie yet."

"Great!" Emma replied. Then she filled her daughter in on the new information about Sergio.

Julie didn't buy it. "Nah. The Mafia theory's just too far-fetched. As for Sergio, I know him. He's a lady's man, not a lady killer. He wouldn't do it."

"In a fit of rage. He *is* Italian after all."

Julie rolled her eyes. "Mom! Where does that come from? The movies? He's a gentle guy. Besides, Natasha wasn't murdered in a fit of rage. If it was poison, it had to be premeditated." Something seemed to pop into Julie's mind. "By the way, how on earth did you wangle an invitation to the party last night?"

Emma waved her hand dismissively. "It was Jack. Jack managed it. Jack knows everybody."

Julie cocked her head to one side and studied her mother. "Speaking of Jack."

"Oh no." Emma sucked in her breath. "What now?"

"Nothing, really." Her daughter hesitated. "I just decided to find out more about him, that's all. So I asked Piers. And then I Googled him."

Emma braced herself. "Go on."

"Well," Julie began, "aside from Harvard and going to the Olympics - I'm sure he told you *that*. He just doesn't sound very likeable."

"Of course he's not likeable, honey. He's a VC," Emma snorted, "whatever that is. It used to mean Viet Cong..."

"Venture capitalist. Really, Mom!" Julie rolled her eyes. "With a physics background, no less. But my point is, *no one* likes him," she persisted. "He spent a ton of money trying to defeat that kooky Cianci guy when he ran for office in Providence. That was in the papers."

Emma shrugged. "Hardly surprising. Cianci sounds Italian. Everyone knows Italians don't trust each other."

"The point is," Julie continued, ignoring her mother's comment, "he failed. Making enemies all along the way, according to Piers."

"Since when is fighting corruption bad?" Emma shot back.

"OK," Julie threw up her hands in frustration. "Have it your way. He's a knight in shining armor. And don't get me wrong. His company has backed a lot of winners. Enough to make him mega rich. But every developer in Massachusetts hates him because he also spent a fortune lobbying against casinos throughout New England. And lost again. That was in the papers, too. Something about a personal crusade against gambling because of his father.

And get this, he just moved here and he's already battling with the owners of Bear Creek."

Emma nodded. "He told me about his father."

Julie crossed her arms over her chest. "How close *are* you two?"

"Not close, Julie! Don't worry. We talk." She paused. "So what about your theory that Jack's part of the Mafia?" Emma cringed as she said it. She sounded so small-minded.

Julie nodded her head vigorously. "Well, actually, there *is* a Mafia connection, Mom. The Mafia *hates* him. Because he was so high profile opposing the casinos. Piers joked that he's probably on some Mafia hit list. He was only *half* joking. One of Piers' partners didn't even want to take Russo on as a client. Until he saw his net worth."

Emma waited a few seconds after Julie stopped talking. Then she said, "Look honey, if you study the soles of anyone's shoes, you're bound to find some dirt."

Julie shot back, "That sounds exactly like something Jack Russo would say. Only he'd probably use the much cruder version that Piers' friends use."

Emma thought for a moment. She still couldn't figure out what version that was.

"Besides, Mom," Julie continued, "the truth is, that's wrong. If anybody analyzed the soles of your shoes, all they would find is a little house dust."

"Unfair!" Emma pouted.

"I meant it as a compliment, Mom. You probably didn't even smoke pot in the sixties."

Emma didn't reply. Yes, she'd smoked pot in the sixties. She'd just never particularly enjoyed it; and she never told her daughter. She stood up to leave.

"Listen, Julie," she said. "I've gotta run. I have a very busy day. But I'd really appreciate it if you'd follow up with Oleg about Lexie. And report back to me immediately if you find out anything of interest." Without saying another word, she marched out of the room.

Emma also didn't mention that she'd decided to check in with Steve at the free legal services clinic to see if there were any new developments with Carmen's defense. She hadn't talked to him since their visit to the jail.

HOUSE DUST INDEED, Emma thought waiting for the electric sliding door to the clinic to open. Who did her daughter think she was? Emma, the independent working single mother all those years!

She scowled at Barbara. "Is Steve around?"

"Isn't this one of your days off?"

"Doesn't matter," Emma barked. "I asked if Steve is here."

Barbara raised her eyebrows. "In fact he is. Do you want me to…"

But Emma had already marched past her straight into Steve's office.

He was on the phone. Emma stood in front of his desk and waited.

"Hey, listen, Rick," he said after it was clear Emma wasn't going away. "I got a meeting. See you at the courts. At Laurel Park. Not the ones at the high school where we played last week. If we get there at five, something'll be open." He paused. "OK. See you then. Bye."

Steve put down the phone, leaned back in his chair, crossed his arms on his chest, and stared at Emma. "What's up?" he finally said.

"I want to know if there are any new developments in Carmen's case," Emma replied. "And if you're still her defense counsel. I'm sure she's innocent. I want to help."

Steve raised his eyebrows. Then he bit his lower lip as though considering something. "That's a gutsy offer, Emma," he finally said, "considering all that bad publicity Carmen gave you. Frankly, I'm surprised."

Emma couldn't help wondering what kind of a selfish wimp people thought she was. She ignored the remark and continued. "Look, Carmen's reaction was understandable *if* she knew she was innocent. And *if* she believed that someone - that someone being me - had framed her. As far as she knew, I was the only person in possession of the kind of information that would lead the police to her door. So, it was natural she would turn on me. She didn't know there were other people implicating her in the murder. In fact, it is exactly her reaction to me that leads me to believe she's innocent."

Steve agreed. "I explained all that to her when she calmed down after you left. Like the fact that Ronnie Fitzpatrick and his father falsely testified about the stuff being in Tonio's garbage can. And that Vera Vasiliev told the police that she saw Carmen eyeing the ring when she first met Natasha Vasiliev. As though Carmen was trying to see how easy it would be to get the ring off. Vera Vasiliev apparently told the police that she believed Carmen stole the ring at the party. Faked being sick to get away. And poisoned Natasha so no one would discover that the ring was gone. By the way, that ring was valued at a hundred grand. Not a bad chunk of change for a Roma."

Emma nodded. She remembered Carmen touching the ring when she held Natasha's hand during the reading. Nothing suggested to *her* that Carmen was planning to steal it.

"That theory is very far-fetched, if you ask me," Emma added.

Steve shrugged. "Chiara Bruno claims she saw the ring on Natasha's finger when Natasha sang during dinner. If that's true, the murderer must have stolen the ring after Natasha was dead, not before. No one has corroborated it. Anyway, by the time I'd explained all this to Carmen, she believed that you did nothing to betray her. I told her that you never even told *me* what she said when she visited your office the day after Natasha died. And that I even bawled you out for it."

Steve took a deep breath and blew it out slowly. "Look, Emma. Carmen's really sorry about everything. She wants you to know that. I was gonna call you but I figured, after that embarrassing news coverage, an apology wouldn't do you much good. I guess I should have called, though. You're a bigger person than I realized."

Enough with the selfish wimp, Emma thought. "It's all water under the bridge, Steve. The point is, I believe that Carmen and Tonio aren't involved in the murder and I want to do everything I can to stop this...," she paused to think of the right words, "rush to justice. The only way I can see to do that is to find the real killer."

"I agree," Steve said. "The murder evidence against them is very weak. We have a good chance to beat this. But even if they get off, until the real killer is found everyone will still believe Carmen and Tonio did it. Frankly, Emma, I've had my hands full just building a defense. I haven't had time to do the police department's job finding the killer. And the police are so sure they've found the killers, they're not doing their job."

"Exactly my thought," Emma replied. "That's why I've been poking around."

Steve motioned for her to sit down in the chair facing his desk.

"So here's what I've found." Emma proceeded to summarize everything she, Julie, Piers, and Jack had found out about their list of suspects.

When she finished, Steve nodded. "You're right. Lexie's gotta top the list. Aside from Chiara Bruno whose alibi, according to the police, is that she spent the whole evening with this Massimo conductor guy." He snorted, "Her lover, right? Aside from Chiara Bruno, Lexie B. appears to have had the most to gain from Natasha Vasiliev's death. Especially if we can show that her husband was giving away his assets to the singer."

Steve paused for a minute and closed his eyes like he was trying to remember something. "Buchanon Vineyards. Lexie Buchanon. Wait a minute."

He opened the file drawer behind his desk and started leafing through some papers. After a couple of minutes he pulled something out.

"Here," he flipped through a file. "About a year ago, a gardener up at the Buchanon Vineyards contacted us about her. Wanted to file some sort of complaint. He was a good looking guy." Steve stopped talking to scan a piece of paper. "According to this report, she propositioned him and when he wouldn't cooperate, she fired him."

"Wow! What happened?" Emma asked.

Steve studied the file some more. "It looks like the poor guy never came back after the intake meeting. He was probably illegal and got scared." He shrugged and continued reading. "But, whoever followed up on this initially - I can't read the signature. Annie? Anton? People come and go here all the time. Anyway, whoever it was ran a search on Lexie Buchanon and found DUI's, an assault, even some shoplifting charges, later dropped. All of them going back to when the then Lexie Grankowsky lived in Connecticut."

"Still, that doesn't make her a killer," Emma answered.

"No, but she's not sympathetic. And nothing rules it out. You said your daughter's following up on this with someone who worked with Lexie Buchanon at the Honorage Spa?" Steve asked.

Emma nodded.

"Good," Steve said. "Now, what about the sister? The unstable twin. Surely she had an axe to grind. Sibling rivalry? Definitely a known cause for murder going all the way back to Cain and Abel in the Bible."

Emma considered that for a minute. Cain and Abel did provide compelling historic precedent.

She nodded. "I agree. It could. But nothing points there. She's clearly devastated by her sister's death. I've seen her. I don't think she's faking. And what did she have to gain? Everything she had she owed to her sister. Alive not dead." Emma paused. "Last night, I got the feeling she's carrying some sort of torch for Sacha Kuragin, the bass. He was all over Natasha at the fundraiser. But he certainly wasn't in love with her. Sacha is only in love with himself. So was Vera jealous enough about that to kill her sister, her sole source of support and the only reason Sacha ever gave her the time of day?" Emma shook her head. "It doesn't add up."

"What about this Sergio character, the celebrity chef?" Steve asked. "Jealous lover? Desperate for money? I don't buy the theory that the Mafia killed Natasha Vasiliev to get back at him. But who knows? Anyway, is anyone following up on that?"

"Can't we just go to the police with Sergio's story? Shouldn't *they* follow up on it?" Emma asked.

Steve looked at her skeptically. "First of all, the police want to believe they already have the killers, right? And second, put the police on him and this Sergio guy will clam up. Or worse, go missing. I say, someone should talk to him informally. He was in love with Natasha Vasiliev. He had every reason to be jealous. Let's hear what he has to say. Sound him out. Do you know anyone who could do that?"

Much to her own surprise, Emma answered, "Me. I know Sergio. I'll do it."

15

WEDNESDAY NIGHT – A LITTLE TENDERNESS

When Emma got home there was a message on her land line from Julie.

"Mom, it's your loving daughter. I'm sorry about the house dust comment. Piers is furious with me. He says you're like Nancy Pelosi compared to his Mom when it comes to getting out of the house. Except, I told him, Nancy Pelosi is in the House which I thought was very funny. Anyway, we both want you to come over for dinner tonight. Harry has been asking when he can see you. Besides, with all that's gone on, Piers and I don't think you should be spending time alone. Piers'll pick you up at 6:00 on his way home."

Emma figured the Piers pickup was Julie's way of ensuring Emma didn't back out. Emma had half a mind to do just that after the house dust comment. But she missed Harry. She looked at her watch. It was already 5:00. Piers would be there soon.

Emma walked into her kitchen, filled her teakettle with water and set it on her Viking range – perfect for testing recipes. Then she pulled her favorite floral mug off the open wood shelving and placed it on the butcher block counter. Julie originally chose Persian Crème granite for the counters, but Emma nixed it as not in character with the old historic home.

The tea kettle had just begun to whistle when she saw Piers' silver Porsche Carrera glide under the flowering white magnolia tree that shaded the small yard between her front porch and Julie's office. Piers was early. She'd barely had time to catch her breath.

She turned off the stove, grabbed her purse and parka off the coat rack in the hall, and raced out the front door, waving at Piers as she locked up. Then she ran down the front stairs to the car and settled into the soft leather interior.

I could get used to this, she thought as Piers drove away. He had even turned on an oldies station for her. Or maybe he actually liked Otis Redding. She closed her eyes and let *Try a Little Tenderness* roll over her.

"Sorry Julie's so hard on you sometimes, Emma. The house dust comment was really out of line."

The sound of Piers' voice jarred her. She'd dozed off.

"I know you know how much she loves you. And values your opinion about everything," he continued.

Valued her opinion? That was a stretch, Emma thought. She squeezed her eyes more tightly shut and listened to the music.

"You've been her rock, what with all the Andy troubles. I think," Piers hesitated, "I think her, well, her abrasiveness for want of a better word, is all part of her defense mechanism. You know how deeply she was hurt. First the divorce. Now the conviction."

Emma tried not to open her eyes. This wasn't a discussion she wanted to have with Piers.

"Anyway, she doesn't mean it," he continued. "She doesn't mean to hurt you is all I meant to say."

Emma tried to keep concentrating on Otis Redding's bittersweet lyrics.

"I know," she said. Then all of a sudden Emma felt tears leaking out of the corners of her eyes. Why did that song always make her cry?

"Oh Emma," Piers looked over at her. "I didn't mean. I'm sorry. This is terrible."

Emma sat up and wiped her eyes. "No. It's not you, Piers. It's not what *you* said. It's that *song*. It always makes me cry."

Piers hand went straight to the radio button. "I apologize." He clicked it off.

Emma wanted to tell him, no! She loved the song. But what was the point?

"Anyway," he added, "while I have you alone in the car, I wanted to mention something about Jack Russo. I know Julie's been giving you a hard time about him. But honestly, I just think she's jealous. I mean, since Andy left, you've never had anybody else in your life and it's going to take her some time to get used to it. That's all."

Emma ignored the "never had anybody else in your life" part. It was what she'd always wanted Julie to believe. In the twenty-five plus years since Andy left, of course there'd been others. Just not anybody Julie knew about. There was the hunky contractor who redid her bathroom after the pipe burst. Awfully good with his hands. But a no go from the start. It was the summer Julie was with Andy's parents in Maine. She didn't need to know.

And, later, there was the old college classmate whose wife abruptly left. And then just as abruptly returned. Julie was on her high school semester in Italy. At the time Emma thought her heart would break. In hindsight, it was just one more bullet dodged.

"Piers," Emma finally replied, "let's get one thing straight. Jack Russo is *not* in my life! We had coffee together. He asked me to the Ormon thing. We're going to the Opera Friday." Darn! She wished she hadn't said that.

"Opening night?" Piers asked. "You know how much that costs?"

"No," she answered. "And I don't care. I mean, seriously Piers, I wouldn't even call him a friend. He's an acquaintance, of sorts."

"OK," Piers shrugged his shoulders. "All I want to add is this. Speaking objectively, more objectively than Julie, he is nice enough personally. If you're on his side. He's smart. Maybe savvy is a better word. But I'll warn you, if you cross him, he can be a very difficult man. He's aggressive and determined to have his way. All the time. Of course, that's not necessarily a bad thing. And sure, he's Italian. Apparently he even likes opera. But despite the Harvard education," he hesitated, "well, he just doesn't seem like our type. Maybe what I'm saying is, Julie and I just don't get what you see in him, that's all. Of course," he added, "that's your business, not ours."

Darn right, Emma thought. She answered, instead, "Piers, what I'm trying to tell you is that you're right. He's *not* my type. I don't see *anything* in him. But that doesn't mean I can't go to the Opera with him."

By then they'd pulled into the driveway of Piers and Julie's elegant, 5000 square foot mansard roofed mini Versailles on elegant Silver Creek Road. It had a huge pool, sat on two acres of lawns and gardens, and was surrounded by vineyards. Yes, Piers had done well for her daughter, Emma noted as she opened the car door. And she liked Piers. So she decided not to end the ride on a strident note.

"Piers," she touched his shoulder before he got out of the car. "I just want you to know that I appreciate the fact that you and Julie always look out for me. I couldn't ask for better children."

The minute she passed through Julie's front door, Harry threw himself at her.

"Nonnie, Nonnie! Yay, Nonnie's here," he shouted. "Come on. Let's play Go Fish in the living room."

That was reward enough for coming to dinner with nothing but house dust on the soles of her shoes.

Go Fish it was. For an hour. Along with a glass of wine and some local goat cheese. Emma played with her grandson, sipped the wine, savored the cheese and figured that if the Big D came that night, she'd die happy.

Then the phone rang. Emma heard Julie's voice. Something in

her tone activated Emma's antennae. Her reaction was justified by the look on Julie's face the minute she walked into the living room.

"I'm sorry, Mom, but," she began.

Emma knew immediately what was coming. If only by now she'd been able to convey to her daughter that it was OK. She really didn't care anymore. In fact, it was all sort of amusing in a zany Fox sitcom sort of way. Her completely mismatched marriage to a philandering felon. It really didn't matter.

Or did Julie want it to matter? Emma considered this for a moment. How could Julie not want it to matter? How could she think that something so hurtful *did not* matter?

"Dad's coming over," Julie explained. "He wants to see Harry. I told him you were here. Of course, that only made him want to come more. Like if he didn't, he'd miss out on something. Is that OK?"

"Of course," Emma answered. "It's fine."

"Sure?" Julie asked.

"Sure."

Twenty minutes later, Andy arrived.

"Emma, so good to see you," he greeted her with a hug. "My don't you look well? By the way, I saw you on the news. I almost called. But I thought, everyone will be calling her. Then Julie explained that those poor Roma, the ones the police have been trying to pin Natasha Vasiliev's murder on, were people you know. It's terrible how the police have scapegoated those Roma, isn't it?"

Emma had noted that, since his conviction, Andy had become an expert on scapegoats. .

"I read all about it in the paper," Andy continued, becoming more and more agitated as he spoke. He turned to Piers. "How can they hold those people? They have no proof. It's obvious they were framed. The real killer probably poisoned Natasha Vasiliev *before* the dinner. Otherwise, how did she have time to digest the poison?"

Emma and Piers exchanged amused looks. Apparently Andy was now a toxicology expert as well.

"What kind of poison was it, anyway? Have they done the final toxicology report?" Andy asked.

"It's due Tuesday," Emma answered.

Andy shook his head as if to say what bozos. "Anyway, it doesn't take a toxicology report to see that the killer poisoned Natasha Vasiliev, then took the ring off the body after she died, and planted it in that poor Roma's trailer."

"What about the stolen stuff in Tonio's trash?" Piers asked.

"Allegedly in his trash," Emma corrected him.

"Trash, smash," Andy dismissed it. "Don't you see? This was premeditated. The killer stole the stuff and hid it in Tonio's trash. The same person probably alerted the police to it. All to frame those poor defenseless Roma." Andy was in tears now. He took out a Kleenex and wiped his eyes. "It makes me sick just to think about it."

Andy checked his watch and looked at Julie. "By the way, when are we eating? I have to pick something up at Target on the way home. And *this*," he pointed to his ankle bracelet, "goes off at eight o'clock. If I'm not home, the darned thing calls my probation officer and snitches on me. Is there time for dinner? Or should I just munch on this cheese and paté?"

"Better load up on the cheese and paté, Dad," Julie answered. "Dinner won't be ready for at least a half hour."

Half an hour later, Andy waved good-bye from the front door. "Sorry I have to run. Great to see everybody. Especially you, my little munchkin." He reached down to give Harry a hug. "Handsome, isn't he?" he said to Piers. "Kinda looks like me, don't you think?"

It wasn't till they'd finished eating and Piers took Harry upstairs for his bath that Julie motioned her mother into the kitchen to discuss her day at the Honorage Spa.

"I found a few things out," she began. "Piers doesn't buy any of it. He still thinks the Roma did it. But even allowing for Dad's paranoia, there might be some truth in what he said."

Emma nodded. "Go on."

"Here's what I learned today. First of all, Oleg, my well informed masseur at the Honorage Spa, adored my eyewitness account of Lexie's drunken show last night. He hates Lexie more than I knew. Going way back to when she first worked at the Honorage. I mean, Oleg used words to describe Lexie like conniving, scheming, stop at nothing to get her way. By the way, she grew up in Connecticut. Oleg thinks she left under some kind of cloud."

Emma remembered the shoplifting charges the free legal services clinic had dug up. She kept that to herself for the moment and nodded.

Julie continued. "Right after the Honorage hired Lexie as a masseuse, she bragged that she'd snag a rich husband and quit her job in three months flat. Well, you can imagine how Oleg reacted to *that*. He's worked at the Honorage for twenty years looking for a rich sugar daddy without a bite."

"*Then*," she continued, "Barry Buchanon cancelled his regular appointment with Vera Vasiliev, Natasha's twin sister. Vera had worked at the Honorage since she and Natasha moved to California three years ago when Natasha won an Ormon Rising Young Star Fellowship. By the way, Oleg says Vera's the best for deep tissue. I believe him after wrestling with her at Jardin last night. So that's when Lexie started doing Barry and figured she'd just got her chance to marry a billionaire."

"She had, right?" Emma asked.

"Not exactly," Julie replied. "According to Oleg, Lexie didn't know that Vera Vasiliev had already made other plans for Barry's nuptial bliss. A few months before, when *Vera* started doing him, strictly massage, Vera discovered that Barry *loved* opera. So she set him up with her twin sister, Natasha, hoping Natasha would marry rich Barry, who would pay off their debts and kick start Natasha's career. Who needed an Ormon Fellowship with Barry footing the bill? For a while Vera's plan for her sister seemed to work. Barry fell head over heels in love with Natasha."

"Onassis and Callas," Emma sighed, "like the rich Greek tycoon and his mistress, the ill fated diva."

"Right," Julie nodded. "But then, just when Vera thought her sister had sealed the deal and would marry Barry Buchanon, something unexpected happened. At one of Barry's parties, Natasha met..."

"Sergio, our handsome celebrity chef," Emma completed the sentence. "And *Natasha* fell head over heels in love."

"Exactly," Julie nodded. "Natasha dropped Barry like last year's Prada flats. And her sister's carefully laid plan to marry her to the rich Barry Buchanon, completely unraveled. Lexie saw the opening to lure Barry to her well made bed, and married the old fool on the rebound a few months later."

"Wow," Emma exclaimed. "Vera and Lexie must hate each other. They were rivals, of sorts, at the spa."

"Of sorts," Julie agreed. "But Vera had only told her co-worker, Oleg, about her plans for her sister's marriage. Lexie never knew. Oleg and Vera even went to Lexie's wedding. After all, it wasn't Lexie's fault that Natasha chose a gorgeous celebrity chef over an old billionaire. Then Natasha's career took off and she moved to New York."

"So why didn't that end it?" Emma asked. "With Barry, I mean."

"Well," Julie resumed, "according to Oleg, what *Lexie* never expected was that Barry would carry a torch. A few months ago, when Natasha returned to San Francisco for the *Trovatore* rehearsals, he wanted Natasha back."

Emma threw up her hands in confusion. "What about Sergio, our hunky celebrity chef? Wasn't she still in love with him?"

Julie rocked her hand back and forth. "Not really. By then, Sergio didn't look so attractive anymore. According to Oleg, he was deeply in debt. And Natasha was famous. Of course, Barry was married to Lexie. And Sacha Kuragin, the sexy basso, was in Natasha's life. Not exactly a Barry Buchanon in the finance department, but a famous and attractive man. And they both spoke Russian. They understood each other in more ways than one."

By now, Emma's head was swimming. "So where does all this leave us?"

"It leaves us here," Julie concluded. "According to Oleg who heard it from Vera, Barry Buchanon had been using every financial inducement he had to lure Natasha back to his bed. Paying off loans. Buying her expensive jewelry. Even slipping her wads of cash. If Lexie knew about that - and obviously she did - well, as we've said before, it's a motive."

Emma blew out a long exasperated breath. "That's all very interesting, Julie, in a confused sort of way. But we need *proof*. Carmen's sitting in jail with a 100K stolen ring found hidden in her trailer. What concrete proof have we got that Lexie Buchanon committed the murder?"

Julie's face fell. "I guess you're right. Nothing yet," she agreed. "Oh," she seemed to remember something. "Oleg had another interesting tidbit. It doesn't incriminate Lexie, though."

"What?" Emma asked.

"It's about his co-worker and confidant, Natasha's twin, Vera Vasiliev. Oleg said Vera had a huge crush on Sacha Kuragin, Natasha's lover, the basso."

Emma nodded. "I know. I think she still does. Last night at the party, she practically threw herself at him."

"Well," Julie continued. "At the very end of my massage, which was great, I might add. It did me a lot of good. You should get one. Anyway, at the end of my massage, Oleg told me Sacha complained bitterly about Vera's annoying advances. Oleg got all this from Sacha, himself, by the way. Sacha is one of Oleg's old buddies."

"Like from way back in Russia?" Emma asked.

"Actually, they're both from Ukraine," Julie explained. "According to Sacha, Vera could *not* understand why Sacha wouldn't leave her sister alone when Barry resumed his advances to Natasha.

Vera offered herself to Sacha instead of Natasha, her twin. Oleg says that in Vera's mind, she and Natasha are identical and therefore interchangeable."

"Except, of course, they aren't," Emma added. "And everyone knows that."

"Everyone except Vera," Julie explained. "She was furious when Sacha rejected her."

"Poor deluded Vera," Emma sighed. "Now she has nothing. No sister. No Sacha. She's probably the biggest loser of all."

Julie shook her head. "No, Mom. Face it. Natasha is the biggest loser."

Just then Piers poked his head into the kitchen. "The little man's finally asleep," he announced.

Emma checked her watch. Time to go. She stood up and looked at her son-in-law. "Can you give me a ride?"

"I'll drive you," Julie offered.

They were almost home when Julie turned to her mother. "Any chance you can babysit Friday? Piers and I need to be at Opening Night. Clare is announcing Barry Buchanon's big donation. It seems he and Lexie have reached some sort of agreement, according to Clare."

"Sorry, honey. I'm busy Friday night," Emma said.

Julie looked disappointed. "Is it something you can change?"

Emma took a deep breath. "Jack asked me to the Opera."

Emma could almost see Julie bite her tongue. "Great," she managed. "You'll have fun." She paused. "What are you going to wear? You can borrow something if you need to."

Emma let her breath out slowly. "Thanks, honey, but no. I'll make do."

Emma got out of the car and climbed the front steps to her door. Otis Redding's song echoed in her ear. Yes, she mused, even old girls get weary wearing the same old dress.

16

THURSDAY MORNING – OUTLETS

Emma woke up Thursday morning unable to get Otis Redding out of her head. She put a sweater over her green fleece muumuu and made her way downstairs to the bright country kitchen where she brewed a small pot of coffee. Yes, she reminded herself as she foamed up a pitcher of milk, the legendary mountain man's farmhouse that Piers and Julie had fixed up for her suited her just fine.

The best part of all was the backyard. One third of an acre of fruit trees, flowers and lawn abutting a small wildlife preserve. The large redwood deck off the kitchen had a picnic table for grilled dinners on hot summer evenings that in Blissburg lasted well into the fall. What more did she – what more did anyone – need?

It was early September. The sun was out. Birds were singing in the fruit trees. Emma brought a tray of the coffee, milk and Claud's biscotti out to the deck to enjoy the warm morning air. When the phone rang inside the house, Emma didn't even bother to get up to answer it.

Then her cell rang inside the pocket of her muumuu. It was Julie. Just checking in. Emma assured her daughter that she was fine. That the tears Piers saw in the car were for Otis Redding, not for herself. And that yes, she was all set for Opening Night.

Or was she?

Emma hung up her cell. Then she mentally searched her wardrobe to see what was there.

First she pictured the brilliant red and orange Missoni sweater, but she'd already worn it with Jack to the Ormon thing. There was the black velvet skirt she got on sale ten years before; but the last time she tried it on it was way too small. The flowered dress she wore to Julie's wedding was too summery and already looked dated. Her own wedding dress wouldn't fit her left thigh.

Pants of any kind didn't feel right, especially if Jack's seats were in the orchestra section. At the one Opening Night Emma had attended, many years before when Mary's husband got stranded in New York, every woman from the orchestra to the mezzanine wore an evening gown. The last time she looked, the San Francisco newspapers still covered Opening Night in the fashion column.

Of course, she reminded herself, Jack had assured her that he didn't care if she wore sweat pants Opening Night. Sweat pants indeed!

Suddenly Emma realized that it didn't matter whether *Jack* cared what she wore. She had a date for Opening Night at City Opera. With a man who looked vaguely like Robert de Niro and who was more or less her age. The music would be great. The food good. The company posh. All that mattered was that, for the first time in months, *she* cared.

She checked the time on her cell phone. It was already 9:15. The day before, she had told Steve she'd find a way to talk to Sergio. The sooner the better. Carmen was rotting in jail. The police, sure of their suspect, were unlikely to turn up any new leads.

Emma thought for a moment. Sergio's chic restaurant in downtown Blissburg only opened for dinner. He probably didn't even start cooking until noon. By the time she got dressed it would be 9:30. It took an hour and a half in traffic to drive to Petaluma and back. That left almost an hour to get the job done. Yes! She pumped her fist. There was time to hit the outlets.

Emma showered, threw on jeans and a T-shirt, and got in the car. She told herself that driving fast, with *no* traffic, she could complete the trip to the stores in a little over half an hour. The stores opened at 10:00. With luck, she'd have time to spare.

She pulled out of her driveway on to Blissburg Avenue and drove by the fire station towards the center of town. Passing the tree-shaded plaza with its chic wine bars and upscale boutiques, she realized she hadn't *really* been shopping in years. Shopping? Why bother, she'd asked herself every time she passed the outlets on her way into the City or heading south to San Jose. The clothes, now, were too expensive. Besides, nothing fit. Even if it did, the clothes were not appropriate. Who wanted to look like a senior slut?

But that morning, driving south on 101 at a reckless 80 miles an hour, Emma realized that something was different. *She* cared. She *wanted* to shop. She felt it. The rush. The longing. Desire. The thrill of, once again, wanting to possess! She hadn't felt those things in years.

Thirty minutes south of Blissburg, the Saks Off Fifth outlet sign loomed into view. Emma quickly decided that would be her first stop. At Saks she hoped to find a kind of overview of a market she'd abandoned seasons ago. She swerved her Prius across two lanes and made the exit. Then she pulled into a parking space in front of the store. As she stepped through the sliding glass doors her heart was full of hope.

And she was right to hope. The first thing she saw started her heart racing. A plain, floor length black satin strapless Armani sheath. It graced a dummy at the very front of the store. With the green paisley pashmina that Julie and Piers brought back as a gift from India almost eight years before, Emma knew the gown would look stunning. She approached the Armani rack crossing her fingers they'd have her size.

An eight. She found it immediately. She grabbed it, then stood in line for almost half an hour waiting for a vacant dressing room. By the time she found one, it was 10:40. But she assured herself that if the dress fit, she'd be back in Blissburg on time.

In the make shift dressing room, however, Emma immediately wished she'd thought to bring the right underwear. The comfort ultra support bra just didn't work with the strapless gown. Given the minimal privacy afforded by the makeshift dressing room, taking everything off seemed risqué. She took it all off anyway. And wriggled into the elegant dress in record time. What's more, it fit! She twirled. No major tears or stains. A miracle! Who knew shopping could be so easy?

A saleswoman peeked her head round the curtain.

She started to say, "Need any help?" Then changed it to, "Wow! You look great."

"I'll take it," Emma cried and quickly dressed, meeting the young lady at the register minutes later. Still marveling at her good luck.

"Do you want this treasure in a travel bag?" the young woman asked.

Emma nodded, surprised at the outlet's great service, and handed the salesgirl her card. She checked her watch. She'd be home by half past eleven.

The girl rang up the purchase. "Sign please," she said and handed Emma the slip of paper.

Emma had just poised her pen above the signature line at the bottom of the receipt when some numbers caught her eye. 3232. She was sure the price tag on the dress had said $300. Was 3232 the date, she wondered? No. Couldn't be. It wasn't March. Nor was it 2032.

She put down the pen and rooted through her purse for her reading glasses to study the receipt more closely.

"What's this?" she asked the salesgirl.

"The price?" the girl answered, raising her voice in another question. As if to say, and what planet do you come from? "It's three thousand two hundred and thirty-two dollars," she said. Then a sympathetic smile crossed her lips. "Are you from out of state? The two hundred and thirty-two is the tax. It's high in California."

"No," Emma answered. "I just...I must have misread the tag." She laughed but the sound she made was more like a sob. "I thought it said," she was about to say '$300 not $3000'. Instead, she said, "Never mind. This isn't gonna work. Reverse the charges."

After that, it was back to the drawing boards. All of them were bad. The Carolina Herrera was too expensive and full of feathers. She'd look like a jungle book cartoon. The Versace had too many zippers. Why, she wondered, would someone her age want to shed her clothes *that* fast? And Nanette Lepore was way too short and sexy. The Prada was covered in pale blue sequins. She had never looked good in fish scales. When she finally slipped through the sliding glass doors to the parking lot empty handed, it was just past 11:00.

She had given up all hope of finding a suitable opera gown when she noticed the Ralph Lauren outlet located across the street. She hadn't been in a Ralph Lauren store in years. But the clothes used to fit. Emma checked her watch. At most she had fifteen minutes.

Unfortunately, when she entered Ralph Lauren she immediately realized that season's wannabe chic was Imperial Russian winter and fur. All of the evening gowns glittered in fake jewels embroidered on yard upon yard of heavy thick velvet. Fine for Julie Christie in a Russian horse drawn troika out for a snow ride with Omar Sharif, but definitely not Emma's style. Her heart awash in despair, she had turned to leave when, out of the corner of her eye, she noticed a sign at the far side of the room.

"Clearance," it said.

She hurried over to take a quick look.

The clothes were clearly last season's. Mostly sundresses and bright summer slacks. She looked at her watch again. Better run.

Then a swath of cloth at the very end of the rack caught her eye. She pushed back six hangers, and there it was. The most beautiful skirt she had ever seen. Mid calf with of layer upon layer of paisley silk chiffon. Her heart fluttered. She was in love.

The size was a ten. With luck, it ran small. She whisked the skirt into the dressing room along with the sleeveless gold cashmere blend tank top hanging beside it.

Only then, alone in the dressing room, did she dare look at the price tags. The sweater was $200 reduced from $800. The skirt, from $1500 down to $600. It was all way over her budget. But what the heck, Emma thought to herself. She had gold sandals and an ancient gold shawl.

She ripped off her clothes and kicked off her Nikes to try on the sweater and skirt. They fit like a glove. Then her eyes caught sight of her toes. She would need a pedicure. No doubt about that.

She dressed. Grabbed her loot. Charged it on her credit card. And was back in Blissburg by 12:05.

Once inside her door, Emma hid the skirt and top way in the back of her closet. Then she laughed at herself and wondered exactly whom she was hiding it from. She rushed back downstairs. No stopping for lunch. It was time to confront Sergio.

17

THURSDAY NOON - WHAT'S ON THE MENU?

As she walked to Sergio's restaurant, located on one of Blissburg's main streets bordering the plaza, Emma rehearsed the approach she would take questioning the hunky young celebrity chef.

First of all, Emma agreed with Julie that Sergio had nothing obvious to gain by killing Natasha, his former lover, except revenge. According to Jack, even stealing a $100,000 ring wouldn't settle Sergio's debts. He was too far under, financially, for that. And of course there was nothing to show that Sergio ever stole the ring. Or anything else, for that matter. Quite the opposite. The ring turned up in Carmen's trailer.

Which left her with Sergio's theory that the Mafia killed Natasha to scare him into paying his debts. But that theory didn't make sense, either. As far as she knew, Sergio was plain out of dough. She smiled at her pun. Killing Natasha didn't change that. And if the Mafia was ticked off, why hadn't they killed *Sergio* by now? No, if Sergio was involved, it had to be a crime of passion. The question was, how to expose it.

Emma had already decided that trying to guilt trip Sergio about the Roma scapegoats probably wouldn't work. Most of the Italian men she knew just weren't susceptible to guilt trips – except by their mothers. So she decided to play the small-town-gossip card first.

She approached the sleek modern redwood and chrome restaurant front whose sign proclaimed, in bold raspberry red script, *Ristorante Sergio*, and tried the front door. It was locked.

She peeked inside, then knocked. From an alcove behind the empty reception desk where the hostess usually greeted customers, two very dark brown eyes peeked through a grey velvet curtain. Seconds later, Sergio emerged. He recognized Emma, then shrugged, lifting his elegant tanned hands, palms up, as if to say, please, *Signora*, don't make me have to come out.

Emma rapped harder on the door. "My books, I've come to collect my cookbooks." She'd planned that opening line in advance. It offered a credible excuse for her visit.

Sergio rolled his eyes. Then all muscular, trim six feet of him emerged from behind the curtain and he tiptoed – yes, Emma laughed, he actually tiptoed like some clown from a *Commedia dell'arte* pantomime show – to the front door. He opened it just wide enough to poke his head of black curls out far enough to survey the street - right and left. Then he motioned for Emma to enter quickly through the narrow opening of the door.

"*Entra Signora*." Like most well bred Italian young men, Sergio used the word *Signora* when addressing someone his mother's age. "What is it you want? The cookbooks?"

Sergio actually said, "What ees eet you want." He spoke with the clipped accent of an Italian who'd learned English in England. Which Emma knew was true. Sergio's apprenticeship at the famed *Uccellino* in Bologna, was followed by a stint in London – too cold, she'd heard him complain – before he found Blissburg, California and opened his own restaurant.

Emma nodded. "I'm collecting the ones I gave to friends around the plaza. What with all that bad publicity."

"The bad publicity," he nodded. "Yes. It's a shame. The book is good. Very good. The *salsa di pomodoro, magnifica*. But under the circumstances, I understand," he agreed. "Wait here."

He cast another exaggerated glance over his shoulder out to the street, and then went to look for the cookbooks which, Emma noted, had disappeared from their featured place at the bar.

"I'm on foot, Sergio," Emma called after him, seating herself at a table just inside the dining room. "I hope you don't mind if I sit down." She intended, in this way, to avoid a curt dismissal once he gave her the books. Without waiting for a reply, she added, "Would you mind bringing me a glass of water?"

Sergio glanced over his shoulder again. The expression on his face signaled he *clearly* minded. But he didn't object and soon disappeared through the door to the kitchen. He returned minutes later with a stack of her cookbooks in a shopping bag and a full glass of water.

Emma took the glass of water from him and set it down, uncertain whether to drink it. After all, if Sergio *were* Natasha's killer, who knows what he might do? Then she dismissed the thought as silly, sniffed the water, and took a tiny sip, trying not to swallow.

Sergio must have observed this. He got right to the point. "*Signora*," he said, "if you think that *I* had anything to do with Natasha's murder, then," he thrust his chin forward and threw up his hands, "*Boh*! You are *pazza*, crazy."

Emma hadn't expected to get to the point so fast. She decided to stick to her script.

"Sergio, look," she began, "I'll admit. I didn't come here just to collect the cookbooks. Though I *am* getting out of the food business."

Sergio nodded.

"The truth is, I came to inform you - and I mean this as a friend." Emma cringed when she told the lie. "Blissburg's a small town, a very small town, and I've heard some rumors. That's all they are, rumors. But I thought you should know about them."

Sergio sucked in his breath. He waved his hand in a tight circle. "Go on, *Signora*," he said.

"First of all," Emma began, having rehearsed this part over and over on her walk to the plaza, "there's talk that you ordered a book on poison from Annemarie's just a couple of weeks ago."

"Did Annamaria tell you that? Awwww," Sergio pounded the table top hard enough to make the silverware jingle. "She promised me she wouldn't say anything. Something like that is very bad for business. I'd have ordered it on line, but Amazon closed down my account when the credit card company refused to honor..." He stopped speaking abruptly, seeming to think better of finishing that sentence. "What I mean is, how was I to know two weeks ago that buying a book on rodent poison would turn me into a murder suspect? What was I supposed to do? I saw a rat in the kitchen one night when I was closing up. It probably surfaced because of all the renovations at the new olive oil tasting room going in next door. Personally, I'd have rathered the dress shop stayed, but..."

Emma interrupted him. "Let me get this straight, Sergio. You had rats in your kitchen and you blamed *me* for dropping a spoon and then using it to stir my pasta sauce? Which, by the way, didn't even happen. I was just knocking on wood for good luck. But you had to make a big deal out of it, claiming your kitchen was clean*issimo*. You can imagine how I felt when the soprano died and everyone thought it was my cooking. Why," she got even angrier now, "I always wondered who fueled all those nasty jokes about my sauce. I bet it was you."

Sergio looked embarrassed. He bit his lower lip and shrugged. As if to say, could you blame me?

"*Signora*," he replied. "I had to deflect any suspicion from me. I already had the rat problem. If the health department got wind of it I'd be sunk. The city was on my back." He abruptly stopped talking again and switched course. "I mean, my restaurant, my livelihood was at stake. Not my hobby. Like you, *Signora*."

"Emma," Emma shot back. "Call me Emma. And it wasn't my hobby. It was my future. What little is left of it," she added.

Sergio appeared to be taken aback by what she'd said. "*Scusa, Signora*. I mean, Em-ma." He distinctly pronounced each "m" Italian style. Then he looked at his watch. Emma knew he wanted her to leave.

She continued quickly. "There's more, Sergio."

He leaned back in his chair and pouted like a sullen teenager.

"There are rumors," she said, "that your restaurant is in deep financial trouble. That you've taken some unwise risks, up at the casino, and that certain unsavory individuals are after you to collect a big debt. There is even a rumor that you're worried the Mafia killed Natasha Vasiliev to get back at you. Though personally," she added, "I think that's far-fetched."

Sergio leaned forward as she spoke.

"Who told you that," he shouted. "Was it Piers?" He nodded. "Sure. It was Piers, wasn't it? And I thought he was such a nice guy. But of course, he's a lawyer. He hears that kind of thing." Sergio pounded the table again in frustration. "Still, I didn't see *that* coming."

Suddenly, Emma felt she had to clear Piers' name. Jack had told her the rumor. Piers wasn't to blame. But if Sergio suspected him, who knew what Sergio might do? She shook her head. "It wasn't Piers. I promise you, Sergio. He's not the one to blame."

"Then who is?" Sergio shot back.

Emma didn't like the direction their chat had taken. Her heart started pounding. "I...I can't tell you," she stammered.

Sergio leaned way back in his chair and folded his arms across his chest. A cagey smile replaced his frown. Then he waved a forefinger at Emma, mimicking her in a sing song voice.

"Em-ma," he began. "I think I should inform you – as a friend, of course. Blissburg is a small town, small*issimo*. And there are rumors I thought you should know."

Emma felt her body tense up. She sucked in her breath.

"People here…I won't name names," he added. "Some people say you are sleeping with…" His voice got loud and angry. "That fat, arrogant Sicilian *cafone* Jack Russo! I know that's whom you heard that *cazzo* of a rumor from."

Emma jumped. *Cafone* meant boor. Her grandmother had used the word a lot. But Emma didn't exactly know what *cazzo* meant. They hadn't covered it in the Spoken Italian class she took before her trip to Italy to research her book. The word was used a lot in that epic Italian movie, *Best of Youth*, that she saw with her class. All she knew was that, whatever *cazzo* meant, it was bad.

Then suddenly something occurred to her. Emma's shoulders relaxed. She exhaled, one long cleansing breath. And thought to herself - *I'm sixty-five years old. What do I care if everyone thinks I'm sleeping with that arrogant, multi-millionaire, cafone VC?*

"Maybe I *should* sleep with him," she muttered out loud. *Except that he's obviously still in love with his dead wife*, she thought but did not say. "Maybe, it would be fun!" she added out loud.

Suddenly, Emma started to laugh. She sat back in her chair and laughed so hard tears sprang to her eyes.

At first, Sergio just stared at her as though she were crazy. Then the volatile Italian's expression swiftly changed to a smile. Followed by a few silent guffaws. Finally he erupted in explosions of laughter that left him gasping holding on to his sides. When he caught his breath, he stood up, reached across the table and hugged Emma.

"*Signora*," he cried. "You're so cute. You make me laugh. You remind me of my grandmother. How can I be upset with you?"

Emma made a conscious decision to take that as a compliment.

Sergio sat back down, kissed his fingertips and saluted. Either his grandmother or herself, Emma couldn't tell which.

Then, just as quickly as his expression had turned from anger to mirth, his face got serious again. He stared across the table at her and said, "Look, *Signora*. Why are we arguing like this and making all these veiled threats? We've both got problems, right? We've both got bills to pay, reputations to rebuild. But as soon as the police convict those two *zingari*, the fortune tellers, we can relax, right? I'll figure out some way to repay my debts. I'm looking for more backers right now to refinance me. You can get back in the food business."

Emma marveled at how quickly the sun chased away the storms in the man's brain. She shook her head. "It's not quite *that* simple, Sergio," she said.

"Why not?" he replied.

That's when Emma told him. Way more than she expected to. About all the holes in the police case against the Roma.

"Holes?" he asked. "You mean problems? Like that case in Perugia against the American girl?" He shrugged. "So this could go on forever."

Emma nodded. "Based on what I know, I don't think the Roma killed her."

Emma went on to relate all she'd heard about Lexie. And why Emma believed Lexie was the one person with all the qualifications to be the murderer: motive, opportunity, lots of malice, and the means to kill.

Sergio considered everything she said for a few moments.

He nodded slowly. "You know, Em-ma, in the back of my mind, I always thought it might be Lexie. Natasha had told me things about Lexie that, at first, made me suspect her. Natasha went out with Barry, before I," he stopped. "Well, you know. Anyway, Lexie hated Natasha. Natasha told me things."

"Like what?" Emma asked.

"That Lexie bad mouthed Natasha all over the Honorage Spa. Called her a whore. Natasha was scared of Lexie. Some bouncer in the City even followed Natasha home one night from rehearsal when Natasha was an Ormon Fellow. The guy told her he'd mess up her pretty face if Natasha didn't leave Barry Buchanon alone. Natasha was sure Lexie put him up to it."

"Could Natasha prove it?" Emma asked.

Sergio shrugged. "She didn't need to prove it. She was sure of it. But not sure enough to prove it to Barry. Who ended up marrying Lexie. Of course, once Natasha fell in love with," he paused, "you know, we fell in love. Well, what did she care who Barry Buchanon married? Until a few months ago when he started acting like he *wasn't* married. Not that she could have stopped Barry from hitting on her when she returned to San Francisco for *Trovatore*. I warned her, Em-ma. I warned Natasha, when she returned, not to take all those gifts from Barry. They could only lead to trouble."

Emma nodded, but something worried her. "So you were in touch with Natasha, then? When she came back here a few months ago? I thought she dropped you...," she blushed.

Sergio winced. "Yeah, she dropped me," he said. "She was famous. Got her big break in New York. I didn't want to move. Besides, by then I'd hooked up with Beth. She owns a bakery in Petaluma. But Natasha and I stayed friends. I still care," he stopped for a second, "cared for her. But once she came back here to sing *Trovatore*, all she did was use my shoulder to cry on when her new lover, Sacha Kuragin, treated her bad. Which was most of the time. As for Barry Buchanon, I think she was just using him for the money. I told her, Em-ma. I warned her. As somebody said, sooner or later, the piper has to be paid. And when Natasha died, I thought the piper was Lexie. Then the police found the ring and charged the fortune tellers with the crime. So I thought I was wrong. I thought, hey, just like in Italy. The gypsies are always to blame."

Emma thought of something. "Did Natasha ever talk about her sister?"

"That poor dog?" Sergio shook his head. "No," he pronounced the word in the clipped Italian way, waving his forefinger back and forth again. "These opera singers? They only talk about themselves. Nobody else."

"Look Sergio," Emma replied. "I *still* think Lexie's the murderer. That it wasn't the Roma."

"You think they were framed," Sergio stated. "Yeah. I can see why you might think so. But what do *I* do about it?"

"Go to the police with what you know," Emma replied.

"Are you crazy?" Sergio exclaimed. "It would be my word about what my dead ex-lover said about the wife of one of California's most powerful men." Sergio's tone became defensive. "Why would I do that? What would I have to gain, except to expose myself? And, as you know, *Signora*, my past. Well, it's not exactly on the up and up. Including my visa." He leaned back in his chair and folded his arms across his chest again. "Go to the police? No, *Signora*, that's not happening. Never."

Emma nodded. She couldn't blame him.

"OK," she agreed. "I get it. But will you do this, at least?" Emma had decided on her final request well in advance. "The toxicology report hasn't been submitted yet, but someone," she didn't say her ex husband Andy, "suggested that depending on what poison killed Natasha, it may have been ingested well *before* dinner was served."

Sergio held his hands up in the surrender position. "*Signora*, I don't know anything about human poison. I just read a little bit about rat poison."

Emma rushed to explain. "I'm not asking about the poison, Sergio. All I want is for you to help me remember everything that was served at the party from the time people first arrived for cocktails."

Sergio nodded, seemingly relieved that this was all he was being asked to do. "Sure, let me go back to my office to get the menu plan and receipts. All the information should be there."

He stood up and walked back to the kitchen, returning a few minutes later with a big white binder, neatly arranged with tabs that appeared to represent his catering jobs.

Emma was impressed. The man was well organized when it came to food.

"Let's see." He opened the book. "Today is Thursday. It was," he thought a moment. "It was just last Friday. Not even a week ago." He glanced sideways at her. "It seems like longer. So much has happened."

Emma rolled her eyes. "Or hasn't happened, depending upon how you look at it."

"I have the menu, right here." Sergio unclasped the binder rings and removed a neatly printed menu that he showed to Emma.

"Can I have a copy?" Emma asked.

"Keep it," Sergio answered. "I have three or four. But, Em-ma, even if we know what was served, someone, the killer, obviously slipped the poison in. Or maybe someone brought something into the party from outside. What does this prove?"

"Nothing," Emma replied. "The menu proves nothing we don't already know. I'm hoping," she hesitated. What was she hoping? "I'm hoping that remembering what was served and when, will help us remember something that might lead us to the killer."

Sergio didn't look convinced.

"The dinner menu lists all the ingredients of everything we served for the sit down dinner, except your pasta sauce," he explained. "But you know the ingredients for that. Besides," he laughed, "I've watched you make it. It's so elegant, simple: butter, chopped onion, chopped garlic, salt, chopped parsley, whole tomatoes, tomato sauce, tomato paste. You cook it for two hours until it tastes like velvet. *Buonissimo!* The *tagliatelle* are easy: flour, eggs, and sometimes I put in a little nutmeg."

Emma smiled, "My grandmother did too."

"Next was the *saltimbocca*," Sergio continued, reading from the printed menu. "Not much there: veal from Wagner Farm, prosciutto, sage, olive oil, butter, wine. Served with green beans, fresh from the farmer's market this morning. Tasso's. The best. Then the dessert:

raspberries from Simon's, meringues from Claud's and whipped cream."

Emma looked up from her copy of the menu. "Hardly anybody tasted the dessert. Sacha started that food fight. Most people left."

Sergio nodded, "And nobody else got sick. That's it for the dinner."

"Don't forget the breadsticks and the olive Sacha rolled down the front of Natasha's dress," Emma reminded him.

Sergio shrugged. "I didn't see that. I was in the kitchen. Good thing too. I'd have punched that *basso* in his face."

"Barry tried to," Emma added.

"So I heard." Sergio looked back down at the menu. "The olives were from Leaping Lizards. I make the breadsticks myself from left-over pizza dough: flour, olive oil, water and sesame seeds."

"Scrumptious," Emma said. "Who wants bread anymore?"

Sergio studied the ceiling. "What else was there? Barry provided all of the wine from his vineyard."

"The vodka?" Emma suggested. "Sacha Kuragin was circulating at the auction, pouring vodka from a bottle in each fist."

"Right," Sergio agreed. "Wine, and vodka from Nesson. That was the only alcohol served." He thought of something. "Wait, Lexie opened that special bottle of wine for Barry and took him a glass with hors d'oeuvres. She pulled something out of the refrigerator for him to eat. But I didn't see it. Too busy with the veal." He stopped to think. "Cheese. Was it cheese? Or maybe the walnut spread with peppers that Barry wants me to serve at the restaurant. I ask him. Why? It's Turkish."

Emma sighed. "I'd sure love to know what Lexie put on that plate. What about the other hors d'oeuvres? The ones *you* served."

Sergio thought for a moment. "They were simple. Barry balked at spending more dough. We settled on," he leafed through the binder. "Here it is, water chestnuts wrapped in bacon. I prepared it myself. Water chestnuts from Little Pete's wholesaler. Bacon from

Pig Heaven. I tasted it. It was all fine. Then I made mushroom caps stuffed with dry bread crumbs, chopped almonds and spinach, basil, a little sherry and cream. I got the mushrooms and spinach from Tasso, and all the rest straight from Little Pete's wholesaler. And finally, I made miniature blinis: yeast, milk, flour, butter and eggs."

"Stuffed with Beluga caviar for the Russians," Emma added.

Sergio looked at her puzzled and shook his head.

"Beluga caviar?" he asked. "Are you crazy? Barry wouldn't even spring for domestic caviar, much less Beluga! And he keeps a tin of Beluga in his refrigerator for himself at all times. Barry and Lexie love the stuff. For that matter, Natasha did too. And I told him he'd better serve caviar at the party or the Russians might trash the place. Happened to me when I ran out of caviar one New Years Eve."

Sergio shrugged apologetically. "Don't get me wrong. I like Russians. But they like their caviar even more." He shook his head. "No, I stuffed the blinis with creamed chicken: chopped onion, tarragon, minced chicken breast, cream, salt, pepper and a hint of mustard. Simple. Cheap. It's what Barry wanted."

Emma was shaking her head. "Sergio, I know there were blinis with caviar. Lexie was holding one. I remember. First she said she loved it. Then she put the plate down."

"A chicken blini, not caviar," Sergio repeated.

Emma shook her head again. "I'm sure it was caviar. Somebody said Beluga."

Sergio thought for a moment. Then his face lit up. "I know. Maybe *that* was what Lexie brought out as the special treat for Barry. A Beluga blini. I'd made the blinis. They were sitting on the counter when Lexie came into the kitchen before dinner. I'll bet she got the Beluga out of the refrigerator, took one of the blinis off the counter, and made a Beluga blini for Barry, herself."

Emma didn't think that sounded like Lexie. She closed her eyes, trying to remember. Then it came to her.

"It was Vera, Natasha's sister!" she said. "Vera had the blini and she gave it to Lexie. Vera's the one who said it was a Beluga blini."

Sergio scratched his head. "Vera would know chicken from caviar. But where did she get it? Not from me."

"We need to find out," Emma answered. "If Lexie prepared it, she had motive, opportunity, means. But how did the blini end up in Vera's hands? And who ate it?"

Sergio shook his head slowly from side to side. "I'm confused. If Lexie prepared it for Barry, then Barry probably ate it. And Barry's not dead. So what does it prove?"

Emma didn't know. But she couldn't help feeling that she had stumbled on to something important.

"Sergio," she said, "I'm going to pay the Buchanons a call and try to find out. If I can, I'll even check their refrigerator to see if the caviar's still there." She stood up to go. She'd have to call Julie to set something up. Quick. "This has really been helpful," she added. "Thanks." She stuck out her hand.

Instead, Sergio gave her a hug. "Thanks for taking me into your confidence, *Signora*."

He showed her to the door looking way more relaxed than when Emma first arrived. Which reminded her of something.

"Sergio?" Emma stopped. "Can you explain one thing? Why are you so paranoid about the Mafia? Isn't that a little far-fetched? I know about the gambling debts but..."

Sergio lowered his voice to a whisper. "You've been honest with me, *Signora*. So, I'll tell you a little secret. My mother's from Bologna, but my father? That's another story. His family is from a little town just outside of Palermo, in Sicily. When he was young, he crossed swords with the Mafia there. That's why he fled Sicily as a young man and moved north. I'm half Sicilian. The family's been afraid of the Mafia ever since." He folded his hands together in supplication. "But, *Signora*, no one else here knows I'm Sicilian. That's just between you and me."

Well, what do you know, Emma thought to herself. The Bolognese chef was really half Sicilian! She put her index finger to her lips, nodded, and backed out the door.

On her way home, Emma pulled out her cell phone and dialed Julie.

"Hi," she said. Without waiting for her daughter to reply, she continued. "I want you to set up a meeting with the Buchanons tonight. Tell them you really need to discuss the publicity for City Opera's announcement about their big donation tomorrow night."

She paused.

"I don't care, Julie," Emma cut in. "Piers can handle it. He's not a baby. Just tell me you'll set up the meeting tonight. It's important. Leave me a message about the time and when you'll pick me up." Emma hung up the phone and power walked home.

18

____

THURSDAY AFTERNOON - BLINIS ANYONE?

Once back home, Emma checked her watch. It was well past 2:00 p.m. She grabbed a tub of yogurt out of the fridge and toasted a slice of whole wheat bread. She took the lunch out on the deck. The sun that had flooded the yard a few hours before, had moved west. In the midday heat, the deck sat in comfortable shadows. No need for a hat. She'd only be exposed to the killer rays for a few more minutes. Didn't the sun used to be good for you, she mused? Along with air, water, fish, cheese.

She ran through the rest of her day. Soon, she hoped Julie would call her with the time for their Buchanon meeting. And she still had to check in with Steve at the free legal services clinic to report on her meeting with Sergio.

Of course, there was also that pedicure she needed to fit in. Emma remembered the catty remarks by a local San Francisco columnist when a well-known movie star showed up Opening Night in a Valentino, sandals and unpainted toes. Based on the outrage *that* caused, you'd have thought the woman mooned the audience from the stage. Not that anyone would even notice Emma's feet tomorrow night. She slapped her hand at the thought. Whether anyone else noticed was irrelevant, she reminded herself. All that mattered was, *she* noticed!

Furthermore, Emma wanted the pedicure *that day*. It was Thursday. Friday, every mani-pedi operator in Blissburg would be booked. And she'd made up her mind to spring for an appointment with someone at the Honorage Spa. Why not mix business with pleasure? Who knew what additional gossip she might pick up visiting Lexie's old employer? Oleg, Julie's regular masseur, wasn't Lexie's *only* co-worker there. Emma made a mental note to call the spa for an appointment just as soon as she heard from Julie about the Buchanon meeting.

Meanwhile, it was time to head for the legal clinic. Emma brought her empty yogurt tub back into the kitchen and locked the back door. Then she stared at the three trash receptacles lined up in the hall. And studied the plastic tub. Trash or recycle? Why couldn't she ever remember?

She threw the tub in the recycle. As she grabbed her purse, she remembered she hadn't rinsed it. No time. She raced out the door.

By the time she reached the free legal clinic it was 3:00 p.m. For the first time ever, she found the parking lot full. There were even two news trucks with satellite dishes. She had to drive all the way to the other side of the quasi-abandoned mall to find a lone free spot in front of the vacant Borders. Then she sprinted back to the clinic, sweating in the intense Indian Summer heat. When she opened the door, the lobby for the clinic was jammed.

Somebody actually recognized her.

"Hey," a young woman waved, "aren't you that lady...?"

Emma shook her head, sped through the lobby past Barbara who, unlike her, clearly enjoyed the attention, and burst into Steve's office. To her surprise, it, too, was jammed with people. Though in the case of Steve's small office, jammed meant a total of five sweating souls conferring around his desk. Emma had forgotten just how hot Sonoma County could get in September.

Steve looked up when she stormed in. "Emma," he said. "Glad you're here. Gimme just a minute."

That was an improvement on Steve's usual greeting, Emma thought. She noted that his attire had improved, too. He wore a rumpled suit and tie, instead of his usual hot day Dudewear: baggy shorts, T-shirt and sandals.

The other men in the room were dressed in suits. And the one, cute young woman among them wore what Emma would have worn to a cocktail party. A short, fitted, gray silk dress, along with four inch, black patent, stiletto-heeled pumps. The girl's strawberry blond hair fell straight to her shoulders, perfectly coiffed. Emma glanced down at her own blue jeans, Nikes, faded GAP blue-striped T-shirt - and green dinosaur socks from Harry - and wondered, who looked like the Dudette now?

Nobody else in the room seemed to notice her. But a few seconds later, Steve broke away from the conference and motioned her out into the hall. It was full of people. So he pulled her into the vacant Men's Room, and locked the door.

"Did you talk to Sergio?" he asked.

Emma nodded. Somehow the small room made her feel disoriented. Must be the urinals, she thought. Training her eyes back on Steve, she asked, "Who are all those people?"

"Reporters," he shrugged. "They've been camped out all day."

Emma shook her head. "I mean all the people in your office."

"Oh." He glanced at her sideways. "Haven't you heard? It was on the morning news. Roma Rights International. They've gotten involved in the Havleks' defense, along with Mitchell, Young + Roberts in San Francisco who are handling their defense *pro bono*."

"For free? Great!" Emma raised her eyebrows at that.

It's high profile because of Natasha Vasiliev, the victim. Turns out she had fans all over the world. Look," Steve continued, "I need your help."

He stopped as though remembering something. "Before I get to *that*," he said, "did you talk to Sergio Santagrata? I gotta tell you, that guy is beginning to smell. Turns out he was the victim's former lover. There's Mafia connections in Sicily, too. OK, they're from a while ago. The family's Sicilian going way back. But the connections are still *there*. Along with the gambling debts. Building code violations. And, of course, the visa problems. So what did he have to say?"

Emma winced. "First of all, I gotta say that I really don't think Sergio did it."

She told Steve her hunch about Lexie Buchanon and the poisoned caviar blinis.

"Sergio agrees, Steve," she explained. "She had the opportunity to poison the blinis when she made up a dish of special hors d'oeuvres for her husband, Barry, an hour and a half before dinner was served."

Steve interrupted. He didn't seem interested in her poisoned blini theory. "'Sergio?' he said. "You two are on a first name basis? Suddenly he's a friend of yours? Emma, I need objective information. Instead, you're reporting on your hunches?"

Fair enough, Emma admitted to herself. With Roma Rights and Mitchell, Young involved, she'd better stick to the facts. So she related everything she and Sergio had discussed. Mentally noting that someone, from the look of things *she*, had better find the killer fast. Or else Steve might bury Sergio eyeball deep in very hot red sauce.

When she was done, Steve raised his eyebrows. "Very interesting. Can you write all that down? Quick and dirty. Don't bother cleaning it up. It's privileged and confidential. Part of our defense strategy. I want to share it with co-counsel."

Emma nodded, wondering whether she had just traded one scapegoat for another. Was there a Sicilian Anti-Defamation Defense League to fund *Sergio's* legal bills? And why did that sound like an oxymoron? From what she could see, America had declared open season on Sicilians a long time ago. To heck with her North Italian grandmother, she thought. She was starting to like Sicilians.

"I'll go write it up now," she replied, turning to open the Men's Room door.

"Wait a minute," Steve grabbed her arm. "Don't go yet. I have another assignment. Co-counsel and I put our heads together early this morning and made a list of all the people the police haven't questioned in their, so-called, rush to justice. That's the way we're portraying the sloppy investigation in our press releases. You'd have heard it if you watched any news."

"I've been busy, Steve," Emma interrupted. A little voice in her head whispered, *at the outlets.*

Steve ignored her. "Here's what we need from *you.* The police interviewed Vera Vasiliev, Natasha Vasiliev's, the victim's, twin sister."

Emma nodded. "I know who Vera Vasiliev is, Steve. I've met her."

"Met her?" Steve's eyebrows shot up. "Great. That's perfect. I need you to follow up with her." He took a deep breath. "Here's the thing, the police interviewed her right after the murder. She had an alibi. She says she was with that Alexis Kuragin character all night. By the way, he's someone else we need to investigate. Don't suppose you know *him*, do you?"

Emma shook her head. He'd been on her original list of suspects, but she'd never gotten around to him. How could she, she thought. It was only Thursday, for goodness sake!

Steve shrugged. "That's OK. Someone from Roma Rights is already looking into him. He had a run in with a Roma back in Ukraine. He claimed she framed him on an assault charge."

Boy, Emma thought. The souls of some people's shoes really were mired in mud.

"Anyway," Steve continued. "When the police questioned Vera Vasiliev, Natasha Vasiliev's sister, *we* didn't know, and therefore hadn't told the police, that *Vera* Vasiliev." Steve stopped and scratched his head. "This is worse than *War and Peace* with all these frickin' Russian names. Anyway, the police didn't know because *we* didn't know until Carmen Havlek told us a few days ago, that Vera Vasiliev, the victim's twin sister..."

Emma nodded and waved her hand in quick circles. "I know, Steve. I know. Get to the point."

"The victim's twin sister," Steve repeated, "visited the suspect, Carmen Havlek, early the morning after the murder allegedly to have her fortune told. Cards read. Whatever. According to Carmen Havlek, she, Vera Vasiliev was so freaked out by the murder she didn't actually stay to have her fortune told. She started crying, and told Carmen Havlek that whoever killed her sister probably wanted to kill her too. Then she raced out the door before Carmen Havlek had time to read the cards."

Emma finally interrupted him. "Steve, I know all this. Remember? *I'm* the one who told you. After Carmen came to my office and related it to me before she was arrested. What's your point?"

Steve got defensive. "Carmen told *us* the same thing after we interviewed her. I forgot about her talking to you first. Anyway, the point is we need someone to pay Vera Vasiliev a visit and get her story. Corroborate what Ms. Havlek told us, and see if this Vera Vasiliev remembers anything that might help us prove the suspect is innocent."

"And don't forget," Emma reminded him. "As I just told you. Vera was the one with the Beluga blini. I could also find out who gave it to her. That would be interesting."

"Sure, Emma. If you think the blini is important, why not?" Steve was clearly not impressed with the blini angle. "I mean, of course. Find out anything you can. Do you think you can handle that? I mean find some excuse to pay Vera Vasiliev a visit? She lives right here in Blissburg."

Emma nodded. "Yeah, I'll do it. I can make an appointment to have her give me a massage. She works at the Honorage Spa. She's one of the masseuses."

Steve frowned, obviously annoyed with her plan. "Yeah, why not get a mani-pedi at the same time?"

Where did he get mani-pedi, Emma wondered? Oh, right. He was married.

"Emma," he continued. "This is serious. It's work. Not just an excuse to get a massage. Are you up for it or not?"

"Yes, of course I am, Steve," Emma shot back. Now *she* was annoyed. Then she thought of something. "I'll call my daughter. She's handling all the publicity for City Opera's big announcement on Opening Night. Barry Buchanon is making a huge donation in memory of Natasha Vasiliev. The victim," she added. "In case you're mixed up."

She realized how bitchy that sounded and softened her tone. "We'll tell Vera that we need to talk to her about the presentation in memory of her sister. I'm sure she'll want to cooperate. To make sure she approves of everything that's said."

"Sounds like a plan." Steve turned. Clearly his mind had already moved on to other things. He swung open the bathroom door and ran into the hall.

Leaving Emma to face the surprised newsman who had entered the Men's Room right after Steve left.

19

THURSDAY AFTERNOON - MANI-PEDI

By the time Emma wrote the report for Steve and drove home, it was well past 4:00. She checked her messages.

There was a text from Julie. "Pick u up @ 6:30. Mtg @ BB's home. LB'll b there. U o me."

Emma blessed the day she'd learned how to text. It was the only way, now, to communicate with her busy daughter. She answered, "1 + favor. Need meeting with Vera V. Same xuse – dnation."

Julie texted back, "Sched massge."

"NO! Mtg. High importance!" Emma spelled that out.

"I'll let u no."

Emma assumed Julie meant 'know' not 'no." She texted back, "VVHI."

She looked at her watch. There was just enough time to schedule the pedicure before the spa closed. She dialed the Honorage Spa's number and crossed her fingers that someone would be available.

When Emma explained to the voice on the phone that she needed an appointment that very afternoon, the girl sounded skeptical.

"Wow," she sighed. "We close at six. It's been a madhouse here all day. Lotta people going to Opening Night tomorrow. Can I put you on hold?"

There was a long pause. Emma heard laughter and something about a birthday party after work. Then the girl's voice was back on the line. "You're in luck. I found you an opening at 5:15. Dolores had a cancellation."

Emma thought for a moment. Five fifteen. That was barely enough time for her toes to dry before she had to meet Julie. But she had no choice. "OK. I'll take it," she said.

"Did you say just pedi, or mani-pedi?" the girl asked. "Pedi's $35. Mani-pedi's a better deal. It's only $50."

"Make it a mani-pedi," Emma replied. "A deal's a deal."

"OK." The girl reviewed the order. "That's a mani-pedi with Dolores at 5:15. You know where we are?"

Apparently, she didn't sound like a regular, Emma thought to herself. "Yeah," she answered. "I know how to get there."

"Don't be late," the girl cautioned. "It's Dolores' last appointment for the day. She likes to be out of here at 6:00."

"I'll be on time," Emma assured her.

In fact, when Emma checked her watch again, it was later than she thought. She dashed out the door and into her car. Traffic was backed up heading north in the direction of the spa. And that day, Honorage's main parking lot was full. She had to park in overflow.

By the time the greeter opened the glass doors giving entry to the posh spa's serene, air conditioned, marble foyer, Emma was sweating, out of breath, and two minutes late. The relaxing sound of the foyer's drop-from-the-ceiling water sculpture, however, immediately put her at ease. She wiped the sweat off her brow and approached the front desk.

"I have an appointment for a mani-pedi with Dolores at 5:15," she said.

The tall, blond, poker faced receptionist – surely not the same girl Emma had just spoken with on the phone – glanced quickly at the clock behind her, then back at Emma. It was 5:18. Emma couldn't subdue a surge of gratitude when the woman actually nodded and motioned her into the mani-pedi room.

There she was offered lemon water from a chilled pitcher and a green apple while she waited for Dolores.

Dolores turned out to be a short, dark haired woman who was about Emma's age, somewhere in her sixties. Emma guessed that, unfortunately, Lexie Buchanon probably hadn't hung out much with Dolores during her employment at the spa. So it was unlikely that Dolores would have information regarding the murder case. For some reason, however, Emma was relieved to find a contemporary to assist her at the spa that day.

That's why, when Dolores took Emma to choose a color for her nails, Emma didn't expect a lot of push back regarding her selections: a pale Pearl Blush for her fingernails and, after lengthy consideration, Flamenco Red for her toes.

Dolores offered Emma a weak smile when Emma handed her the bottles of polish.

"Are you sure? Dis is so *bor*ing," Dolores sighed. "Wouldn't you like something more fun? More *young*?" She glanced at Emma's nails.

They'd grown alarmingly long, Emma noticed with surprise. Except for two she'd bitten down almost to the cuticle.

"If you don't mind my saying," Dolores suggested, "it looks like you don't treat yourself often." She added, "Is dis for a special occasion?"

Emma nodded and smiled back, reminding herself that the woman was only trying to be helpful.

"So, if I may ask, what are you wearing?" Dolores continued.

Emma checked her watch. Time was awasting. She had to leave the spa by 6:15 to be home when Julie picked her up for the Buchanon meeting. Emma quickly described the paisley skirt and gold top.

"Opening Night. Right?" Dolores' eyes lit up. "A lot of my customers today are going." She paused. "Let me make you a little suggestion." She lightly touched Emma's arm. "No pressure, honey. Just see if you like it."

Dolores walked back to the case full of polish and selected a turquoise blue. It was, in fact, one of the colors of the new skirt's paisley print. She handed it to Emma in exchange for the red.

"Keep the finger nails conservative. Pearl Blush is more you," Dolores explained. "But the toes?" She raised her eyebrows and smiled. "You gonna take a risk. Go a little *crazy!*"

By then, it was 5:30. Emma just didn't think she had time to argue about it. "Fine," she agreed. "Great. I'll go with the turquoise toes. Thanks." But her heart sank. Turquoise toes? What was she doing?

A few minutes later, however, after a soothing warm cuticle soak, Dolores' complimentary foot and calf massage began to dispel Emma's unease. Then, Dolores motioned for a gorgeous young woman named Bing to scoot over on her wheelie stool, to help with the mani.

"Do you mind, Bing?" Dolores asked the willowy, dark haired girl. "Otherwise, I'm gonna be late getting out of here."

Bing shook her head. "Can you believe it? My 5:00 arrived early." She giggled about that behind her latex-gloved hand.

The two worked quietly and efficiently. Emma began to relax believing that the timing all might work out. She quickly forgot about Lexie Buchanon.

They were almost done when Bing turned to Dolores. "Did you see Lexie today? Flower cut her hair. For Opening Night. She and Barry will be up on the stage. They are giving the City Opera a big donation."

Dolores nodded. "I saw her. It's in honor of that dead singer. Vera's sister."

"The one Barry was bonking?" Bing asked, giggling behind her glove again. "If he were *my* husband," she continued. Then she made a chopping motion with her right hand aimed somewhere south of her navel. "I'd have cut it off. Like that...what was her name? The lady who did that?"

"Bobbitt," Emma heard herself blurt out the answer. And wondered why that name had stuck in her brain all these years. Sometimes she couldn't even remember what she'd had for breakfast. "At least, I think her name was Bobbitt," she added, embarrassed. "Or something like that."

"Bobbitt?" Bing repeated. She looked up at Emma and giggled behind her glove.

Dolores shook her head. "But not our little Lexie. She would never do that." She tapped her heart a few times, rapidly. "Alexita's a saint. I mean it. I wish she was my daughter. I feel like she is. We've known each other a *long* time."

"How long?" Emma asked, more embarrassed at having interjected herself twice into the two women's conversation.

"Since she first started working here," Dolores replied. Then she looked up at Emma from her wheelie stool. "I'm sorry. Maybe you think we shouldn't talk like this. About another customer. But, it's all good. What we're saying. I mean, about Lexie Buchanon. She's had some hard times, poor girl. But she has a heart of gold. I'm gonna tell you something. Maybe, I shouldn't. What's your name again?"

"Emma," Emma answered.

"Well, Emma, when my little daughter, Teresita, was in the hospital for an operation, this rotten sp...," she bit her lip. "Let's just say the health insurance plan I had here wouldn't pay. Dolores nodded grimly. "You know who gave me the money? It was Lexie Buchanon. No questions asked. No strings attached. That's the kind of person she is. And if I can't say something good about a customer like that?" She shook her head. "Well, I don't care what I can't say. I'm gonna say it anyway. Alexita's a saint." Then she looked up at Emma again. "Honey, I'm all done. Now come over here and I'll put the blowers on you."

Dolores ushered Emma to a different seat where she arranged Emma's hands on a clean white towel on the counter and her toes on the floor. Both in front of little white heaters that she clicked on to blow hot air onto her nails.

"You sit here for at least half an hour," she explained. "You hear that, honey? I gotta go at 6:00. Bing will bring you the bill, so you can pay up now before I leave. But don't *you* leave before 6:30. Otherwise your nails not gonna be dry. And you know what that means." She wrinkled her nose. "Smudge! By the way, where're your flip flops? Over there in your purse?"

"Flip flops?" Emma asked. She shook her head. "I...I didn't bring any."

"Sandals?" Bing suggested. She had returned with the bill and handed it to Emma.

"No flip flops. No sandals?" Dolores said, giving Emma a stern look.

Bing giggled behind her hand.

"Honey," Dolores said. "You gotta wear flip flops home. Otherwise you gonna ruin all my work." Then she smiled. "It's OK. I'll bring you some flip flops from the sauna room. They're gonna be big; but you gotta wear them."

Dolores returned shortly carrying a pair of flip flops the size of snow shoes. There was no way Emma could drive home in them.

Dolores must have caught Emma's look of dismay. She stared down at Emma's turquoise toes.

To Emma, they looked like a set of ten miniature Easter eggs.

Dolores pointed to the flip flops again. "You gotta wear them, honey."

By then, Bing had processed Emma's credit card with a fancy mobile credit machine.

Bing handed Emma back her card and thanked her for the generous tip. In seconds the two mani-pedi women were packing up to leave.

Dolores pointed a finger at Emma when she left. "Don't forget the flip flops."

It was 6:05. Emma decided that the best she could do was give her toes until 6:15. But waiting the full ten minutes seemed endless. At 6:12 she tested her right big toe with her forefinger.

Big mistake, she realized.

She should have tested the pinky toe. Her finger left a half inch wide smudge smack in the center of her toenail. Emma groaned. The woman sitting beside her looked over and raised her eyebrows in horror.

It was going to be a mess. But Emma knew she couldn't wait any more. She had to leave.

To the shock of her blow dry companion, Emma gingerly lifted her dinosaur socks over her bright turquoise toes and pulled them on her feet. She stuffed her feet into her Nikes, and tied the laces. Then she stood up, waved goodbye and ran out of the spa.

20

THURSDAY EVENING - CUPCAKES ANYONE?

Traffic was slow. When Emma pulled into her driveway, she noted Julie's BMW was already parked there. She braced herself and got out of her Prius.

"Nice goin', Mom. We're late," Julie greeted her when she opened the door of her daughter's car and started to get in. Julie's eyes shifted from her mother's face, down to her faded striped T-shirt, blue jeans, and finally to the dinosaur socks. "Frankly, Mom, and I say this lovingly. The whole outfit is scary, but are you really wearing *those* to a business meeting with the Buchanons? I know they're from Harry but, a business meeting?" She pointed to the socks.

Emma tried to defend herself. "It's not exactly a business meeting, is it? I mean it's about PR not an IPO, right?"

"It's *my* business," Julie reminded her angrily. "No matter how superficial and pointless you think my work is for a bunch of spoiled, socially useless parasites."

"Your words not mine, Julie," Emma interrupted.

"Oh forget it," Julie sighed. "Just tell me this. What possible reason can I give for your even being at this meeting? Much less dressed like *that*?"

Emma had to admit. *That* was a good point. Her initial response, that since moving to Blissburg she pretty much went *everywhere* with her daughter, wasn't going to fly. She thought for a moment while Julie drummed her fingers on the steering wheel.

"I think I've got it," Emma finally said. "We'll tell them I've lost a ring. That after days of searching for it, I remembered taking it off while I was cooking the pasta sauce on Friday, and putting it on a shelf in their kitchen. I happened to hear you were meeting them tonight and suggested I might come along to see if I'd left the ring where I thought I had. Of course we'll add that we're terribly, terribly sorry for the inconvenience."

Julie started the engine. "That's good," she said, sounding surprised. "I'm impressed. Do you always lie that well?"

"Whatever works," Emma replied.

When they were on the highway, heading out of town, Julie resumed the conversation about the Buchanons.

"Funny thing is, Mom," she said, "Barry was glad I called. He said that he and Lexie had wanted to clarify a few things about the press announcement I was drafting. Before its release tomorrow night. Specifically, Barry wanted to explain that Lexie was back on board with the gift. That I could forget everything that happened at Jardin. The gift was from the Buchanons, plural. In fact, the official designation for the Russian opera series will now be 'Produced with Funds from The Baxter and Alexandra Buchanon Russian Arts Archive.'"

"Is it an archive?" Emma asked.

Julie shook her head. "I don't know. I guess it is. *Now.* Apparently both Baxter and Alexandra love the name. It sounds so, I don't know, presidential or something. Less crass than: the Buchanons are giving a ton of money to City Opera to ensure their social salvation." She paused. "My guess is, the name change was all Lexie's idea."

"Why?" Emma asked.

"It takes away the sting of donating a lot of money in memory of her husband's dead mistress. Personally, I think that after the scene at Jardin, Lexie and Barry reached some sort of well-insulated, rich couple, breakfast table agreement. Barry can do whatever he wants with whomever he pleases, in return for a separate Swiss bank account for Lexie and her promise never to embarrass him like that again. And the donation becomes an archive so that Lexie can chair its board for credibility. You know," Julie took her hand off the steering wheel and swatted the air with it. "One of *those* deals."

By then, they had pulled up to the first gate of the Buchanon Estate at the Buchanon Vineyards.

Julie opened her window and punched some numbers into a keypad stationed well back from a huge metal barrier. A few seconds later the gate slowly swung open and they began the initial approach to Middle-earth. It was a well maintained, winding road surrounded by vineyards. Emma had marveled at the setting on the day of the fundraiser when she first visited the Buchanons' home to make her sauce.

After what seemed like a mile, Julie stopped the car in front of another keypad, opened her window and punched in more numbers. An even more ornate iron gate swung open and the car continued for another mile up a much steeper, more winding stretch of road. This time bordered by a forest of sequoias and pine trees.

Finally, they arrived at what looked like a piece of sculpture. Layer upon layer of multicolored metal formed into clouds. Emma remembered loving the sculpture the first time she saw it the day of the party. This time, in the fading light, she noticed that the colors of the clouds looked completely different.

Once Julie entered the right numbers into the nearby keypad, the clouds magically parted and the car entered a lush plateau. A midsummer night's dream of gardens set amid ancient redwood groves. The other side of the plateau, the side opposite where they entered, sloped off into another vineyard. The one where Natasha Vasiliev died almost one week before.

The Buchanon's house was situated beside a man-made bubbling brook. At first sight the old, two story brown shingle appeared deceptively modest. But as Emma had already discovered, the building had been completely redone. The living space almost doubled in back by the addition of a cluster of semi-attached guest houses surrounding the herb and flower garden where the silent auction had been held.

The Buchanons must have heard the car approaching. Or, more likely, they'd seen it on a surveillance screen inside the house. They stood on the front porch, hand in hand, when Julie pulled into one of several guest parking spots serving the main house and cottages. True to Julie's prediction, waiting for them on the porch, the Buchanons looked the picture of marital bliss.

Barry even draped his arm around Lexie's shoulder and gave her a squeeze before they descended the steps. Then he dropped his arm from his wife's shoulder, smiled at Julie and stuck out his hand.

"Glad you could fit into our time slot," he said, before cocking his head and staring at Emma.

Julie gave the explanation for Emma's presence that they had rehearsed in the car.

That's when Lexie leaned forward to give Emma a hug. "I'm *so* glad you're here," she whispered. "I was mortified when I heard all that cheesy gossip about your yummy spaghetti sauce." She sighed. "Boy, I hope it didn't hurt sales of your book. I'm ordering a copy for everybody I know for Christmas."

Barry waved them through the open front door to their home. "C'mon in. Have you eaten? Morena can fix you something. Lexie and I have a dinner engagement, or I'd have suggested you stay with us for a bite. You'll at least have a glass of wine, I hope."

Julie good-naturedly refused. "No thanks. We have work to do. And our time is short. Besides," she laughed, "I have to drive home."

"Let's get started then." Barry ushered them through the living room into a study. It boasted a lovely view of the rear side of the house overlooking a swimming pool built to look like a series of natural springs flowing into enormous granite bowls.

"Sure you don't want any wine?" Barry asked pouring himself and Lexie each a glass out of a magnum bottle labeled Reserve.

He handed Lexie her glass and motioned for Julie and Emma to sit down on one of two couches arranged facing each other across a narrow marble coffee table. "Now about the press release," he began.

That's when Lexie interrupted him. "Wait a minute, Barry." She turned to Emma, "I'm sorry. You don't need to hear all this boring stuff, Emma. Do you want to go into the kitchen and look for your ring?" She shook her head apologetically. "Honestly, I haven't seen it. But then, I don't spend a lot of time in the kitchen." She and Barry exchanged amused smiles.

"And Morena didn't mention it," she continued. "Oh, don't worry. Morena's honest as the day is long. I mean," she glanced at Barry for confirmation, "we leave all kinds of stuff around and she's never taken a thing. Of course," she snorted, "Barry pays her well enough." She linked her arm around Emma's. "I'll show you the way to the kitchen. I hope the ring's there."

While Barry and Julie reviewed the draft of the press release, Lexie led Emma into the kitchen where Emma began her charade.

"I remember taking it off so I wouldn't get it covered with tomato sauce," she began. "And I put it," she glanced around the kitchen. Her eyes landed on a high shelf that held two decorative Provencal faience pitchers. "I think I put it up there on that shelf."

She walked over to the shelf, raised herself up on tippy toe and slid her fingers along the stainless steel surface. Then she turned to Lexie, "Darn! It's not there. The ring's not very valuable," she added. "But it was my mother's so I hope I can find it."

She and Lexie spent a few minutes searching the kitchen. Then Lexie said, "Wait a minute. Morena's in the den watching television. She sleeps downstairs," she explained. "Why don't I go ask her if she saw the ring?"

"That's so kind of you," Emma answered, somewhat taken aback by the woman's thoughtfulness.

"As I said," Lexie repeated, "I know Morena wouldn't *take* it. But she might have seen it and put it somewhere thinking it was mine."

Lexie was about to leave the kitchen when Emma thought of something. This might be her only chance to ask Lexie about the blinis.

"Oh, by the way," she said, "Before you go, I've been wondering something. What was that you served in the blinis on Friday? It was delicious. Was it some sort of caviar? I don't think I've ever had it before."

Lexie shrugged. "It was chicken. Don't get me wrong. Personally, I love caviar. Beluga, I mean. The rest of it's yucky. But Barry wouldn't spring for caviar. Even when Sergio told him to be careful or the Russians might trash the place."

"But I thought," Emma hesitated. "Didn't Vera hand you some caviar?"

Lexie seemed to think for a minute. She frowned as though she'd remembered something unpleasant.

"Oh, you mean right before that drunken bass singer dumped my wine all over my dress?" she said. "Yeah. You're right. Vera did hand me something. Did she say it was caviar?" Lexie shrugged. "Maybe she did. If so, Barry must have given it to her. I brought him out a really good glass of wine. Not that junk we served. And a little plate of special hors d'oeuvres for us to share. I put some of our own stash of Beluga on Sergio's blinis. I hate those bacon things. Too much fat! Anyway," she swatted her hand at Emma. "Let me go down and ask Morena about your ring."

The second Emma heard Lexie on the stairs, she raced to the refrigerator and opened it. There, way in the back, was a tin labeled what? Yes! Beluga caviar. Emma almost grabbed it and stuffed it in her purse.

But she stopped herself. Steve was right. What was the point? The Buchanons had Beluga caviar in their refrigerator. So what? Lexie said she loved Beluga. The Buchanons could afford it. What did that prove? Nothing. Except that Lexie, who everyone knew hated her husband's lover, Natasha, had the motive, opportunity and means to poison her.

The caviar was the one thing served at the party that, according to Sergio, was not on the menu. Lexie was the one suspect in the kitchen that night who had access to it. Along with Sergio. Emma thought about that. Wait a minute, she said to herself. What about Barry? She shook her head. Why would Barry kill Natasha?

Emma heard a door close somewhere downstairs. She softly shut the refrigerator door and walked back into the living room. When Julie and Barry looked up, Emma shook her head at them.

"No luck," she sighed. "I must have left the ring somewhere else. I hope I didn't wrap it up in a paper towel or something, and put it in my purse." She assumed a worried look. "I did that once, and threw away a favorite earring."

Julie rolled her eyes. Then she stood up. "I think we're just about done."

Barry motioned her to sit back down. "Wait, Julie. I want Lexie to look over the revisions to the press release. She's practically adopted the Russian Arts Archive. It's her baby. She'll be president of the board."

Julie shot Emma a knowing look. As if to say, what did I tell you? Then she sat back down just as Lexie entered the room.

Now Lexie was shaking her head. "Sorry, Emma. Morena says she didn't see it." She looked at her husband. "Barry, Emma can't find her ring. She thinks she put it on a shelf in the kitchen. Could you come in there with us and check? We couldn't see up on the top shelves."

"Sure," Barry smiled benevolently at his wife. "But after you approve this, honey." He handed her the marked up draft of the press release.

Lexie took the press release from him. She read it over two or three times, making one minor change that Julie duly noted. Then she reread it. Smiled. And handed it back to Julie. "All done," she said.

Whatever the Buchanons' bargain was, Emma noted that Lexie took her part very seriously.

Emma and Julie were about to leave when Lexie reminded her husband of her request. "Just one last look." She motioned with a nod of her head towards the kitchen.

Barry looked at his watch. "I'm warning you. We're going to be late."

"It won't take a minute," Lexie persisted. She looked at Barry and pouted. "I just know that if *I* lost a ring my sweet dear mother gave me, I'd be sick. No matter how little it cost."

They walked quickly back into the kitchen and Barry dutifully checked all the top shelves. Of course, no ring was found.

"Darn!" Lexie looked genuinely crestfallen. "I really hoped we'd find it," she said.

They were walking from the kitchen through a small breakfast room that led to the front hall, when Lexie suddenly stopped like she had noticed something. She turned around, walked back a couple of steps, and stared at the breakfast room wall for a full minute, her arms crossed on her chest. Then she glanced around the room before she asked, "Barry, where's my cupcake?"

Emma and Julie traded confused looks.

By then, Barry had joined his wife staring at the wall. "Lexie," he said. "You're right. It *is* missing. Rasputin's Cupcake." He stopped and seemed to correct himself. "I mean, the little cupcake. It's missing."

Lexie was already combing the room looking for it everywhere. On the walls, under napkins, behind furniture, on the floor. "Come on!" she shouted. "Where *is* it?"

But hard as the couple searched, the cupcake simply was not there.

"Get Morena in here," Barry ordered.

Lexie went to summon Morena. When she appeared in the doorway, Barry pointed to a space on the wall. "Morena, what happened to Rasputin's Cupcake?" he shouted.

The poor girl blanched. "Raswho? Raswhose cupcake?" she asked, clearly having no idea what the man was talking about."

Lexie explained in a gentler voice. "The painting of the cupcake by Wayne Thiebaud, Morena." She glared at Barry and then continued. "You remember, Morena. The one I was so upset about. The one Barry gave me for Christmas and then wanted to give to Natasha Vasiliev for her birthday."

"Oh. Jes." Morena's eyes got wide. She looked down at the floor and nodded, as though remembering something she would rather forget. "The leetle cupcake painting. The one jou say was so baluble. Ayayay!"

Emma watched Morena and wondered how many things Morena saw in that house and wanted to forget.

Suddenly the girl looked frightened. Like visions of ICE enforcement operations were dancing in her head. "I don't know Missy Lexie. I...I didn't touch." She shook her head. "I didn't do..."

Julie and Emma exchanged more puzzled looks.

Barry glanced at them. He must have thought he needed to explain.

"It's a little Wayne Thiebaud painting of a cupcake," he said. "I bought it for Lexie for Christmas last year. She'd seen a similar one at the museum in San Francisco and liked it." He flashed Lexie a conciliatory smile. "It has a special meaning. I called Lexie cupcake when we were courting. I thought I'd surprise her with a cupcake of her own. Actually," he noted unnecessarily, "it's worth quite a bit."

"I'll say," Lexie added.

"Well," Barry continued. "Natasha saw it one night when she and Vera were here for dinner. For some reason, she loved it, too. Kept laughing and calling it Rasputin's Cupcake. You know, because of that Russian. Lexie and I thought it was funny." He glanced warily at his wife. "Didn't we, dear?"

"Sure. Until last month when you suggested giving the painting to Natasha for her birthday."

Emma thought she saw Morena shudder.

"I was *joking*," Barry cried, his eyes darting from Lexie to Morena.

"Right," Lexie replied. Then, as if by force of will, her demeanor resumed the composure Emma had noted when they arrived. Lexie forced a laugh. "I know. You were just joking, sweetie. And I got offended. It was silly of me." She paused. "But gosh. What do you suppose happened to it? It's worth a mint. It's gotta be here some-where. Unless."

"Honey?" Barry cut in. "Are you *absolutely sure* you didn't put it somewhere? Up in your bedroom?"

Emma wondered if he really meant, in your Swiss bank vault.

Lexie assumed a very innocent look, shook her head and replied. "No, sweetie, did you do something with it?"

Emma figured *she* really meant, did you give it to your Russian mistress anyway?

"OK," Barry looked around the room. "When's the last time anyone saw the thing?"

Emma and Julie both put their hands up, palms forward.

"I've *never* seen it," Julie answered.

"Me either," Emma agreed.

Lexie's tone turned matter of fact. "Barry, the truth is, I *wouldn't* have seen it. I never use the breakfast room. The last time I was in here was when Howard and Lilah spent the night. But that was almost three weeks ago. We had breakfast in here. Wouldn't we have noticed if it wasn't on the wall?"

"You're right," Barry agreed. "Of course we saw it. Howard pointed to it and said that prices on Thiebaud oils have gone through the roof. But after that, I don't recall."

All of a sudden, Barry seemed to remember that Emma and Julie were still standing there. He smiled. "Look, you two don't need to hear all this. I'm sure the painting will turn up." He looked at his wife. "And we're going to be late."

Julie shook her finger at him. "In light of all that's happened, my advice is to file a police report if you don't find the painting tonight. So you can collect some insurance money if it doesn't show up."

Barry nodded. "Yes. Of course. You're right." Then he showed Julie and Emma out the door.

"What was that all about?" Julie asked as she started the car.

Emma shrugged. "I guess somebody stole their expensive painting."

"Yeah, but what was all that about Rasputin's Cupcake?"

"Oh." Emma swatted the air with her hand. "Natasha was talking about Rasputin, that Russian mystic who was councilor to the last tsar. He got so powerful, his enemies tried to kill him with cupcakes poisoned with cyanide."

"Tried to? What happened?" Julie asked. "Didn't he die?"

"No," Emma explained. "Legend has it he ate the cupcakes but didn't die. Finally his assassins shot him in the head and dumped his body into the Neva River."

Julie wrinkled her nose. "Ewww! Why didn't the cupcakes kill him?"

Emma threw up her hands. "Probably because they cooked the cupcakes and the poison vaporized at high temperature. They should have mixed the poison with some caviar and served it with blinis instead."

Emma laughed at her own joke. Then she noticed the alarmed look on Julie's face.

"What? I heard that in the Russian history course I took last year at the Foundation for Senior Studies. Don't worry. I'm not the murderer."

21

THURSDAY NIGHT – SMUDGE

Julie and Emma stopped at Zah's for a pizza before Julie dropped Emma home.

"By the way," Julie asked after the waiter had brought them each a glass of Zin, "did Lexie say anything that actually *supports* your poisoned blini theory?"

Emma shook her head. "No. Not really. In fact she acted surprised about the caviar. Even though she's the one Vera gave the Beluga blini to. Lexie says that Barry must have given Vera the Beluga. She says that she and Barry were the only people eating caviar that night. Lexie said she brought him a plate of special hors d'oeuvres. Including Beluga from their private stash. And a glass of their special reserve wine. Not the junk they were serving at the fundraiser. Her words. Lexie confirmed exactly what Sergio said. Barry would not spring for caviar, even though a couple of people apparently suggested it."

"Except that you said Vera gave Lexie some," Julie added.

"Or thought she did," Emma shrugged. "Yes. From Barry, according to Lexie."

"Could Lexie be covering her tracks?" Julie asked.

Emma shrugged. "If Barry gave Vera the caviar, maybe he's the killer. Has anyone focused on him? I surely haven't."

Julie covered her face with her hands. "I feel like we're back where we started."

The television over the bar caught Emma's attention. One of the news shows was playing a clip of Steve, from the free legal services clinic, standing outside the jail with a crowd of Roma Rights advocates. They looked angry.

"I hope the Roma Rights confrontation doesn't get ugly," Emma commented. "The Roma have been living in California for years. Despite what Piers said, they're very peaceful. They do their thing. Fly under the radar. There's never been any trouble; but this kind of publicity could change that." She shuddered. "Julie, we have to figure out who really killed Natasha. It's the only way the police are going to let Carmen and Tonio go."

Julie nodded. Then she thought of something. "Oh, I almost forgot. I talked to Vera. I told her we wanted her to review the press release. She agreed to, but...," Julie hesitated.

"What?" Emma asked.

"Well," Julie continued, "the only time she can get together tomorrow is at her house at 9:00 a.m. The problem is, I have a parent teacher meeting at Harry's preschool at 9:00. And Piers has a court appearance in Santa Rosa. Barry told me tonight that he *really* wants Vera to review the press release *and* his remarks at the ceremony. Given the bad blood there's been lately between Vera and Lexie, Barry wants to make sure there's no trouble on Opening Night. He's added some complimentary language about Vera to his speech to try to smooth things over. About what a big support she was to Natasha since their parents died."

"Both of their parents died?" Emma asked.

"Yeah," Julie nodded. "I guess poor Vera really was Natasha's sole support for years. Until Barry Buchanon came along."

"Wow," Emma sighed. "They had tough lives."

Julie nodded. "Barry is putting Vera on the archive board. Assuming she can patch things up with Lexie, of course. Barry thinks she can. He said Lexie and Vera were friends when they worked together at the Honorage Spa. Before Barry Buchanon entered their lives. He says he'd like to make things right for Vera. Of course, she'll get Natasha's estate. Recording rights, etc. But Barry says he wants to give her something she can do, now that Natasha's gone. Something to remember her sister by."

"Hope it works," Emma mused.

"The point is, Mom, I can't go see Vera with you at 9:00 a.m. And Barry's asked me to make sure she reviews his written remarks and the graphics for the commemorative program. So," Julie shot her mother a pleading look. "Do you mind going alone? Just drop off the stuff. Then you can ask her whatever it was you wanted to know. Tell her to call me on my cell with any revisions to Barry's remarks."

Emma felt her shoulders tense. She'd promised Steve she'd ask Vera about her visit with Carmen the morning after the fundraiser. Now, for some reason, she didn't want to go alone.

"I don't know..." She hesitated. "I guess something about how she grabbed Lexie by the throat at Jardin scared me," she explained. "I mean, what if she doesn't like the remarks. Is she gonna fly into a rage and grab *me* by the throat?"

The minute Emma said it, she knew how silly she sounded.

"Not exactly the same as throttling someone who trashed the memory of your dead twin sister and only living relative," Julie said. "After all, that's what Lexie did. It was really out of line."

"You're right," Emma agreed. "Sure. I can go by myself. Where does Vera live?"

"I'll text you the address," Julie said.

They'd finished the pizza. A few minutes later, Julie dropped her mother off at home.

Emma climbed the stairs to her front porch. By the time she'd opened the door, Julie had texted her Vera's address: "362 Morningside Drive". It was close by. One of the luxury townhouses in the brand new complex next to the post office. Emma wondered if Barry Buchanon had bought that for Natasha as well.

Emma was changing into her fleece muumuu to get into bed when she remembered her pedicure. She glanced down at her hands. The manicure looked OK, she noted. So far, she'd only chipped the Pearl Blush polish off the tip of her right index finger opening the door to Julie's car. But the toes? She winced. That would be another matter.

Emma took off her shirt and underwear, and pulled the fleece muumuu down over her head. Then she sat down on her bed and unlaced her Nikes. The minute she pulled off her shoes, she realized that her turquoise toenails were stuck to her dinosaur socks. If she pulled the socks off, most of the polish would surely come with them.

She closed her eyes, pulled off the first sock, opened her eyes, looked at her toes and thought, maybe not so bad. The smudged turquoise blue and white pattern looked kind of Pollock. Assuming he had a turquoise blue phase. She pulled off the second sock. The toes looked the same. She looked again and shook her head. Who was she fooling? Her toenails looked ridiculous. She'd stop at CVS the next morning, pick up more polish, and touch up her toes.

22

FRIDAY MORNING - RUSSIAN I SPY

Emma woke up the next morning to the sound of pounding. At first, she thought maybe it was Julie, trying to get in. Then she realized it was rain. Hallelujah! It was September. Blissburg hadn't seen rain since May. The river was so dry you couldn't even swim in it during the recent autumn heat wave. The city was threatening water rationing if rain didn't come soon.

The hammering got louder. Emma thought, too bad the storm hit on Opening Night. There'd be rain all the way to San Francisco. Everyone's fancy shoes and pretend-to-be-fake furs would get wet. When it rained in Blissburg, the sky dumped buckets of water. Like some god had turned on a giant fire hose. If the storm continued, the front yard would be a swamp by late afternoon.

Emma got out of bed and checked her cell phone. It was already 8:30. She'd overslept. She barely had time for coffee before her appointment with Vera to drop off the stuff. Which reminded her. Where was the stuff Julie was supposed to drop off? She'd promised to deliver the press release, a copy of Barry's remarks and the program on her way to Harry's preschool.

Emma ran downstairs and checked the front porch. Sure enough, Julie had deposited a brown manila envelope at her front door. It was wrapped in two plastic bags against the rain. Inside the bags, on top of the envelope, she'd even attached detailed directions to Vera's townhouse, signed with a big heart and a lot of Xs and Os. Emma shook her head. Julie really was a dear under all those quills.

But Emma couldn't ponder that for long. She needed coffee. Strong coffee. Fast. There was no way she was facing the mercurial Russian twin without bracing herself with that!

While the coffee was brewing, Emma quickly dressed. For Julie's sake she decided to try to look professional. She found her black slacks in her bedroom closet. Then she noticed the beige silk sweater from Julie draped on the back of a chair. She hadn't washed it since she wore it the night of the fundraiser. What if Vera noticed, she thought. And it reminded the poor girl of Natasha's death?

Emma put on the sweater anyway. Natasha had died one week before. To the day. *Everything* must still remind Vera of her twin sister's death. Emma stepped into her old loafers and looked in the mirror. What on earth, she wondered, was that huge spot of pasta sauce doing smack on the front of her sweater? Emma ripped it off and threw on the vintage Missoni top lying on the old painted trunk at the foot of her bed.

Then she raced back downstairs to grab some coffee, gulping it down without even stopping to eat a biscotti. She'd have to get breakfast *after* the Vera visit. By 8:50 she was in the car congratulating herself on her fast getaway.

Vera's townhouse was located deep inside one of Blissburg's new developments. This one was named Aria! Fitting, Emma thought as she drove a few blocks up Blissburg Avenue past the post office. By then, the rain poured down in such thick gray sheets she almost missed the complex's discreet sign. She turned into a narrow drive lined with drought resistant shrubs.

Once inside the drive, Julie's instructions told her to turn right, continue on a curving lane for three blocks, turn left and then make a quick right onto Morningside Drive. By now it was raining so hard

Emma couldn't even make out the numbers on the townhouse doors. In desperation she parked the car and got out to study the house fronts on foot.

By the time she located number 300 on a gate down a path that had turned into a river of mud, she was sopping wet. She dashed back to the car, drove a hundred yards and re-parked the car by the curb. The rain had not let up. In her haste to leave her house, she forgot to bring an umbrella. Her ultra thin fuchsia parka was soaked through.

Undaunted, however, Emma grabbed her purse, stuffed the plastic wrapped papers inside and stepped out of the car. Then she made a dash for a covered porch from which she could reconnoiter, jumping puddles as she went and hoping not to become one more senior statistic.

"She never got back on her feet after she broke her hip," a voice in her head mocked her. "Then the bed sores got infected and the pneumonia set in."

"Oh, shut up," she spoke the words out loud. And surprised herself by thinking next, *maybe I will sleep with that arrogant cafone! Maybe it would be something to look forward to.*

But she quickly reminded herself that Jack, the arrogant *cafone*, had never even actually made a pass at her. Still mourning his wife. The thought only made her madder. Pathetic old goat! For a split second, she remembered the agony of watching Mary, her best friend, die. What was it like for Jack watching his wife of forty years die, she wondered? She chased the thought away. Too painful. TMI.

When Emma finally reached the covered porch, to her relief she saw that the number on a nearby door read 362. She wiped some of the rain off her face, removed her soaking wet jacket, slicked back her sopping wet hair with her hands, and reached for the bell.

Vera answered. She was dressed in what looked like a Japanese kimono transformed into an elegant tunic. Vera wore it over tailored green pants the color of her eyes. Emma couldn't help wondering if the outfit had once belonged to Natasha. It fit Vera perfectly, its v-neckline exposing her impressive cleavage. Unfortunately, Emma noted, the outfit did nothing to hide the poor girl's thick neck, or to soften her horse like features.

"Thank you for coming, Emma," Vera said leaning forward to give Emma a hug. Then, apparently noting how wet Emma was, she backed up a few paces.

Emma lifted her shoulders apologetically and pointed to her jacket. "Where should I put this? It's sopping wet."

"No problem," Vera replied, taking the parka and disappearing, for a moment, down a hall and into another room.

Seconds later, she reappeared and motioned Emma into the living room.

"What a beautiful home you have," Emma exclaimed walking from the elegant marble foyer of the townhouse into a cathedral living room. From its two story high windows, Emma observed a breathtaking view of the adjacent wild life preserve set against a backdrop of miles of rolling vineyards. Even in the pouring rain, the effect was spectacular. She added, "I had no idea these townhouses had such amazing views."

Vera smiled. "Only a few of them do."

Then Emma watched the young woman's eyes tear up.

"Barry bought this. For Natasha," Vera explained before covering her face with her hands and quietly beginning to sob.

Emma started to reach for the girl's shoulder.

But Vera quickly pulled herself together. "I'm sure I don't need to tell you, Emma. He loved her so much. They were made for each other. It was obvious," she shook her head sadly. "Everyone knew."

Emma nodded uncertainly.

"Of course," Vera continued, "I was a sort of beneficiary of," she hesitated, "of Barry's generosity, if you will. I lived here. And Natasha visited me often. I was her sister; it was natural. I had a beautiful home. She had a...a fitting place where they could meet. And now," she broke down again. "Look who has it all?" She gestured around the lavish home. "What do I want with it? Natasha's gone." She sobbed silently again.

After taking a few seconds to collect herself, Vera changed the subject. "Look. You didn't come to listen to me cry. Here," she motioned to a plush purple decorator sofa arranged in front of a marble coffee table to take advantage of the view. "Sit down. You were kind enough to bring the papers. I'll look at them quickly. I'm sure they're fine. Then I'll give them back to you and you can go. That way I don't have to bother Julie with another call." She grinned her goofy, toothy grin. "I know this is a busy morning for everyone, what with Opening Night. I have a hair appointment at 10:00, and the nails, and makeup."

Emma had removed the papers from her purse and just sat down on the couch when Vera's cell phone rang. She had set the phone on the coffee table, as though she were expecting a call.

Vera glanced down at it. Emma, who was already seated in front of the coffee table, was close enough to see the name that appeared on the cell phone's face.

"Sacha," it read.

Vera quickly bent down and grabbed the phone off the table. "Excuse me," she said. "I have to take this call."

"Hello," she answered, quickly walking away into an adjoining room. Before Vera closed the door, Emma heard one side of a rapid exchange in Russian.

The call lasted quite a while. So long, in fact, that Emma wondered if Vera might miss her hair appointment. At first, all Emma heard through the closed door was the soft murmur of Vera's voice.

Emma waited, her eyes first absorbing the extraordinary view. Slowly, however, her gaze shifted to the contents of the large room. It was beautifully, if somewhat sparsely, furnished. Not to Emma's taste which ran more to the personal, informal, handmade.

The furnishings of the townhouse were the opposite. Expensive, mass produced time share. The parquet floors were covered in thick grey wool carpets. And the contemporary Louis XIV style side chairs, tables, and buffet had all obviously been selected by a decorator from the same line out of a high end catalogue. There was nothing personal about the place at all. Except, Emma noted, for the Steinway grand piano and some photographs.

Emma stood and walked over to the piano on whose closed lid the photos were displayed. There were four of them, lovingly framed in ornate silver. The first was of a radiant Natasha and Vera standing with their arms around each other in front of Carnegie Hall in New York. Natasha's name was clearly visible on the theater's marquee. The photo was obviously taken recently. No doubt during Natasha's critically acclaimed, sold out debut the previous spring.

The second photo was of Natasha and Vera as teenagers. It was worn and faded. In it the twins, dressed in bathing suits, stood arm in arm on a beach. The photo looked like it was taken somewhere in Russia.

The third was some sort of family photo. Two little girls in pigtails stood with six adults of various ages behind a dining room table. The photograph was so faded and creased, it was hard to recognize anybody in it. Emma guessed, however, that the girls were the twins and that two of the adults were their parents, along with some other relatives.

The final picture was of a serious young man and a beautiful smiling woman. The black and white photo was obviously taken in a studio somewhere long ago. Emma guessed the two young people were Vera and Natasha's parents. The photograph, which had been blown up well beyond its original size, sat on top of the piano behind a small vase of fresh roses. The effect was something like a shrine.

Emma had picked up the photograph to study it more closely, and was replacing it on the piano, when she heard Vera's voice rise in the adjoining room. She quickly returned to the couch and sat down. Soon Vera's voice got so loud, she was shouting. Of course, she spoke in Russian, so Emma had no idea what the shouting was about. Whatever it was, the argument lasted a long, long time, until finally Emma heard a crash. As though Vera had thrown the phone against a wall. After that came the heart wrenching sounds of sobbing.

Emma checked her phone. It was already 9:40.

About five minutes later, Vera emerged from the adjoining room. She had dried her eyes and looked composed, but she was still sniffling.

"I'm so sorry about that," she apologized. "Sometimes, people say things. They mean well," she hastened to add, "but they say things that, well," she paused. "That make me so, so sad. I mean, that remind me of my sister. And then I start crying all over again."

Emma nodded. But she couldn't help thinking that Vera and Sacha had not been talking about Natasha on the phone. Whatever the handsome Russian tenor said, it had not made Vera sad. It had thrown her into a rage.

Vera had brought a plate of cookies into the room with her. She set them on the table and offered Emma one. "In case you didn't have time for breakfast before you came," she said with a timid smile.

Emma took one of the cookies. It looked delicious. But when Vera opened the manila envelope that Emma had placed on the table, and began to examine its contents, an uneasy feeling made Emma slip the cookie into her purse. Then she laughed at herself.

Vera glanced quickly at the press release and the program. She spent a little more time reviewing the text of the speech Barry would make from the Opera House stage when the Opera's Director announced the creation of the Baxter and Alexandra Buchanon Russian Arts Archive. Emma noticed Vera's eyes tear up again as she read.

Vera wiped the tears away with one hand and put down the text. "It's so beautiful. What Barry said about me." She sniffled. "It's true. I supported Natasha. After our mother and father died, I was all she had left. She was so beautiful. So talented. Mamma always said she would go far. Very far. It was my parents' dream. So, after they died, I was determined to make it come true for *them*. Well," she quickly added, "for us, too."

Emma couldn't help wondering what burdens Vera shouldered as the less beautiful – and possibly less loved – twin. The poor girl had certainly worked hard to make up for not being as good.

"Anyway," she continued. "Barry has always been kind. Very kind." She nodded her head. "But I don't know. This thing about being on the Board of the Russian Arts Archive? You see," she shrugged. "I was never really interested in Russian Arts. I was only interested in...in Natasha."

Emma glanced at her phone. It was almost 10:00. "Well," she said, "you don't really have to decide about that now, do you Vera? See how you feel in a few months."

"You're right," Vera agreed. "Why spoil the generous donation with doubts. We are meant to celebrate Natasha tonight. I'll decide about the archive later. Thank you." Vera checked her watch. "Oh my goodness," she cried. "It's late. I'd love to chat more, but I have to get to that appointment." She stood up.

Emma stood up too. She was also glad to get away. She followed Vera back to the front door.

Then Vera looked out the window. It was still pouring rain. "Oh, your coat. I almost forgot." She turned.

Without thinking, Emma followed her down the hall and into what must have been her bedroom.

"I put your coat in my powder room. On the tile," she called over her shoulder as she opened the door to the adjoining bath. "It was so wet, I didn't want it dripping on the wood floor."

Emma heard Vera shaking out her parka. While she waited, she glanced around the bedroom. A powder blue jewel box with blue silk damask drapes and a king sized bed covered in a poufy quilt of matching material.

And that's when she saw it. Out of the corner of her eye. Just as Vera walked back into the room. It sat on the nightstand next to the bed.

It was a small painting. But it wasn't hanging on the wall, the way a painting would be. Instead, it was propped up on the nightstand. As if put there hurriedly. It looked out of place. Not exactly the picture you'd stick on a nightstand next to your bed. It was more like art you'd hang in the dining room. The painting looked like an oil. It was *very* good. So good you wanted to eat it.

It was the picture of a cupcake. One solitary cupcake. Vanilla with pink frosting and a cherry on top.

Emma looked from the painting to Vera. Vera caught her eye. Something in Vera's expression told Emma that Vera had seen her studying the painting.

"Cute," Emma said, pointing at the painting while trying to disguise any alarm in her voice. Then she added, "I saw one like it at the Blissburg Arts Fair this weekend. I almost bought it myself."

Vera seemed to let out her breath. "That's funny," she smiled warily. "That's exactly where I got it. At the Blissburg Arts Fair. I guess we have the same taste."

Vera shoved Emma's coat at her. Emma wondered if she imagined it, or was Vera pushing her out of the room? At the front door, Vera barely even said goodbye.

23

FRIDAY - HIGH NOON

Emma didn't bother going home. She went straight from Vera's to the free legal services clinic. Her hands shook on the steering wheel the whole drive there.

That morning, the parking lot at the mall wasn't very crowded. Apparently Carmen and Tonio – and Roma Rights – had had their fifteen minutes of fame. As far as the news channels were concerned, without more drama, the Roma's entertainment value was gone. Emma prayed she could wrap up the case before someone took more drastic steps to spotlight the Roma plight.

Once again, Emma raced past Barbara at the reception desk, barely nodding. And barged into Steve's office. That day only one other person was with him in the room. Dexter Young, the *pro bono* lawyer from the downtown San Francisco firm who represented Carmen for free. Dexter had taken off his suit jacket and rolled up the sleeves of his starched custom pin striped dress shirt. Steve had resumed wearing T-shirts. Another sign the press was gone.

Dexter was on his cell phone and Steve was on his computer when Emma burst in. Steve looked up, a flicker of annoyance crossing his face when he recognized Emma.

"What's up?" he greeted her. The look on his face signaled he had better things to do. Dexter stayed on his call.

"I hope it's good," Steve added. "We've got problems, big problems. Tonio says he got manhandled being transported to the jail. He kicked in a window in the holding area. The police have now added felony assault and felony destruction of property to the charges. With his word against the police, those will be hard charges to beat."

Emma sucked in a deep breath and let it out slowly. "That's not good." Then she looked at Steve and shook her head. "But if I were held for a murder I didn't commit, I might do worse."

Steve cast her a skeptical look bordering on incredulity.

"C'mon Emma," he said. "This is serious. We're running out of time. The Roma Rights people are planning a big demonstration on Sunday. Peaceful, of course. But agitators will try to spin things out of control and blame it on the Roma. Anti-Roma bigots have been coming out of the woodwork. Besides," he added, "we haven't come up with one bloody thing to prove that Tonio and Carmen *didn't* do it." He rubbed his forehead. "We need solid evidence either that someone *else* committed the murder, or that Carmen and Tonio *didn't*. Absent that, we can only do our best to beat the rap on a technicality."

Emma paused for dramatic effect. Then she leaned forward and said, "That's why I'm here, Steve. That evidence you want? I have it."

Steve cast her an appropriately awed look. "OK," he said. "Let's hear it."

Dexter Young, who had been half listening to her while on his call, quickly hung up his cell phone.

You could have heard a pin drop. Emma began her story.

"It's Vera," she said. "I met with her, this morning, like I promised. I've got the evidence. I'm sure of it. Vera Vasiliev murdered her sister."

Steve's jaw dropped. "No way!"

"Way," Emma nodded. "I don't know exactly how or why yet. But I have the evidence."

"What?" Steve and Dexter asked at once.

"Rasputin's Cupcake," Emma announced before she realized there was such a thing as *too much* dramatic effect.

Steve and Dexter rolled their eyes at each other.

Steve shook his head. "Emma, not another…"

She interrupted him. "OK. I guess I never told you about the Buchanons' missing painting. I learned of it last night, when I went to their house. So when I was at Vera's, we walked into the bedroom because I'd soaked my parka in this downpour trying to find her townhouse in the new luxury complex behind the post office. When she got the parka for me, right before I left…"

Steve started waving tight circles with his hand for her to get to the point.

"OK." Emma stopped and took a deep breath. "The point is, I went into her bedroom and I saw the painting of the cupcake. The one that someone, obviously Vera, stole from Barry's house the same night someone – Vera – committed the murder. It was the painting of the cupcake that Barry gave to Lexie for Christmas. But then Natasha saw it and loved it. She called it Rasputin's Cupcake. So Barry wanted to give the painting to Natasha for her birthday. Of course, he and Lexie had a big row about *that*. Well, now the painting's been stolen; and *that* is the painting I saw on a nightstand next to Vera's bed this morning. If that doesn't…"

Suddenly, she noticed that Dexter was back on the phone; and Steve was shaking his head at her.

"Emma." Steve spoke very slowly. Like he was talking to a child. "I have no idea what you are talking about."

"I'm talking about Vera," Emma almost screamed at him, angry with herself for not having rehearsed her announcement in the car. "Vera stole the paining. Vera is the murderer!"

By then, Steve was holding his head like he had just gotten a migraine.

"Emma," he said, "last time you barged in here, you were sure that Alexandra Buchanon poisoned Natasha Vasiliev with caviar blinis. Now you seem to have developed another theory. The poisoned cupcake theory. According to *that* theory, without any logical motive, Vera killed her twin sister with a poisoned cupcake. If I understood you correctly, the motive has something to do with Vera and Natasha Vasiliev being Russian. And with the fact that another Russian, Rasputin, was poisoned with cupcakes over a hundred years ago in Russia. Except, I'm sorry to tell ya, unlike Natasha, Rasputin didn't die from eating the poisoned cupcakes. He died of a gunshot wound to the forehead. Then he drowned. In the Neva. Natasha was not shot. Nor did she drown. So, for what it's worth, the parallel does not work."

At that point, Dexter put his cell phone on mute and whispered, "Exactly right, Steve. Except, recent evidence indicates Rasputin may not actually have drowned. The water found in his lungs is a common autopsy finding. The reason the cupcakes didn't kill him, assuming he ate them, is because..."

"They cooked the cupcakes," Emma interrupted.

"Right again. The poison may have vaporized." Dexter resumed his call.

"You don't understand what I'm saying, Steve," Emma protested.

"That's right," Steve nodded vigorously. "I don't understand *at all*. But this cupcake theory sounds to me like one more of your hunches. You've convinced yourself that Vera killed her sister for no good reason. As I said the last time you were here, Emma, we need solid proof to win this case not your..."

Emma guessed Steve was about to say silly, but he spared her.

"Hunches," he repeated. "Look, did Vera tell you anything about her visit to Carmen the morning after the murder? That's what you were going to find out, wasn't it? Did Vera say anything that might help us? Anything that might prove Carmen didn't do it? Like did they discuss the ring, at all? Or did Carmen have her basket? And what was in it?"

Emma cringed. In all the excitement of the rainstorm, Vera's argument with Sacha, the poisoned cupcake, she'd completely forgotten to ask Vera about her visit to Carmen the morning after the murder. There was no way around it. She had to tell Steve. She let her breath out slowly again, and braced herself for his reply. Then she blurted it out. "Sorry, Steve. I forgot to ask her about that."

Steve cast her a withering look and pressed a button on his phone. "Barbara," he said, "would you try to get Vera Vasiliev on the phone. Immediately. I need to set up an interview with her."

"She's at the hairdresser now, Steve," Emma said. "She's gonna be hard to reach."

Steve nodded his head grimly. "That's choice, Emma. You got information about cupcakes and hairdressers. Nothing really about the murder." He pointed towards the door. "Dex and I got a lotta work to do."

But Emma wasn't going to give up that easily. She folded her arms across her chest and stood her ground.

"I know I didn't get off to a good start here, Steve," she began. "I didn't tell my story well. But it's important. I'm going to ask you to hear me out one more time. And," she added. "DO NOT interrupt me."

Then, starting all the way back with her visit to the Buchanons' house the night before, she began. First she quickly summarized the meeting with Barry (omitting the ruse about her missing ring). Then she described the part where Lexie and Barry discovered the missing painting from the breakfast room of the very same home on the grounds of which Natasha was killed. She explained how Natasha had called the painting Rasputin's Cupcake when she saw it. How Barry and Lexie argued about whether Barry could give Rasputin's Cupcake to Natasha as a birthday gift. Finally, Emma described being in Vera's bedroom, noticing the very same missing painting on her nightstand, and Vera claiming she bought the painting at the Blissburg Arts Fair.

"So," Emma concluded, "you see, don't you? I made up the part about *my* seeing the painting at the Blissburg Arts Fair. So Vera's obviously lying about where she got the painting. That proves she has something to hide. That something being that she stole the painting the night she killed Natasha."

"We're talking about a missing picture of a cupcake?" Steve asked.

Emma nodded.

"And you're assuming that Natasha's killer stole the picture of the cupcake the night he, or she, committed the murder.

"It's what the police have assumed about Carmen," Emma replied. "That she stole the ring the night she murdered Natasha."

Steve shook his head. "No. Not quite. The police are assuming Carmen killed Natasha Vasiliev *in order to* steal a 100K ring. Are you proposing that Vera Vasiliev killed her own sister in order to steal a painting of a cupcake that belonged to Baxter and Alexandra Buchanon? Why?"

Darn! Emma thought. Steve was right. Her theory really didn't make sense.

Dexter looked up from his iPad. "How big was the painting?"

"Not big," Emma replied. "It fit on the nightstand. Maybe eight inches by eight inches."

"And Baxter Buchanon said it was really valuable?" Steve asked. He sounded skeptical. "We're talking about a little picture of a cupcake? Like the kind you see at that tacky Blissburg Arts Fair? The kind people hang in their kitchen over the stove?"

"Well, not exactly," Emma objected. "Barry said his cupcake was a Wayne Thiebaud. The kind that hangs in the de Young Museum in San Francisco."

Steve shook his head. The name Wayne Thiebaud obviously didn't mean anything to him.

But Dexter looked up again from whatever he was reading on his iPad.

"Wayne Thiebaud?" he asked. "Did you say the Buchanons had a Wayne Thiebaud stolen out of their house? And you saw it in Vera Vasiliev's bedroom?" He looked Emma over carefully. "Are you sure? I mean, do you know exactly what the Buchanons' Thiebaud looked like? I've seen the ones at the museum. That retrospective they did was great. I actually *have* a signed Thiebaud lithograph. One of the famous gumball machine series. The price of *that* has sure skyrocketed. By the way, did the Buchanons' file a police report on the theft? Someone better tell them. They'll need a police report to collect any insurance."

Emma nodded. "We told them."

"So, Emma," Steve cut in, "answer Dex's question. Do you even know what the Buchanons' painting looked like? I mean, how could you? It was stolen right? So, did one of the Buchanons show you a photograph of it?"

Emma's heart sank. She shook her head. "No," she answered warily. "The Buchanons just said that the stolen painting was a picture of a cupcake. One cupcake. And that it was a Wayne Thiebaud. I've seen Wayne Thiebauds at the museum. So I sort of remember what they look like."

"Sort of," Steve repeated. "So, maybe, I mean *maybe*, it is within the realm of possibility that the painting in Vera Vasiliev's bedroom *wasn't* a Wayne Thiebaud? That, perhaps, it was, I don't know, a copy? Or someone imitating a Wayne Thiebaud? Or someone who just liked painting cupcakes? And Vera Vasiliev, knowing that her sister liked cupcakes, purchased one for her at the Blissburg Arts Fair."

"Yeah," Emma admitted. "I guess that's possible. But the Blissburg Arts Fair was last weekend. Natasha was already dead. So Vera wouldn't have bought the painting *for* Natasha."

"OK," Steve rubbed his hand back and forth across his forehead. Emma could tell he was losing patience fast. "Then perhaps Vera bought the cupcake painting, or just *a* cupcake painting, to remind her of her sister. In her sister's *memory*, if you will. Or," Steve continued, building up speed, "perhaps she bought a reproduction of the Thiebaud painting at the museum store months ago. Museums *do* make reproductions of their popular paintings and sell them." He smirked. "Even *I* know that. Is any of that possible, Emma? In fact, isn't *all* of that possible?"

Emma's head started pounding. Steve was right. It was *all* possible. So why was she so sure none of it was true? Why was she so sure that Vera, for no reasonable reason she could think of, killed her twin sister whom she obviously loved. Was she crazy?

"Sure, Steve," she nodded. "It's all possible."

Steve turned his back to her and walked to his desk. Like a lawyer who has just demolished a witness's testimony on cross examination. She almost expected him to add, "No more questions, your honor."

But that didn't happen. Because they weren't through questioning her. It was Dex's turn. They were playing good cop, bad cop. Dexter resumed questioning her in a gentler tone.

"Now Emma," he began with the kind of smile some male gynecologists use when they are about to begin an exam. "Even assuming the painting was worth killing someone for, it wasn't Natasha's painting. It was Alexandra Buchanon's. So, what was the point of killing Natasha? Where's the connection between the painting and Natasha Vasiliev's death?"

Emma said nothing. The fact was, she didn't know.

Dexter continued. "And didn't you say that, despite the Buchanons' united front the night of your visit with them, last night to be exact, when they discovered the painting was missing you sensed mistrust between them? Mistrust with regard to the where-abouts of the painting?"

Emma kicked herself for mentioning that. She knew exactly where Dexter was going with the question. In fact, she'd thought of it herself.

She nodded. Then she said, "Yes," even though there was no court reporter there to take it down.

"So," Dexter continued in a very congenial voice. "It's also possible that Baxter Buchanon, himself, *gave* the painting to Natasha. Just as you believe his wife, Alexandra Buchanon, suspected. Isn't it? Possible?"

Emma nodded. This time she didn't bother to answer out loud.

"Isn't it even possible," Dexter added, "that Natasha loved the painting *so* much that Natasha, or Vera, purchased a small Thiebaud painting? After all, Natasha was finally making a lot of money. It is possible – I'm just saying possible – that she had enough to purchase it. Or perhaps, as Steve suggested, one of them purchased a print of it at the museum store. So isn't it possible that the painting in Vera's bedroom wasn't stolen at all? All we're saying is that all of this is possible, Emma," he concluded. "Isn't it?"

Emma nodded her head again. She was devastated. She decided it was time to go. But she added one more thing as she was leaving. "I agree that everything you said is possible." She looked at both Dexter and Steve when she said that. Then she turned to Dexter. "But I'll tell you one thing. If what *you* said is true, then, more likely than not, Vera lied when she told me she bought the picture at the Blissburg Arts Fair. And," she added, "if what you said was true, and Vera had nothing to hide, then why did she push me out of that bedroom so fast?"

Without waiting for an answer, Emma moved towards the door. As she opened it, Dexter called after her.

"Just for the record, Emma," he asked, "what exactly did the painting you saw in Vera's bedroom look like?"

"It was a square painting," Emma answered, closing her eyes to bring the memory back into focus. "It had a whipped creamy background and in the middle was one lone, solitary, cupcake. It looked like vanilla. Or maybe the cupcake was in a white paper holder. And it had pale pink frosting with a red cherry on top."

Emma didn't wait for him to reply before racing out the door.

24

FRIDAY AFTERNOON - BUCK UP

Once inside her car, Emma burst into tears. She felt stupid. Humiliated! Steve and Dexter had torn her theory to shreds.

Was she right about Vera, she wondered? Emma didn't know anymore. What Steve said was true. It was just a hunch. A hunch based on what, Emma asked herself? On how easily Vera flew into a rage? First at the restaurant when she attacked Lexie. Later, that morning with Sacha on the phone.

And what about the painting? Emma was *sure* Vera stole it because Vera lied to Emma about where she got the painting, and pushed Emma out the door after Emma noticed it. Nonetheless, Emma had to admit, there was no proof. Nothing that tied Vera and the stolen painting to her sister's death. It was all just a hunch.

Why, she now asked herself, hadn't she anticipated Steve's arguments? Why hadn't she simply reported the fact of the missing painting, along with the fact that she'd seen a similar one in Vera's bedroom. Then Steve and Dexter, who were clearly so brilliant, could have connected the dots themselves. Or not. At least she wouldn't have let them humiliate her.

Worst of all, Emma wondered why she completely forgot to ask

Vera about her meeting with Carmen the morning after the murder. *That* had been the whole reason Emma arranged to visit Vera.

She started to change lanes and caught a glimpse of her face in the rear view mirror. Old was written all over it. Is that why she forgot, Emma asked herself as the Big D grinned back at her? Was she losing her memory? After all, she was sixty-five years *old*.

Emma glanced at the clock on the dashboard. There was just enough time to squeeze in the visit with Carmen in jail. Before going home to dress for the opera. Maybe, she consoled herself, she'd find some answers about Vera's early morning visit to Carmen. Answers she forgot to get when she visited Vera earlier that day.

As for the opera, Emma realized that she really didn't want to go to Opening Night anymore. Just about everyone at Opening Night was old. She'd call Jack and cancel. One of the Walkie/Talkies would be thrilled to take her place. She even assured herself she could return the new skirt and top. For an enormous store credit at the Ralph Lauren outlet. Enough to keep her in sweatpants and T-shirts for rest of her life.

Emma knew that the sooner she called Jack the better. She pulled her car off the road, located his number on her phone, and hit the talk button. Her call went straight into his voice mail. Bailing on a recording sounded rude. She decided to call him back later.

Meanwhile, she also realized that she was hungry. She hadn't had breakfast. And she certainly wasn't touching Vera's cookie that she'd slipped into her purse. There was nothing to eat at home. When Emma saw the Claud's Bakery sign up ahead, she pulled into a parking space, got out of her car and went in. It was still pouring rain. After *her* morning, she deserved some good food.

Emma had barely stepped in the door, when someone called her name. It was Jack, seated at a table reading the paper.

"Hi. Come join me," he said loud enough for a few patrons to stare at him.

Under the circumstances, she could not refuse.

She walked over to his table and sat down. It would be harder to blow him off in person; but it was what she had to do. She decided to get it over with quickly.

"Jack, I got something to tell you," she began after ordering a bowl of tomato soup and some whole grain bread.

He interrupted her. His face looked genuinely concerned. "Something wrong, Emma? You looked down when you walked in. Otherwise, I might not even have bothered you. Everything OK?"

Tears suddenly sprang into Emma's eyes. She couldn't stop them. All she could do was root in her purse for a tissue.

Jack squirmed in his chair. Clearly, Emma thought, women's tears made this man nervous.

"Please don't cry, Emma." He pleaded. "I hate it when women cry. It reminds me of my mother. Whatever it is, can you talk about it, maybe? *Instead* of crying? I'm a good listener. I promise."

That's when Emma started talking. Her soup had arrived. She talked between spoonfuls of the delicious creamy bisque. She told Jack about the legal clinic, about Sergio, about her conversations with Julie, about meeting with the Buchanons, about seeing Vera that morning, and finally about her cross-examination by Dexter and Steve.

When she finally finished her story, Jack shook his head. He hadn't interrupted her once the whole time she was speaking.

"First of all, Emma," he said. "You know I hate lawyers. They're parasites, going all the way back to the Canterbury Tales."

Suddenly Emma wondered what this guy read for fun. First it was Greek Choruses. Now the Canterbury Tales.

But Jack had covered his face with his hands. "Oh no! I'm sorry, Emma."

Emma looked at him puzzled.

"Your son-in-law's a lawyer," Jack exclaimed. "And he's no parasite. He's terrific. He does great work." Jack leaned back in his chair and continued. "That said, however, it is a fact. Lawyers *are* parasites, vultures living off other people's financial and emotional wreckage. Road kill. My point is, talking to Steve-whoever-he-is and Dexter Dershowitz, what did you expect? Lawyers are trained to tear other people to shreds. At least," he smiled, "that's what I pay *my* lawyers to do, when I can't be bothered doing it myself. So, these two jerks did what they do. That doesn't mean they're right about everything they said."

Here Jack paused. He bit his bottom lip, and tilted his head slowly from side to side as though considering something.

"See, Emma," he shrugged. "The problem is, *you* know they got a point. A point that, in all honesty, they have to point out. Or they wouldn't be doin' their job. There just *are* a lotta reasons that Vera Vasiliev could have that painting in her bedroom. You know that. And, face it, there are a lotta reasons you could be wrong about what you saw. You never actually saw Barry's painting, did you? You can't say for sure that it's even the same one."

Emma's face fell. Another jerk was ripping her to shreds.

"Moreover," Jack continued. "You know and I know. Even if Vera Vasiliev *did* steal Barry's painting, one stolen cupcake doth not a murderess make."

Emma nodded.

"That said," Jack shrugged, "*you* seem to know in your gut that it's the same painting. Right?" He didn't wait for her to reply. "And for whatever reason, *you* believe in your gut that Vera killed her sister. You don't know why she did it, but *you know* she did. Well," he shook a hairy finger at her, "here's what I'd do. You're a smart lady. Go with your gut! Let the lawyers worry about the details. It's what they get paid to do."

Then, without skipping a beat, he added, "Now, what time can I pick you up tonight? Is 5:00 OK? I made us a reservation. Same deal. Appetizers and wine at Jardin. Dinner after the opera at that donors thing." He nodded encouragingly. "Sound good?

In spite of herself, Emma nodded. "OK."

.   .   .

WHEN EMMA LEFT CLAUD'S, it was 2:00 p.m. She realized there wasn't much time to squeeze in a visit to Carmen. But she'd promised herself. She would visit Carmen in jail and find out what happened during Vera's early morning visit.

The women's prison was a good half hour drive from Blissburg. Longer in the pouring rain. Emma stepped on the gas, but it was almost 3:00 by the time she arrived at the jail.

Arranging for a visit with an inmate turned out not to be simple. First there was paperwork. Then a long wait while the administrator found Carmen and determined whether she agreed. He finally located her in the exercise room. Then Carmen had to sign some papers. It was after 4:00 by the time Emma sat down in front of a glass window facing Carmen on the other side. They talked using two black phones. Before she even started the interview, a guard informed Emma she had fifteen minutes. She'd better get to her point fast.

The first thing Emma noticed was that Carman had lost weight. To make matters worse, she began to cry the minute she saw Emma.

"Emma," she said when she had composed herself and picked up the phone. "I'm so sorry." She shook her hanging head from side to side. "I know now I was wrong to blame you. You did nothing but try to help. Please, accept my deepest apology."

Emma tried to stop her. Precious minutes were ticking away. But for some reason, Carmen only wanted to relive that terrible moment when she called a curse down on Emma's head, and labeled her a traitor in front of a couple of dozen photographers and newsmen.

"How could I do that to you?" Carmen asked. "You, who are my friend. Steve explained everything to me. How you were so careful to keep my secret. How you never even told him." Then she added, "By the way, Emma. That curse I called down on you? Don't worry. I've made sure. It's all reversed."

Carmen spoke as though reversing a curse were as easy as reversing duplicate charges on your MasterCard.

"Let me see your palm?" Carmen added. "Hold it up to the glass."

Emma shook her head. "Everything's fine, Carmen. Don't worry about it." Once again she checked her watch. The fifteen minutes were already half gone. "There are just a few questions I want you to answer. As best as you can recall."

That's when Emma asked Carmen about her visit from Vera.

Carmen began her story. She described how, early on the morning after Natasha's death, Carmen and Tonio were awakened by a knock on the door of their trailer.

"We'd had a bad night," Carmen explained. "Tonio and I had seen the old man holding the dead singer's body under the olive tree."

"You mean Tonio returned to the vineyard with you?" Emma interrupted. She didn't remember Carmen telling her that before. "When you saw Barry with Natasha's body, Tonio was there?"

"Yeah," Carmen shrugged her shoulders. "He drove me. Back to the vineyard."

Emma didn't like the sound of that; but she motioned Carmen to continue.

"After we got back," Carmen said, "we couldn't get to sleep. Tonio was worried we'd get framed for the murder. The death or whatever it was. Just like my other husband was framed. Because I was at the party. Anyway, when we heard the knocking we were still in bed. I answered the door and it was the ugly twin. She said she needed help. I told her I was tired. All my psychic energy was gone. Then I tried to get her to leave, but the ugly twin wouldn't go. Finally, I told her to come into the living room. Then, you know what she said?"

Emma shook her head.

"She said that whoever the killer was, he was after her next. She was the twin. They were identical. Interchangeable. Whoever wanted Natasha dead, wanted her dead too. That's what she said.

Which was strange. Because the ugly twin and the beautiful singer obviously aren't identical. One so ugly; the other so beautiful. Then, she begged me to read her cards. So she'd know what her future was. I told her, honey, the cards don't work that way. I wouldn't be living in a trailer if they did." Carmen rolled her eyes at Emma.

"But in my office last Saturday, you did say the cards told you Natasha would be murdered, right?" Emma asked.

Carmen seemed to squirm. "Sure. Earlier that night, something gave me a bad feeling. What can I say? When I held the beautiful singer's hand and felt that big ring."

"You noticed the ring?" Emma asked. This wasn't good.

Carmen nodded. "Of course I noticed the ring. How could I not notice? It was so big. And I'm a psychic. I get feelings about things. When I felt that ring, the feelings I got from it weren't good. They were bad. But," she shifted her eyes back and forth like a trapped animal. "I didn't want to tell you this before, Emma. When I felt that ring, the bad feelings I had were not about Natasha. They were about me." She pointed to her chest. "Something bad was going to happen to *me*. That's why I ran away from the party. And I was right. We got framed for stealing that ring."

Emma felt her heart sink fast. "So, if you weren't worried about Natasha, like you said before, why did you and Tonio return later to the vineyard?" Emma asked.

"Because once I got home, I realized that I'd left my basket of cards on the auction table," Carmen explained. "Tonio and I went back to the party to find it. But we didn't want to use the front drive. After all, they told me I was supposed to leave at 8:00 p.m. So we came up the back, through the vineyard, so nobody would see us. The garden where I left the basket was deserted. I don't think anybody saw me. I grabbed the basket and met Tonio back in the vineyard. That's when we saw the old man with the young singer's body in his arms."

OK," Emma said, wondering why Carmen's new story sounded

so much worse than before. "What happened next? In the trailer, I mean. Back in the trailer, the morning after."

Carmen continued. "The ugly twin insisted she wanted the cards. The cards I'd used the night before with Natasha. The ones Tonio and I went back to get. I got so sick of listening to her, I went to look for them."

"Were they still in the basket?" Emma asked.

"That's the funny thing," Carmen answered. "I couldn't find the cards. Or the basket." She paused. "I need those cards. It's what I do. I have to have the cards. So I went into the bedroom to ask Tonio if he knew where they were. But he'd gone back to sleep. When I woke him he got mad. He's like that. First he said he didn't know. Then he said he remembered he hid the basket under the bed because the kids were playing with it."

"The kids?" Emma interrupted. "Where were the kids? You didn't mention the kids before."

"Oh, I forgot. The kids were at Tonio's cousin's trailer watching TV. Tonio sent them over there so we could get more sleep. They woke us up at 6:00 a.m., Emma."

Emma started to wish she'd never come to the jail. She was getting more and more confused.

"Then we had an argument. Tonio wanted me to send the ugly twin away. But I went and got the basket anyway. Of course, all the cards were in it."

"Was the ring in it?" Emma asked. Then regretted it.

Carmen's eyes narrowed. "Why *would* it be?" she answered, starting to frown. "You think we stole that ring. You think we're gypsies, so we steal things."

"Of course not," Emma replied, though she *was* starting to have doubts. "What happened next?"

The fifteen minutes were over. The guard motioned to Carmen to wrap things up.

"Next?" A sullen look crossed Carmen's face "Next, I took the cards into the living room. But the ugly twin didn't want me to read them anymore. Instead, she said that she felt sick. She wanted a drink of water. That's when I realized Tonio was right. I should never have let her in the trailer. Roma like us have trouble enough. All I needed was for the ugly twin of the murdered beautiful singer to drop dead in our trailer. I went into the kitchen. While I was there, Tonio got dressed. He went into the living room and sent the ugly twin away. She was gone when I returned with the water."

The guard took the phone out of Carmen's hand while she spoke. Then he led Carmen out of the interview room. Carmen never looked back and she never said goodbye.

25

FRIDAY EVENING – LIGHTS, ACTION

That was the trouble with trusting your gut, Emma thought as she drove back home on 101 in a downpour that slowed traffic to a crawl. Sometimes your gut got tied in a knot. Like hers was now.

After talking to Carmen, all Emma's gut told her was that Carmen and Tonio had just as much opportunity and motive to kill as anyone else. As for means, the toxicology report was due out on Tuesday. But what would that prove? Anyone could get hold of poison.

So far, she knew Sergio, the chef, had bought poison to kill the rat in his kitchen. Emma also was sure the police found rat poison in the Buchanons' broom closet the night of the murder. Now that Carmen and Tonio were charged with the murder, she wondered if the police had bothered to ask the Buchanons about *that*. Suddenly, her gut told her everyone was guilty: the Roma, both Buchanons, Vera, Sacha the bass, Sergio the chef, and, of course, Chiara the understudy who still had the most to gain.

Emma's thoughts were interrupted by an advertisement on a commuter bus stopped in the lane next to hers. It was an ad for City

Opera. A photograph of Natasha Vasiliev, in full Trovatore costume, with her mouth wide open.

Emma checked the clock on the dashboard and gasped. It was quarter to five. She tried to remember exactly what time Jack said he would pick her up. Five fifteen, she assured herself waiting for the traffic to pick up speed. It had to be five fifteen.

But when she pulled into her driveway, the dark blue Tesla was already parked in front of her house. She watched Jack descend her front stairs with his umbrella and get back into his car.

Darn! Emma thought, noting the frown on his face. This was *sure* to make a bad impression.

Emma also noted that, wearing his well-tailored tuxedo, Jack looked almost distinguished. In a Hollywood Godfather sort of way. Then she scolded herself for being a jerk; and admitted he looked a *lot* better than most of the old geezers who would be at the Opera Opening Night.

"I was at the jail visiting Carmen," she shouted getting out of her car and running to the house through the rain. She tried to make it sound like she'd been visiting a sick relative. Like it was part of the Sermon on the Mount or something. After all, hadn't Jesus said, blessed are ye who visit the sick and the scapegoats like me unjustly locked up in prison? She thought she remembered something like that.

But Emma could tell Jack didn't buy it. He still looked irritated, and checked his watch before replying, "If there's any traffic we're gonna miss the appetizers. And I get pretty grumpy when I'm hungry."

"Be down in a sec," Emma assured him, sprinting up the stairs and into the house.

In fact, she changed out of her slacks in record time. No shower. Same underwear. She added stockings. She was dressed in the new skirt and top in five minutes flat. She skipped the old gold shawl. Who knew where *that* was? Grabbed her black coat. And ran a comb through her hair. Then she looked for the sandals. Four minutes later she found them. In the closet under her boots.

But when she started to put them on, she finally remembered her toenails. She stared at them. They looked awful. But there was no time to worry about them now. It was also too late for makeup. She found an old clutch purse in the top drawer of her dresser, and stuffed in her wallet, keys and a lipstick. Then she dashed downstairs.

To her surprise, when she opened her front door and walked out on the porch, she heard a loud whistle.

"Wow!" Jack called from the car. "I'm impressed."

Emma blushed. Nobody had whistled at her in twenty years. Except for that valet when she'd forgotten to give him her car key.

"Thanks," she called over her shoulder as she locked the front door. "I know I don't look *that* great."

Jack, she noted, did not get out of the car with his umbrella or open her door. As she slid into the leather passenger seat, flicking the rain drops off her hair, he replied. "I meant I'm impressed at how fast you got dressed." That was all he said.

They were almost in Petaluma when she turned to him. "I really apologize for being late, Jack. I needed to talk to Carmen. I didn't think it could wait until tomorrow. It was about my hunch. The hunch you encouraged me to follow." She glanced at him, hoping he'd buy into this excuse since she gave him credit for it.

Instead, he continued to watch the road.

Emma noted, with relief, that so far traffic had not been heavy. So she took courage, and continued. "Well, for what it's worth, I'm glad I went to visit Carmen. Even though it meant being a little late. I found out some interesting things." She did not add, things that make me more confused than ever.

Jack didn't ask about the interesting things; Emma felt she'd already said more than enough. They sat in silence for almost half an hour.

Then, as if to extend the distance between them, Jack reached for the radio dial to turn on the news.

Emma glanced at his hand. His tuxedo sleeve had pulled above his wrist revealing what, in the darkened interior of the car, looked like a gold bracelet. Emma mentally gagged. Men and gold bracelets! How tacky. Then she realized it was a plain yellow plastic band.

She looked up. Jack was staring at her.

"It's for cancer," he explained. "I always wear it. So I don't forget. That I didn't appreciate her the way I should have. She died of cancer."

"Oh," Emma said. "I'm so sorry."

"Please," Jack replied. "Don't misunderstand. I loved her, of course. But, seriously, I'm not being romantic. All I mean is, I miss her. Selfishly. I miss her a lot. It wasn't until she was gone, that I realized how much I had never learned to do. How much *she* did all those years. She was a wonderful lady; and I never really appreciated her as much as she deserved."

Tears sprang to Emma's eyes as he spoke. Was that the best any of us can hope for, she wondered? To be missed? To be missed by someone like that?

"At least you understand now," was all she said.

Jack turned his head to look at Emma. He must have noticed her wipe her eyes. She felt embarrassed. She motioned with her hand for him to keep his eyes on the road.

"Just like my wife," he laughed, as though to lighten the mood. "My friends think I'm crazy," he continued. "You're rich, they say. If you're lonely find somebody new. And it's true," he nodded, "even some of the young ones. They throw themselves at me. And don't get me wrong, they're pretty. Some of them are downright beautiful. I admit it, a few years ago, once in a while I took the bait. But now, I'm thinkin', what do these babes want with an old codger like *me*? Well, I know what they want. They're thinkin', this old man's gonna kick the bucket real soon, and I'm gonna get all his money."

Jack looked over at Emma again, and added, "That's the Sicilian in me talkin'." He took his right hand off the wheel and pointed his index finger at her. "We're realists."

Emma laughed, thinking of Lexie Buchanon. Is that what Lexie was waiting for, she wondered? Barry to kick the bucket? Was *that* the rich couple bargain Julie had talked about?

Instead of agreeing with Jack, however, she took the opposite tack. "Look," she said, "I don't see anything wrong with someone remarrying if they're lonely. Young. Old. What difference does it make? You only live once."

"What about you?" Jack said.

"Me?" Emma answered.

"Yeah, you. Why didn't you ever remarry? You're a good lookin' woman," he added as if *that* were the test.

Emma shrugged, uncomfortable with the question. "I'm not lonely," she finally said.

Jack ignored her answer. "You wanna know what I think?" he said. "In my opinion, a woman like you would be crazy to get married."

"Why?" Emma asked. Then she added quickly. "I mean, don't get me wrong. I agree with you. I just want to hear why you think so."

"Simple," Jack replied. "See, at our age, men need women way more than women need men. What does that mean?" He didn't wait for an answer. "I'll tell ya. It means that if you marry some old codger now, you're gonna spend the rest of your life taking care of someone who hasn't a clue how to take care of *you*. Because if that old codger was me, and had a wife doin' everything for him, then he never learned how. Why would you want to do that again? You probably been takin' care of people for years."

Emma thought for a moment. "I don't know. Maybe because you loved the old codger?" The answer embarrassed her as soon as she gave it. She blushed.

"Love?" Jack shrugged. "*That* kind of love? The kind that makes you do irrational things? At our age?" He shook his head. "Nah, we're too smart for that. I mean, at this stage of my life, I'm not 'fallin' in love' like in the songs. At my age, I'd have to know someone *really really* well for that kind of love to develop. I don't think I have that many years left."

"You're probably right," Emma nodded. "But people our age don't have to get married. They can take trips together," she suggested, remembering her wonderful trip to Italy researching her book. Her old friend, Mary, went along. Right before she got sick. They had a ball.

Jack disagreed. "Tell me this. Men are tight with their money – except when it comes to food. We don't like to shop. Most of us don't care about museums, sunsets, or cutesy villages. We bring our computers and cell phones with us. And spend hours figuring out which bar has a satellite dish so we can watch the Super Bowl. Face it, we're a pain in the neck. So why would a woman like you want to travel with a man?" He glanced over at Emma. Then something about the look on her face did make him blush.

"Oh-oh." He shook his finger at her. "I know what you're thinkin'. You're naughty."

Now Emma blushed. The man *had* read her mind.

He laughed. "In the old days it was us guys who only had one thing on our minds. Now, I swear, it's you ladies." He shook his head. "Let's get one thing straight, Emma. After losing my wife, I promised myself one thing. I'm not goin' to bed with anyone I might get attached to. It was way too painful. I'm never goin' through that again."

As he finished speaking, he pulled up in front of the parking valet at Jardin.

The maitre d' greeted Jack with an arm around his shoulder. Just like the time before.

"*Ciao bello!*" he said. "*Senti.* Listen to me, Jack. I'm still black and blue from that body check the other night." He turned to Emma and laughed. "Totally illegal! Ever seen this guy play hockey? He's a madman. Blocks like a twenty year old. I can't even roll over in bed. My wife is furious."

"Tell your wife it's not much of a game if you don't take a few hits," Jack replied.

Vince showed them to their table. Jack ordered a replay of the delicious wine and appetizers from the week before. Substituting a 2003 *Dom Perignon Brut* for the *Nuits Saint Georges*.

After the waiter uncorked the champagne, Emma continued to study the menu. One of the appetizers had caught her eye. Beluga blinis. Emma hadn't noticed it before. The price tag was steep. $95. She'd been trying to figure something out ever since she left Carmen at the jail. How could she narrow down her list of suspects? Suddenly she had the answer. It was going to be expensive; but she decided it was worth it.

As soon as the wine came, she closed her menu and gave it to their waiter. Then she excused herself to visit the ladies' room. On her way back to the table she tapped Vince, the maitre d', on the shoulder.

"Tonight," she said, "at the dinner we're attending after the opera. Is there some sort of seating plan?"

Vince motioned with his thumb to the private rooms at the rear of the restaurant. "For the party after the opera?" He nodded. "Yes, you're on the list. There's a chart."

"So, you know exactly where everyone is seated?" Emma asked.

Vince nodded again.

"Great," Emma replied. "Here's what I want you to do." That's when she explained her plan to Vince. "You understand?"

He took his iPhone from his dress suit pocket and made a note to himself. "Yeah," he nodded. "I got it."

Then he read the message back to her. When he finished, Emma handed him her credit card, crossing her fingers that VISA wouldn't reject the charge. A few seconds later, she'd signed the receipt.

"What was that all about?" Jack asked when she returned to the table. "You checkin' up on me? Worried that maybe I play too rough? Seriously, you wanna come and watch me play sometime? The hockey rink's in Santa Rosa."

Emma laughed. "I don't think so. I know nothing about hockey. But I've planned a little surprise for after the opera. I'll tell you about it later."

Emma noticed that, for some reason, Jack looked disappointed. Like a kid whose mother missed his championship game. She thought to herself, some men never grow up.

The oysters were delicious. The champagne even better. In fact, Emma had never tasted such delicious champagne. It was so good, Emma wondered if it really was the taste. Or just that she felt like celebrating her brilliant idea.

Before Emma knew it, it was time to rush across the street to the Opera House. In her excitement, she almost forgot. They needed to get to their seats early. Right before the curtain rose, Clare Blumberg, City Opera's Director, would announce the creation of the Baxter and Alexandra Buchanon Russian Arts Archive in memory of Natasha Vasiliev.

Jack and Emma had just taken their seats when Clare, Barry and Lexie appeared on the Opera House stage. Then Clare announced the breathtaking donation. Each year, the Baxter and Alexandra Buchanon Russian Arts Archive would fund a new production of one of the Russian opera classics. At the end of each cycle, the foundation would commission a new work by a contemporary Russian composer. All this, Clare announced, was dedicated to the memory of their dear friend and highly gifted soprano, the late Natasha Vasiliev.

At that point an image of Natasha was projected onto a large screen behind Clare and the Buchanons. Then Barry took the microphone from Clare and invited Natasha's twin sister, Vera Vasiliev, to join them on stage. Sitting in the third row of the orchestra section, Emma saw all that transpired in vivid detail.

Clare, the director, looked striking in a long black silk suit accessorized with humongous South Sea pearls. Barry looked OK, but old, in his black tuxedo. Lexie, in contrast, looked stunning and trendy in a shell pink taffeta floor length strapless gown. Its tight bodice shimmered with row upon row of cut glass crystal beads and seed pearls. The papers later reported that it was a Gaultier couture.

In the end, however, it was Vera who stole the show. Emma could not imagine how she'd done it. Was it the hair, the makeup? Or just the jeweled choker hiding her fat ugly neck? She looked gorgeous. She commanded the stage like a star. Not exactly her sister's star. The twins simply weren't *that* identical. But, once on stage, some form of magic transformed the horsey nose, the too large mouth, into a face that was handsome. Certainly remarkable. And on Vera's great figure, Natasha's green silk dress with the plunging neckline fit like a glove.

Barry's speech about Vera's selfless dedication to her sister's career, brought tears to many eyes. And to Vera's as well. It was her moment of glory after so much hard work in her sister's beautiful shadow.

All in all, the entire ceremony lasted less than ten minutes. Then Massimo, the conductor strode to the podium amid loud applause. The orchestra began the overture. And the curtain rose on Verdi's *Il Trovatore*. The story of a gypsy scapegoat, a mother's deadly mistake, and star-crossed lovers who meet a tragic end.

Once the singing started however, Emma had to admit that Chiara, the understudy, simply could not fill Natasha Vasiliev's big Russian boots as the heroine, Leonora. Most of the time Chiara's singing was fine. But the understudy's first act aria, delivered flat on her back in the middle of the stage, simply didn't project. Massimo should have restaged it. Of course, Emma thought, Chiara probably sang the difficult aria perfectly in the maestro's bed.

The mezzo soprano in the Roma role, however, stopped the show. At the intermission, the applause for Azucena, the gypsy, continued a full five minutes.

When they stopped clapping, Jack guided Emma into the aisle and upstairs to the Allegro lounge for more champagne. There they shook hands with the usual suspects. Mostly well-heeled seniors with a smattering of trophy wives.

And once or twice they even encountered a member of the young set. Like Julie and Piers. Piers looked handsome in his tux. To Emma's delight, Julie looked adorable in her black velveteen beaded gown.

Emma and Jack had just returned to their seats for the third act, when Emma caught sight of Vera Vasiliev hanging on Sacha Kuragin's arm. Once again, the ugly twin looked radiant.

26

FRIDAY NIGHT - CURTAIN FALLS

When the curtain dropped on the final act of *Il Trovatore*, Emma noted that the audience's response was tepid. Emma wasn't surprised. Even the rousing Anvil Chorus had sounded blah. Only the gypsy got a standing ovation, accompanied by shouts of "*bravo*" and "*bravissimo*" from those who didn't speak Italian. And "*brava*" and "*bravissima*" from those who did like Jack. All this for the poor Roma who threw her own infant into a raging bonfire, instead of the Count's kidnapped son.

Jack left the Opera House shaking his head.

"I'm tellin' you," he said as he and Emma walked to the restaurant. "The music moves me to tears, but the plots are just plain goofy. Like I'm gonna believe this loving mother threw her own baby into a bonfire by mistake? Gimme a break!" He added, "It does, however, make me feel better about my own parenting. I may have worked too hard; but I didn't toss my kid into a campfire by mistake, or even on purpose. And she turned out well, too."

"Where does your daughter live?" Emma asked. Jack rarely mentioned her.

"In Palo Alto. She's a hematologist. She runs her own lab at Stanford," Jack added with pride, even though Emma hadn't asked what his daughter did. "Cara is the reason I moved to California. After her mother died, she didn't want me living so far away. She's the one who suggested Blissburg. Close, but not too close. You know what I mean? I spend one night a week with her and her family at their place in Palo Alto. To be with the grandsons. And they have a weekend place in Calistoga, not so far away from where I live. It's worked out fine."

He seemed to remember something. "By the way, what's that little surprise you're planning? As I told you, Emma, I don't like surprises."

"Don't worry," Emma replied. "It's not about you."

They had reached the restaurant. Vince met them at the door and ushered them into the private room set up for the party. Jack found their table while Emma checked out the seating arrangements.

When she sat down, Jack repeated his question. "So, about that surprise?"

Emma leaned over and whispered something in Jack's ear.

When she finished his eyes got big. "You're crazy, Emma," he said. "Besides, it must have cost a fortune."

Emma swatted his concerns away with her hand. "Don't worry. If they didn't do it, they'll eat it. If they did, they won't. And I will have found the killer."

Jack shook his finger at her. "And if they *all* eat it, you just lost yourself a chunk of money and a big hunk of caviar."

"Beluga caviar," Emma corrected him.

"Tell ya what," he added. "If this crazy plan of yours works, I'll pick up the tab."

"Deal." Emma stuck out her hand noting that, despite his well publicized hatred of gambling, Jack was clearly a betting man.

While they were talking, the room suddenly filled with people bumping into each other trying to find their chairs. When the commotion died down, Jack looked around their table. It had ten places. Julie and Piers sat to Jack's right, next to Chiara, the understudy and Massimo, the conductor. Next to them sat Puss Carleton and her date, a distinguished white haired man with a southern drawl. Between them and Emma, seated to her left, was an older couple who introduced themselves as Friends of Barry. Emma sat next to Jack, on his left.

Emma studied the rest of the tables in the room. All of *her* suspects were seated at the next table.

Jack focused his eyes on Chiara. He leaned sideways to whisper in Emma's ear. "I've sighted target number one. Over."

"Roger," Emma answered. She stared over his shoulder at the adjoining table. "I have targets two, three and four clearly in view."

Finally everyone was seated. Seconds later Emma saw Vince walk toward them carrying two small plates of food. He was followed by another waiter who also carried two plates in his hands. They wove their way around the tables. First, Vince stopped at Emma's table and set one of the appetizer plates in front of Chiara. She stared at it. Something was written on a small card that Vince delivered along with the plate. She bent down to read it.

Meanwhile, Vince and the waiter delivered the three remaining plates of caviar blinis to Lexie, Barry and Vera at the adjoining table.

Emma held her breath, waiting to see what happened next.

Jack kept his eyes on Chiara.

As Jack later told Emma, Chiara giggled when she read the note. She showed it to Massimo. He shook his head. Then the two of them fed each other the blinis.

At the adjoining table, Lexie and Barry read their notes. They briefly looked around their table to see who their secret admirer was, looked at each other, and dove into the blinis.

Which left Vera.

Emma watched the twin's face. Unlike the other blini recipients, her face froze when she saw the blinis. Then she studied the message. Emma repeated its contents silently in her head.

"Hope you like the Beluga blinis. They're just like the ones you served last Friday night. Enjoy!"

Emma held her breath wondering what Vera would do.

All around them, other party goers were getting restless. Wondering why their appetizers hadn't come too. Somebody at the adjoining table yelled, "Why don't I get caviar blinis?"

Emma continued to watch Vera. Her initial expression slowly dissolved. First in confusion. Then into panic. She looked down at the blinis. She looked back at the note.

Finally, Sacha, sitting next to her, reached over and grabbed one of the blinis off Vera's plate.

"If you're not going to eat this, darling, then I will," he said, and started to put the blini into his mouth.

That's when Vera came unstuck. With one strong stroke, she dashed the blini out of his hand. It flew across the table and landed in Lexie's wine glass. Then Vera stood up.

"Stop her!" Emma cried. She was sure Vera would try to run away.

Jack rose from the table.

Vera looked up when she heard Emma's voice. At the same time, Emma saw her remove something from her jeweled clutch. It wasn't a blini.

That's when Vera screamed.

"It's you," she cried, pointing at Emma. "I knew you knew. I saw it in your eyes this morning when you spotted the cupcake!"

Vera's face contorted in an obscene leer. She ran forward and lunged at Emma.

Still seated, Emma watched all this happen in what looked like slow motion. And she said to herself. Wow! This *is* the Big D. This is what it looks like. Then she felt something prick her sweater followed by a sharp pain in her shoulder.

After that, the action sped up. Emma saw Jack slam into Vera, driving his shoulder, upper arm, hip and elbow smack into her and pinning her to the table. It was an awesome body check. Vera crumpled slowly to the floor, still holding the bloody stiletto.

"Mamma, Papa, forgive me," she sobbed. "It was a mistake. It was all a terrible mistake. Please believe me. I meant for Lexie to eat the poisoned blini. So our beautiful songbird could marry her rich lover, Barry. And I," she held her arms out and sobbed louder, "could finally have my beloved Sacha. But Natasha ate the poison instead."

Seated to Emma's right, the Friends of Barry watched stunned.

"My goodness, Harold," the woman exclaimed. Her hand still clutched her chest. "It's urban theater. A takeoff on the mix up when the gypsy in the opera threw her son into the bonfire by mistake. Wow! They really had me going for a minute."

Then she saw blood dripping from under Emma's torn cashmere sweater and let out a scream. "Oh my gosh, Harold. That woman's bleeding. It's not urban theater. It's real. It's real blood. And it's dripping all over that beautiful Ralph Lauren skirt she's wearing."

By then, five policemen had appeared out of nowhere. As they dragged Vera away, she cried, "Sacha. Say you'll still love me. Please say you will."

But Sacha didn't answer. He had grabbed the rest of her blinis and crawled under the table.

A doctor, dressed in a tux, also materialized. "Let me through. Let me through," he cried.

But before attending to Emma's wound, he turned to Jack. "You're Russo, the forward, aren't you? You were on the Olympic Hockey Team? That was some body check!" he exclaimed. "Totally illegal, of course. But hey," he pointed to Emma, "you just saved this lucky lady's life. Another second and she'd have been done for." He reached out to shake Jack's hand. "It's a privilege."

Emma figured she must have passed out then. The next thing she remembered she was lying in an ambulance. Julie hovered over her, holding her hand.

27

SATURDAY MORNING - FRONT PAGE NEWS

hen Emma woke up the next morning, there was a party going on in her hospital room. Julie entered bearing a huge bouquet of flowers. Emma noted that her room was already full of them. Piers, Jack and Barry talked to Sergio while stuffing their mouths from a large platter of food on her nightstand. Barbara, the receptionist, stood in a corner deep in conversation with the police chief's wife and one of the Walkie-Talkies. Andy, her ex, flirted with Lexie over what looked like a glass of champagne. Steve from the free legal services clinic and Dexter, the *pro bono* lawyer, were there with Carmen and Tonio.

Carmen was the first to notice that Emma had awakened. She slipped over to stand by Emma's bed.

"Emma," she said taking Emma's hand and squeezing it. "Why did I ever doubt you? I said to Tonio, what kind of psychic am I who didn't even recognize a saint when I saw one?" She nodded her head vigorously. "It's a crisis for me, you know. Of confidence. I need counseling. I hope it's covered on that Obamacare you guys got for me." She laughed. "Emma, I couldn't believe it. Last night, when the guard came to my cell and said I could go home. Steve..."

She turned to look at him. He'd also seen that Emma was awake and approached the bed.

"Steve," she continued. "He came to the jail late at night. To get us out right away. I am so grateful." She took Steve's hand too. "Grateful to both of you."

Steve shook his head. "Nah. It's Emma's doing. She gets *all* the credit for this one. Emma," he addressed her directly now. "I owe you an apology. Vera Vasiliev confessed everything last night in a signed statement at the police station after her arrest."

Carmen smiled at Emma. "That's how we got out so fast."

Steve continued, "It turns out she was obsessed with Sacha Kuragin, her twin sister's lover. Vera believed that if Natasha married Buchanon, then Sacha would take her as his lover instead. Because she and Natasha were identical. Identical twins."

Emma nodded. "Poor Vera. She never understood why everyone, probably including her parents, loved Natasha more."

"But Vera had to kill Lexie Buchanon so Natasha could marry Barry," Steve explained. "She figured out how to do it the night she and Natasha dined at the Buchanons' home. Natasha saw the Thiebaud painting and called it Rasputin's Cupcake. That's what gave Vera the idea to poison Lexie with the Beluga caviar Lexie loved."

"Instead of with a poisoned cupcake," Emma added. "Because cooking the cupcake vaporized the poison, and that wouldn't happen with the caviar blini."

"Exactly," Steve continued. "So Vera bought some poison, mixed it with some Beluga caviar and stuffed the caviar in some blinis. Then she gave Lexie a plate of the poisoned blinis as an hors d'oeuvre at the party."

Emma nodded. She remembered that. "But Lexie put the plate down," she added.

"Right," Steve continued. "Kuragin bumped into Lexie who spilled red wine on her dress."

"And Lexie went back to the house to try to get the stains out." Emma continued. "Leaving the blinis on the auction table. I'm sure glad I didn't eat those blinis."

Steve nodded. "But Natasha did."

"Then Barry found Natasha dead out in the vineyard where the poor girl probably went to get some air," Emma concluded.

Steve nodded again. "Vera said in her confession that she suggested hiring the fortune teller for the party so she could frame the 'gypsy' for Lexie's murder. She stated that in Russia it's done all the time. So when she found Natasha's body in the vineyard she removed the ring, before she announced over the microphone that Natasha was missing. Later she snuck into the Buchanons' house and stole a few more items to frame the Roma with. She planted the ring in Carmen's tarot basket the morning after the murder. When she visited Carmen and asked her to tell her fortune."

"Stealing the painting of the cupcake was her big mistake," Emma said.

Steve agreed. "As often happens, the killer went too far. See, Vera took Rasputin's Cupcake for herself. Or, as she put it, in honor of Natasha. Vera claimed Barry Buchanon promised the painting to Natasha, but reneged when his wife threw a fit. So Vera stole the painting to avenge the sister she'd killed. And that's what tipped you off. Rasputin's Cupcake was Vera's undoing." Steve pointed to Emma. "And you figured it out. Good going!" Steve gave her a painful high five. "Your hunch was right on the money. And I was too focused on details to see it."

"Don't worry about it," Emma said, looking up at him from where her head still rested on a pillow. "You were only doing what you were trained to do. You were being a lawyer."

Steve nodded. "Right. I was being a jerk." He squeezed her hand and said goodbye.

Emma tried to sit up. She felt good except for the sharp pain when she moved her shoulder. "Can someone help me raise this bed?" she asked.

Six people rushed to her bedside, but Julie got to the control panel first.

"Thanks," Emma said. She motioned Julie closer. "By the way, am I OK?" she asked. "What actually happened last night?"

Julie smiled and kissed her mother's forehead. "You're fine, Mom. We're bringing you home this afternoon. You got a puncture wound in your shoulder. From Vera's stiletto. It's small. We just need to make sure it doesn't get infected. The doctor called you a tough old bird."

"Thanks!" Emma sighed.

Julie laughed. "He meant it in a good way," she said.

Emma wondered what that was.

"The stiletto didn't penetrate your shoulder very far," Julie explained. "Because of Jack. He knocked Vera down before she could get close enough to you to do real damage." She nodded solemnly. "Jack Russo saved your life, Mom."

Then she thought of something and laughed. "The doctor also said something about that sweater you were wearing. The cashmere and chain mail blend? At least, I think that's what the tag said."

Thank you, Ralph Lauren, Emma thought to herself. Expensive but worth every penny.

Julie frowned. "I'm afraid the sweater's ruined. They cut you out of it in the ER. And the skirt, too. Blood stains are hard to get out of silk chiffon. But, I have to say, the photos of you in the papers are gorgeous. There's a big one of you being carried to the ambulance on the front page of the Chronicle. The reporter who writes the social column actually tracked down the designer of your outfit and mentioned it in the column."

"Not exactly the way I wanted to make the society column," Emma shrugged. "But as they say, no publicity is bad publicity"

A puzzled look crossed Julie's face. "What was going on with your toenails, Mom?" she asked. "Did Jackson Pollock have a blue phase? Your toenails looked gross. Thank goodness you could hardly see them in the photograph."

Just then, Andy, her ex, interrupted them with a big, painful hug. Emma finally realized the poor man just couldn't help himself. He was like an Act of God.

"Emma, you look great," he said before turning to Julie. "Doesn't your mother look great? Even in a hospital gown. I told her the same thing the day she gave birth to you. Right after I saw your little hairy head come out of your mother's..."

"TMI, Dad! TMI!" Julie interrupted him, cringing.

"What?" Andy threw his hands up. "What did I say?"

In what could only be termed an intervention, Sergio made his way to the bedside. He looked over his shoulder and started to whisper.

What? Emma thought. Is he *still* paranoid?

"Em-ma," he said. "You won't believe what's happened. I started talking to Jack Russo, a few minutes ago, while you were asleep."

Emma nodded. "You mean that arrogant Sicilian *cafone* boor who probably saved my life?"

Sergio's face fell. He slapped his open hands on his cheeks. "Em-ma," he said. "Don't talk that way. He's *simpatico*, nice-*issimo*. He's a wonderful man. While we were talking, it slipped out that my father's Sicilian. Actually he recognized the southern surname. Anyway, Jack is willing to come in as a new investor. To pay off my debts, in return for a share in the restaurant." Sergio waved his upturned palms in tight circles. "Of course, I have to agree to do a Sicily night. Once a month." He sighed. "Not such a big deal. Right?"

Emma nodded. "Sounds like fun."

"Anyway," Sergio continued. "I have more good news. Little Pete's wants to sell your frozen *salsa di pomodoro*. And, you're really gonna like this, I got a call from the Chronicle early this morning. They saw that blog I wrote about your cooking. When I was promoting your cookbook at my restaurant. By the way," he added hurriedly, "I still am. Promoting it. Well, they want to do an article on you in their cooking section. On your book. They think it'll be a best seller after all this publicity." Sergio shook his head. "What you did was amazing, Em-ma."

As if on cue, the police chief's wife and Emma's walking mate with the Walkie-Talkies rushed to Emma's bedside.

"The chief sent me to convey his appreciation, Emma," she said. "You were such a big help solving the case. Of course, he wanted me to assure you that the department was already closing in on Vera. They just didn't have enough evidence yet to make an arrest."

Closing in? My eye, Emma thought. "Yeah," she said. "That confession Vera made pinned to the table at the restaurant last night must have helped."

"A little," the police chief's wife nodded. She laughed and swatted her hand at Emma. "Silly. Of course it did."

Then Emma remembered something. "How *did* the police show up so fast?" she asked.

Dexter Young, the *pro bono* lawyer, stood beside the police chief's wife. He was dressed, predictably, in his blue pin striped suit, starched custom shirt and Hermes tie. The one with the chickens and the eggs.

"*I* got them there," he announced. "After you left the clinic yesterday, I decided to do some research on my own. About the missing Thiebaud. I got hold of the Buchanons' police report regarding the theft; and determined exactly which cupcake the Buchanons had purchased. Your description of what you saw in Vera's bedroom fit the description in the police report perfectly. As you suspected Emma, that particular painting *was* unique. Thiebaud only did one, and it stayed in the hands of a private collector until Barry bought it. So there wasn't any question of Vera finding a print, or museum reproduction. There simply weren't any."

"When I called Barry," he continued, "he confirmed that he

bought the painting directly from the private collector. Barry also assured me that Lexie hadn't hidden the painting. And he swore that he didn't give it to Natasha himself. After that, I was pretty darned certain that the painting really was stolen. And based on your description, there was reasonable cause to believe that the stolen painting – which is worth *a frickin' huge amount of money* I might add – was in the bedroom of Vera Vasiliev's townhouse."

"Based on Vera's knowing you'd seen it, Emma," he added, "I was also pretty sure the painting was in danger of disappearing if we delayed. Judge Kennedy, my golf buddy, thought so. Turns out *he* has a Thiebaud too. The Boston Cremes lithograph from the '70s. I'd love to get my hands on one of those. He issued a search warrant and made sure the police got over to Vera Vasiliev's townhouse double quick. The property manager let the police in." Dex rocked his hand back and forth and winced. "Probably shouldn't have done that but, since she voluntarily confessed to the murder, it probably doesn't matter."

Boy, Emma thought. This guy really likes to hear himself talk.

"The point is," Dexter concluded, "they found the stolen painting valued at I don't know how many hundreds of thousands of dollars, and sent the police to arrest Vera for grand theft as soon as she left the restaurant last night. Of course, they didn't have to wait because of you, Emma."

He smiled. "All of which is just a long way of saying thanks!" Dexter checked his watch. "Whoops. Gonna be late for that settlement conference. In another matter, of course." That said, he turned and walked out the door.

The crowd in the room had started to thin. Emma had talked to almost everyone. Finally, it was Lexie and Barry Buchanon's turn. They stood together at her bedside to convey their thanks, as well. Barry spoke first.

"Emma," he said. "I can't begin to thank you enough. Or to convey how much we owe you. Especially considering the way I behaved at first. The things I said about you, about your sauce." He shook his head. "I'm ashamed. So, first of all, though I doubt you will need more publicity, we have already ordered your book, *Dining with the Stars*, to sell in the Buchanon Vineyards' gift store."

"And second," he continued, "Lexie and I," he reached out to grab his wife's hand, "are commissioning a new cookbook from you that features food pairings with our wines." Barry smiled. Emma could almost see him buffing his fingernails on his chest. "I've already thought of a title." He paused for effect. "We'll call it *What a Pair!* Good, huh! I talked to our winery's publisher about it already. He thinks it's brilliant."

Emma had to try hard to keep from laughing out loud.

"Thanks!" she replied. "Super title!"

Lexie spoke next. "Honestly, I don't know where to begin, Emma. Between you and Julie."

She turned to Emma's daughter. "You saved my life, Julie. Literally. Last week when Vera had me by the throat? I thought I was dead! I know you were the person who pulled her off." Lexie shook her head. "I don't think I ever thanked you properly for that. So," she paused, "as far as we at the winery are concerned, you are it. You're the only person handling our publicity from now on. And we're recommending you to every other vintner in Sonoma County. In the world," she corrected herself.

Then she turned back to Emma. "Julie saved my life. But, face it, Emma, you saved my reputation. Hard as it is to believe, I have enemies. Right here in Blissburg. Some people spread horrible rumors that *I* was somehow involved in Natasha's death. Like I was jealous of her or something ridiculous like that. Well, thanks to you, Emma, those rumors are dead. Buried. And I don't have to worry about them anymore. That's a big personal debt I owe you. Gosh," her eyes teared up and she leaned down to give Emma a hug and a kiss, "I don't know why, but I feel like you're my mother, or something. You're just so wonderful."

As Barry led Lexie out of the room, she was still crying.

Finally, only Julie, Piers and Jack were left.

Now it was Emma's turn. She motioned Jack closer to the side of her bed.

"Early this morning," she began, "one of the doctors here told me that I had a very close call last night. And that a certain old codger saved my life. That's a serious debt, Jack. What do I do?"

Julie and Piers had stopped talking when Jack approached Emma's bed. They heard what Emma said. When she called Jack an old codger, Emma saw Piers wince.

"Don't worry about it," Jack said.

At first it seemed like that was *all* he had to say. Then he shot Emma a sidelong glance and smiled. "OK. I'll tell you what you do owe the old codger. It's simple. All he wants is," he hesitated. "All he wants is the chance to get to know you a *little* bit better."

Emma smiled. She knew that coming from Jack Russo that was a very big compliment.

THE END

ABOUT THE AUTHOR

AJ Carton grew up in San Francisco eating her grandmother's Bolognese cuisine. She now resides with her husband and children in Sonoma County, California where she enjoys writing about food and drinking the local wine. AJ Carton would be delighted to hear from you. You can reach her at: aj@ajcartonbooks.com.

OTHER BOOKS BY AJ CARTON

Murder by the Mouthful
Plum Gone
Veni Vidi Vin
TakeOut: The Prequel

FICTION DISCLAIMER

This book is a work of fiction. Any resemblance to persons, living or dead, is purely accidental. All of the events, organizations and characters used in this story are fictional and/or solely the product of the author's imagination and invention.